Love Only Me!

Disclaimer

Love Only Me is a work of fiction. All names, characters, schools, organizations, locations, events, and businesses such as Chelseaville Academy, Blossom Adult Day Center, Blossom Youth Camp, and the fictional stage play A Different Echo: Tiny Words are entirely products of the author's imagination or used fictitiously. Any resemblance to actual persons, living or deceased, or real institutions, events, or locations is purely coincidental.

This novel is intended to uplift, encourage, and inspire through storytelling centered on growth, identity, friendship, faith, and emotional healing. It does not claim to represent real individuals or provide professional advice.

Scripture references are quoted from the King James Version KJV of the Bible and are used to support the spiritual and thematic elements within the story.

Love Only Me
© 2025 The Cozy Scratchpad

Scripture quotations are taken from the King James Version (KJV) of the Bible.

First Edition
Printed in the United States of America

Hardcover ISBN: 979-8-9998730-4-0
Paperback ISBN: 979-8-9998730-5-7

Published by:
The Cozy Scratchpad

Dedication

To God, who has been through every step of the way.
To my family and friends,
I love you all.

Author's Note

Thank you for walking through Mya's journey with me.

This story was written for every girl who's ever felt unseen, unheard, or underestimated. For anyone who's struggled with self-doubt, bullying, grief, or comparison, I want you to know: your story doesn't end there.

Mya's courage didn't come from having it all figured out. It came from showing up anyway. It stemmed from choosing forgiveness, finding her voice, and embracing who she was, both on and off stage.

If you've ever felt like your voice didn't matter, I want to tell you right now: it does. You do.

Keep going. Keep growing. You are not alone.

Love God First.

Love Kimberly

Resources & Support

You're not alone. These tools and organizations can help you or someone you love continue the journey toward healing, self-love, and confidence.

Bullying & Emotional Support
StopBullying.gov
Tips and help for students and families dealing with bullying.

STOMP Out Bullying
www.stompoutbullying.org
988 Suicide & Crisis Lifeline – Dial 988 for 24/7 mental health support and crisis care in the U.S.

Self-Esteem & Positive Identity
Blossom Youth Camp (fictional), inspired by real programs like:
Girls on the Run www.girlsontherun.org
The Confidence Code for Girls book & resource site

Self-Esteem Journal Prompts: Write three things you love about yourself every morning.

Faith & Encouragement
Scripture to Carry With You:

"I will praise thee; for I am fearfully and wonderfully made."
Psalm 139:14 KJV

"God is within her; she shall not be moved."
Psalm 46:5 KJV

"Be strong and of a good courage..."
Joshua 1:9 KJV

Disclaimer

The organizations listed are for informational purposes only. The author is not affiliated with these organizations and does not endorse or guarantee the services provided. Readers are encouraged to contact the organizations directly to verify the services they offer.

About the Author

Kimberly Cummings is a passionate storyteller, community educator, and author of faith-based fiction that speaks to the heart. With a background in child development, criminal justice, and logistics leadership, she brings layered insight into the lives of her characters, especially those navigating identity, resilience, and redemption.

Kimberly's stories are known for their emotional depth, relatable characters, and powerful spiritual themes. Her writing draws from real-life challenges, encouraging readers to embrace healing, self-worth, and the quiet strength that comes from faith.

She is the author of several impactful books, including Table of Regrets: What Was Too Much, I'm Not Him: The Stranger in the Mirror Was Me, The Waiting Porch: Finding Your Way Back, Walking on the Sea Sand, A Different Echo: Tiny Words and Cracked Glass Trilogy. Her commitment to uplifting others is evident in her novels, youth mentorship, and her growing collection of personal journals and devotionals.

When she's not writing, Kimberly enjoys crafting, traveling, and building meaningful spaces for growth and reflection. She believes every voice matters, and every heart deserves to know it is loved, chosen, worthy… always!

Connect with the author on her website at kimberlycummingsauthor.com or email her @ scratchpadcreate@gmail.com

I will praise thee; for I am fearfully and wonderfully made: marvellous are thy works; and that my soul knoweth right well.
Psalm 139:14KJV

Table of Contents

Chapter 1
A Different Cry

The sharp cry of a newborn baby pierced the quiet of Room 312 at the medical center, slicing through the hushed anticipation that hung in the air. Nurses bustled with practiced ease, and monitors blinked softly in the dim light of early morning. Outside, the sky was still painted in hues of lavender and soft peach as dawn crept over the city. Inside, however, time had stood still until now.

"She's here," whispered the nurse, her voice catching just slightly, as she turned toward the proud parents. "Seven pounds, ten ounces. Healthy, strong, and full of lungs."

Jenna Carter let out a long, tearful breath and fell back against the pillows, her body exhausted but her heart full. She reached out with trembling arms as the swaddled newborn was gently placed in her embrace. The moment their skin touched, a wave of warmth swept through her. Tiny fingers curled instinctively around her pinky.

"A girl…" Jenna whispered in awe, her voice cracking as she cradled the baby to her chest. "Noah, she's here. We finally have our baby girl."

Noah Carter stood at his wife's side, his eyes glassy and lips parted as he stared at his daughter in amazement. His broad frame seemed to fold inward with emotion as he leaned over and kissed Jenna's forehead.

"You did it, babe," he said, brushing a strand of damp hair from her face. "She's perfect. Just like her mama."

"She's everything," Jenna whispered, letting a single tear trace down her cheek.

Outside the room, the Carter boys, Theo, Levi, and Owen, were practically bouncing out of their sneakers in the waiting room, pestering every nurse that passed with eager questions.

"Did the baby come yet?"

"Is it a boy or a girl?"

"Can we see her or him?"

Eleven-year-old Theo, the oldest, tried to look composed, but his foot tapped anxiously against the linoleum floor. Levi, ten, had been making bets with Owen, who was seven, about whether the baby would have curly hair like Mom or straight like Dad.

A nurse finally smiled and motioned toward them. "Come on, boys. Come meet your baby sister."

"Sister?" They all chorused, nearly knocking over a stack of waiting room magazines as they sprang from their seats.

Back in the room, Jenna had shifted slightly to sit upright, proudly holding the baby girl wrapped in a pale pink blanket with silver stars. Noah held up his phone to record the moment as the boys burst in.

Their expressions transformed instantly from wild energy to stunned reverence. The room fell into a sacred hush as the three brothers approached the bed, peeking over the edge to catch their first glimpse.

"She's tiny," Owen whispered.

"She smells like baby powder," Levi added, leaning in with a grin.

"She's kinda... cute," Theo admitted, though he quickly added, "For a girl."

Jenna laughed softly. "Boys, meet your sister. Her name is Mya Rose Carter."

Noah added proudly, "Mya means 'beloved.' And that's what she is. Completely and loved."

Theo nodded solemnly. "Can I hold her?"

"Not until you wash your hands," Jenna said with a chuckle, already slipping back into Mom mode.

As the nurse helped sanitize their hands, Noah wrapped his arms around Jenna and looked down at the tiny miracle they had prayed for. After three rough-and-tumble sons, a daughter felt like a quiet sunrise after years of chasing storms.

There was a deep peace in the room, one that seemed to settle not just over Mya but over the entire Carter family. She had arrived not just as the youngest sibling but as a sign of new beginnings, softness, and hope.

Noah whispered a prayer under his breath: "Thank You, Lord, for this gift. For this little girl, you've placed in our care. Help us raise her strong, safe, and never doubting how loved she is."

And with that, Mya let out another soft cry, not one of pain or need, but the cry of life declaring, I'm here.

And everyone in the room knew: the Carter family would never be the same.

Two days later, the hospital bracelet was cut, and baby Mya was wrapped in a thick blanket for the chilly ride home. Jenna nestled her gently into the car seat while Noah triple-checked the straps. The boys sat quietly in the back row of the van, peering over the seat with awe-struck faces, as if the ride might rattle them too much.

Home greeted them with the smell of lavender spray and freshly vacuumed carpets. The "Welcome Home Baby Girl!" sign, drawn by Levi and Owen, was taped crookedly above the doorway with bright pink crayon hearts and glitter glued across the top.

Noah set the baby carrier on the coffee table while Jenna shuffled slowly to the couch, moving like someone whose body still remembered labor. She leaned back with a groan and winced when her lower back met the cushions.

"I'll get your pillows," Noah offered, dashing toward the hallway. "And water. And do you want a snack? Or maybe tea?"

Jenna smiled. "A nap would be nice."

Theo appeared with Mya's diaper bag slung over his shoulder like a backpack. "I got it, Mom. I'm the oldest, remember?"

Jenna nodded, amused and exhausted. "Yes, baby, I remember."

But the next few hours revealed what Jenna had suspected all along: Noah was overwhelmed. Between unloading the car, keeping the boys from bickering, trying to sterilize bottles, and overthinking every diaper change, he looked like a man juggling with one hand.

"Where do we keep the burp cloths again?" he asked, halfway through changing Mya on the kitchen counter.

"In the basket on top of the dryer," Jenna called weakly from the couch.

"That's not a real place, Jenna. That's a made-up place."

Jenna chuckled softly. "Welcome to my life."

That night, sleep became a game of shifts. Noah tried his best to take the midnight feeding, but he fell asleep standing up next to the bassinet with the bottle still in his hand. At 2:43 AM, Mya began crying again. Jenna sat up before he even stirred.

By the morning, the sun crept through the blinds, and the house was in chaos. Levi couldn't find his sneakers, Owen spilled orange juice on the counter, and Theo kept asking if Mya could come to his class for show-and-tell.

"I need help," Noah muttered, more to himself than anyone else.

Help came just before 9:00 AM in the form of Grandma Rose Watkins, Jenna's mother, who appeared on the porch wearing her favorite lavender coat and carrying a tray of blueberry muffins, a diaper bag, and what looked like a planner.

"Move out of the way, Noah," she said with a kiss to his cheek. "This house has too much testosterone and not enough common sense."

He stepped aside gratefully as Grandma Rose swept into the kitchen and immediately began restoring order. She packed the boys' lunches, found Levi's sneakers under the couch, of course, wiped down the juice mess, and even convinced Owen to stop licking the baby's pacifier.

By the time Noah was ready to head out for work, the house looked somewhat normal again. Jenna stood in the doorway, Mya cradled in her arms, while Grandma Rose adjusted her robe and eyed her son-in-law knowingly.

"You've been in over your head, huh?"

Noah laughed. "I was ready for football practice and spelling tests. Not bottle warmers and breast pumps."

"You'll adjust," she said with a wink. "Girls don't break easily. They just come with more feelings."

He kissed Jenna goodbye, then knelt to hug each boy before walking them to the van.

In the stillness that followed, Jenna sat down on the couch with Mya on her chest. Grandma Rose sat across from her with her cup of herbal tea and sighed.

"She's beautiful, baby," she whispered. "You got your girl."

"I did," Jenna said, her voice trailing off. "But now what? I'm used to loud. Wrestling. Mud. Now there's... pink."

Rose leaned forward and touched Jenna's hand. "You raise her just like the boys with love. But don't forget she'll see herself first through your eyes."

Jenna nodded slowly, her gaze falling to the bundle in her arms. "I want her to know she's enough. No matter what."

"She'll know," Rose said, sipping her tea. "As long as you don't forget it yourself."

Outside, the sound of the van backing out faded, and inside, the Carter house settled into a new rhythm. Life would never be the same. And deep in her blanket, Mya let out a soft, sigh-like cry, peaceful, unaware that the world around her was already bending, shifting, and preparing to shape her identity one word, one look, one day at a time.

At six months old, Mya Carter was a force of nature wrapped in pink footie pajamas. She had recently discovered that crawling opened an entirely new world of freedom, and she was determined to explore every inch of it.

This morning, the house felt unusually still. Jenna had gone to get her hair done for the first time since Mya was born, a well-deserved break that Noah insisted she take. He promised her everything would be fine.

"It's just a few hours," he had said, waving her off confidently. "Go get pampered. I've got the kids."

Now, in the living room, Noah was comfortably sunk into the couch, watching a basketball game, one leg crossed over the other, remote in hand. His soda rested on the end table next to a baby bottle that had rolled slightly under the lamp. The boys were outside playing tag in the backyard, occasionally shouting through the screen door for water or to tattle on each other.

And Mya?

Well, Mya had her agenda.

She had been on the floor with her favorite plush bunny, gnawing on one ear, but the moment she spotted the family cat, Whiskers, slinking silently across the hallway, her tiny body reacted. She dropped the bunny, planted both hands firmly, and took off after him like a soldier on a mission.

Whiskers flicked his tail and darted up the staircase.

Mya followed.

One hand, one knee. Wobble. One hand, one knee. Climb. She made it to the second stair. Then the third.

Noah's laughter boomed from the living room as a player made a ridiculous shot. He reached for his drink and took a long sip, his mind completely absorbed in the game.

It wasn't until halftime that he blinked and looked at the empty baby blanket on the floor.

"Mya?" he called out casually.

Silence.

He leaned forward slightly and looked around the living room. "Mya, girl, where'd you go?"

No answer.

He stood quickly and glanced toward the kitchen. No sign of her. He peered into the laundry room, then turned sharply toward the front door, still locked.

The smile drained from his face.

"Boys! Is Mya outside with y'all?" he shouted through the screen door.

"No!" Theo called back. "She was with you, Dad!"

Panic rushed through Noah's chest like a shot of adrenaline. "Oh no... oh no no no..."

He began searching the house as if possessed. He checked under tables, behind the curtains, in her crib, and in the bathroom. His breathing became short and shallow. His heart thudded against his ribs as images of worst-case scenarios flooded his mind. What if she'd gotten outside somehow? What if she'd pulled something down on herself?

"Noah, think!" he snapped to himself, slapping his forehead lightly. "She was crawling. Where would she go?"

Then he saw it, the faintest smudge on the carpeted stairs. A small trail of spit or drool. A soft, almost invisible path.

His chest seized.

He sprinted up the stairs, two at a time. "Mya?! Baby girl?!"

And then, there she was sitting proudly in the boys' room, chubby legs splayed out in a V, cheeks flushed pink, babbling happily as she smacked one hand on an action figure. Whiskers sat smugly nearby on Theo's bed, licking a paw.

Noah dropped to his knees and scooped Mya into his arms, pulling her close against his chest.

"Oh my God, baby girl," he whispered, voice breaking. "You scared me half to death."

Mya cooed, oblivious to the fact that she had just shaved five years off her father's life expectancy.

He rocked her in place, letting the adrenaline work its way out of his system. For a moment, he didn't move. He just held her. His hands trembled against her back.

When Jenna got home an hour later, her hair newly trimmed and curled, she found Noah standing in the kitchen installing a baby gate with a drill that looked like he had never used it before.

"Hi, babe," she chirped. "Where are the kids?"

"The boys are outside. Mya is napping in her crib." He didn't look up.

Jenna set down her bag and tilted her head. "Why do you look like you haven't slept in three days?"

Noah turned around slowly, sweat on his brow and a look of stunned exhaustion in his eyes.

"She climbed the stairs, Jenna."

Jenna blinked. "What?"

"While I was watching the game... I looked away for, I don't know, maybe five minutes. She followed the cat to the boys' room. I found her just... sitting there like she owned the place."

Jenna's hand flew to her mouth. "Oh, my goodness. Noah!"

"I know, I know," he said quickly. "She's okay. She didn't fall. But I swear, my heart stopped. I ran through the house like a madman. I thought... I thought something had happened to her. I thought I lost her."

She crossed the room and hugged him tightly. "It's okay. You found her. She's fine."

"I should've been paying attention," he said, guilt lacing his words. "I let my guard down. And now we're getting a gate. One for the top and one for the bottom of the stairs. I already ordered another set online just in case."

Jenna leaned against his chest. "You were doing your best. We're both learning. But yes, a gate. Multiple gates."

He nodded. "She's fast, Jenna. Like... sneaky fast. Like a mini ninja."

She smiled despite herself. "Takes after her daddy."

Noah chuckled, then exhaled slowly. "I just keep seeing her little body... halfway up the stairs. All I could think was, 'This is on me.' I didn't know it was possible to love someone so small so much."

"You're a great dad, Noah," Jenna whispered, brushing a strand of hair from his forehead. "And it's okay to be scared sometimes. That means you care."

That night, after everyone was asleep, Noah stood by Mya's crib watching her chest rise and fall. Her tiny fingers twitched in her sleep, and she made a soft sucking noise, still dreaming.

He placed a hand gently on her back and closed his eyes.

"God," he prayed in a whisper, "please help me protect her. This world is already full of things that'll try to pull her down. Keep her safe when I'm not looking. Help me be the kind of father she can always run to, even when she climbs too far."

And somewhere in the quiet, the fear finally softened into something:

Love unconditional, clumsy, panic-inducing, fierce-as-a-bear kind of love.

Chapter 2
The Edge of Trouble

The sun beamed down on the zoo like a warm invitation. It was the kind of spring day that made families spill out into the sunshine, in search of adventure and overpriced slushies. The Carter family had decided it was the perfect day for a family outing, a rare Saturday where everyone's schedules aligned.

Mya was now a full-blown toddler, bright-eyed and constantly on the move. With her tiny pigtails bouncing and a juice box in hand, she marched beside her brothers as if she were the same age and size.

"Mya, stay close to Daddy," Jenna called, her voice patient but strained. She pushed an empty stroller with one hand while checking her phone with the other. Mya rarely wanted to ride anymore; she wanted to run.

Theo, now twelve, held the zoo map like a field commander. "The giraffes are next. If we go past the aquarium, we can loop around near the bird house. It's faster."

"No! I want to see the elephants!" Owen shouted, already skipping a few feet ahead.

Levi shrugged. "We'll see it all. Just chill."

Noah adjusted his baseball cap and gripped Mya's little hand. "Let's stay together, team Carter. One unit, remember?"

But the moment Noah paused to grab a sip of water, Owen saw his chance.

He darted forward quickly, wild, untamed, toward the giraffe overlook. A wooden rail separated the crowd from the lower feeding platform, and a red "Do Not Climb" sign was posted. But Owen, ever the curious one, leaned in far too close.

It happened in seconds.

"OWEN!" Theo shouted.

The people nearby gasped. A few pointed.

Jenna turned in time to see her son's foot slip along the wooden ledge. Her scream cracked the air.

"Noah!"

Noah dropped Mya's hand and ran. "Owen!"

Before the boy could tip fully forward, a khaki-clad zookeeper, tall, fast, and experienced, lunged forward and snatched the back of Owen's shirt, yanking him safely away from the edge.

Gasps echoed through the giraffe exhibit as several onlookers clapped and murmured in response. One elderly woman placed a hand over her heart and whispered, "Thank God."

Jenna ran to Owen and collapsed to her knees. Her hands trembled as she inspected him from head to toe.

"Are you okay? Are you hurt?"

Owen, wide-eyed and pale, nodded. "I was just trying to see if the giraffe's tongue was purple."

Jenna blinked through tears. "You could've been hurt, Owen. You could've..." Her voice broke. "Don't ever run off again. Ever!"

Noah wrapped his arms around them both, trying to mask his shaking hands as he kissed the top of Owen's head. "Son... you scared me half to death."

Levi and Theo stood frozen nearby, both speechless. Theo's map had crumpled in his hand. Levi's eyes brimmed with unshed tears.

A small crowd had gathered now. Some offered comfort and relief.

"That could've ended so badly," a mother of three said quietly.

Others weren't so kind.

"Where were the parents?" one man muttered to his wife.

"Kids running wild these days," another whispered.

A younger couple nearby exchanged glances before one roared, "Some people shouldn't bring that many kids out if they can't handle them."

The comments stung more than Jenna wanted to admit. She stood up slowly, brushing dirt from her knees. Her cheeks burned not from the sun, but from embarrassment. Noah's jaw tightened.

Theo stepped forward, his voice trembling. "It's not their fault. Owen's just... fast. It happened quickly."

The zookeeper, still kneeling near Owen, looked up at the murmuring crowd. "He's fine. No harm done. That railing is secured, but it is still a good reminder for all of us that kids move fast. No judgment here."

Jenna looked at the man, tears welling in her eyes. "Thank you. Thank you so much."

"You're welcome, ma'am. Happens more than you'd think."

Noah stood taller, trying to regain control of the moment. "Alright. Everyone okay? We're good. Let's move on."

They stepped away from the crowd, strolling toward a shaded bench near the flamingo pond. Noah carried Owen in his arms while Jenna pushed Mya, who had finally agreed to sit in the stroller after all the commotion.

Theo walked beside them, unusually quiet.

"Dad?" he asked after a moment.

"Yeah, buddy?"

"I thought he was gonna fall... I thought..." His voice cracked

Noah stopped walking and turned to face him. "I did too, son. But he's safe. That's what matters. And you were brave to yell."

Theo nodded, wiping his eyes quickly when no one was looking.

Mya kicked her feet in the stroller, chewing on a fruit snack with no idea what had just taken place. Her world was still simple with shapes, colors, and movement. She reached up toward her dad with sticky fingers.

Noah bent down and kissed her forehead. "You keep both feet on the ground, little girl. Please."

Later that evening, Jenna would replay the scene over and over in her mind: the slip, the gasp, the crowd. And the fear.

But in that moment, all she could do was thank God for second chances.

And hold her babies just a little tighter. Noah didn't say a word at first.

As he guided the family back toward the parking lot, his jaw was clenched so tight it looked like he was grinding his teeth. One hand rested on Owen's shoulder the entire walk. Jenna pushed Mya in the stroller, her knuckles white as she gripped the handlebars. Her eyes darted back and forth at Owen, at Noah, at the faces still watching them as they passed. Some offered sympathetic glances. Others... not so much.

She kept hearing those words echoing in her head.

"Some people shouldn't bring that many kids out if they can't handle them."

She wanted to scream. But her voice was still caught somewhere in the panic that hadn't worn off yet.

Owen, usually full of energy and questions, was quiet. His sneakers scraped the sidewalk as he walked, head down, too ashamed or shaken to look anyone in the eye. His little hand kept brushing his dad's, but he never asked him to hold it. He just stayed close.

Theo and Levi walked in silence behind them, unusually subdued. Theo had stuffed the crumpled zoo map in his pocket, and Levi clutched the reusable cup he never even got to fill. None of them said what they were all thinking.

By the time they reached the van, the air had shifted. The excitement from earlier was gone. The laughter, the sibling jokes, the dreams of ice cream on the way home, all of it had evaporated under the weight of what had almost happened.

Noah opened the van doors. "Everyone in. Seatbelts."

His voice was low, but firm. It wasn't a suggestion. It was a command.

Mya whimpered as he buckled her into her car seat. She was tired, confused by the sudden quiet, the change in energy. She kicked her legs a little, whining until Jenna handed her a pacifier. It calmed her enough to stop the fussing.

Jenna slid into the passenger seat and sat staring at the dashboard, her hands still trembling.

"Owen..." she said softly, turning around. "Are you hurt anywhere? Do you feel okay?"

He shook his head. "I didn't mean to scare you."

"You didn't just scare me," she whispered, her voice tight with emotion. "You almost gave me a heart attack."

Noah climbed into the driver's seat and pulled the van into reverse.

The ride home was painfully silent.

No one dared touch the radio. Mya drifted off to sleep somewhere between the giraffe exhibit and the city exit sign. Levi kept his eyes on the passing trees, and Theo stared at his lap, fidgeting with a loose string on his shirt sleeve.

Every so often, Jenna would glance over her shoulder to check on Owen, making sure he was still buckled, still breathing, still there.

Noah kept both hands on the wheel, his eyes never leaving the road.

Finally, after nearly ten minutes, he spoke. "That could've gone differently."

Jenna turned to him quickly. "Don't say that. Please don't say it. I know. I know."

"I'm not blaming you," he said calmly but firmly. "But we need to talk about what happened. About how fast things can go wrong."

Her voice cracked. "You think I haven't been replaying it in my head on a loop?"

"I'm saying we can't afford to be casual anymore. Not with Mya crawling toward the stairs, not with Owen disappearing at the zoo. I'm not trying to scare you, Jenna. I'm already scared enough for both of us."

She covered her mouth with one hand, trying not to cry. "I keep seeing him leaning over that rail. I keep seeing what could've happened. I wanted today to be special…"

"It was almost tragic."

That silenced the van again. Even Theo looked up briefly, his face somber.

Owen finally spoke, barely a whisper. "I'm sorry, Dad."

Noah inhaled deeply and exhaled slowly. "I know you didn't mean to. But son… when we say stay close, we mean it. Not to ruin your fun. Not to keep you from exploring. But to keep you safe."

Owen's voice cracked. "I just wanted to see if the giraffe's tongue was purple…"

A long pause followed before Noah nodded and whispered, "It is."

Everyone chuckled, even Jenna, though her laugh came with a tear.

By the time they pulled into the driveway, the tension had softened, but it hadn't fully lifted. Not yet.

As Noah parked and turned off the engine, he reached over and squeezed Jenna's hand.

"We'll get through it," he said. "We're learning."

She nodded. "And we're buying another gate." By the time the Carter family pulled into the driveway, the sun had dipped low behind the rooftops, casting soft orange light across the front yard. The van doors opened with a familiar creak, and tired feet shuffled up the steps.

Jenna carried a sleepy Mya against her shoulder while Noah grabbed the stroller from the trunk. Owen, still unusually quiet, followed closely behind, while Theo and Levi exchanged looks that were just a little too mischievous.

As soon as the front door shut behind them, the teasing began.

"So…" Theo began, dragging out the word dramatically as he flopped onto the couch. "Should we start calling you 'Giraffe Boy' now?"

Levi grinned. "Or maybe 'Long Neck.' You know, since you almost became one of them."

Owen rolled his eyes, a faint smile tugging at the corner of his lips. "Ha-ha. Funny."

"You're lucky you didn't fall in," Theo said, nudging him with a pillow. "That giraffe probably would've thought you were a snack."

Jenna walked by, shooting the boys a playful glare. "Ease up, you two. He learned his lesson."

"But Mom," Levi said with mock seriousness, "he almost joined the zoo's animal cast. You can't expect us to ignore that."

"Goodnight, not-so-funny children," Jenna called over her shoulder, disappearing into the hallway with Mya.

Inside the nursery, the soft lavender walls were dimly lit by a star-shaped nightlight. Mya blinked sleepily as Jenna placed her gently into the crib and tucked a plush bunny beside her.

Jenna sat in the rocking chair, pulled out her favorite story of a yellow cloud, and read softly.

"Yellow bird, Yellow cloud, I love you! Do you love me?…"

Mya's tiny hands played with the edge of her blanket as her mother's voice lulled her. Her eyes began to flutter closed.

When the last page turned, Jenna leaned over and kissed her forehead.

"Sleep sweet, baby girl."

She turned on the white noise machine and tiptoed out, leaving the door cracked open just a sliver.

In the main bedroom, Noah had already changed into his T-shirt and gym shorts. He was lying on his side of the bed, scrolling mindlessly on his phone, though he wasn't reading anything. Jenna slid under the covers next to him, her body finally starting to relax.

But neither of them spoke at first. The weight of the day still sat quietly between them.

Finally, Noah broke the silence.

"I can't stop thinking about it."

"Me neither," Jenna replied, staring at the ceiling. "It keeps playing in my head... his foot slipping, the way he leaned in. My chest still feels tight."

"I keep wondering what would've happened if that guy wasn't there," Noah said, his voice low and thick. "I froze for a second. That's the part I hate the most. That second, I froze."

"You didn't freeze," Jenna said softly. "You ran to him. You grabbed him. You were there."

"But I was a second too late. That attendant..." Noah stopped and swallowed hard. "He got there first. God knew we needed him."

Jenna turned her head toward him. "We didn't even get his name."

Noah nodded. "Doesn't matter. God sent him."

A long pause settled between them, not heavy this time, but reverent.

"Could've been so different," Jenna whispered.

"But it wasn't," Noah said, reaching over to take her hand. "Owen's in his bed right now. Safe. Breathing. Laughing about giraffes. That's grace, Jen."

Tears welled in her eyes, not from fear this time, but from gratitude.

"I told God thank you when I laid Mya down just now."

"Me too," Noah said, squeezing her hand gently. "We're not perfect parents. But we're trying. And I think... I think He sees that."

They lay in silence, side by side, fingers intertwined.

In the next room, the hum of the baby monitor filled the quiet. The house, finally, was still.

And as sleep began to settle in, Jenna whispered one final thought into the soft darkness:

"Thank you, Lord... for watching what we can't always see."

Chapter 3
A Voice Unfolding

Saturday mornings at the Carter household, it smelled like pancakes, maple syrup, and competition.

In the heart of suburban Chelseaville, the family home buzzed with energy as sunlight poured through the expansive kitchen windows. Jenna stood at the stove flipping golden pancakes while Noah, dressed in sweats and a T-shirt from last year's Turkey Trot, poured orange juice into tall glasses. The boys were already halfway through their second plates.

"Don't eat like wolves," Jenna warned, eyeing Levi as he shoved a syrup-drenched bite into his mouth.

"We have practiced this morning, Mom," Levi mumbled through a mouthful, "we're fueling up."

"We don't eat like animals just because we have sports," she replied with a smirk. "We still chew like humans."

Theo, now fourteen and taller than Jenna by nearly a head, laughed as he reached for another pancake. His dark curls flopped over his forehead, and he smelled faintly of grass and sweat even before morning drills. Levi, thirteen, was all muscle and motion...always in a hurry, always hungry.

Across the table, Owen, ten, sat with perfect posture, meticulously cutting his pancake into perfect squares. Golf had taught him patience and precision. He wore his Chelseaville Elementary golf hoodie like a badge of honor.

And then there was Mya, sitting at the end of the table in her booster seat, legs swinging back and forth, pink bows perched in her soft curls. At just three years old, she already had a flair for the drama. Her breakfast pancake had been rearranged into a smiling face with blueberries for eyes, and she was humming softly to it, utterly oblivious to the noise around her.

"Do you hear that?" Jenna asked, pausing at the stove.

Noah looked up from his seat beside Mya. "She's humming again."

"I'm not humming," Mya said proudly. "I'm singing hello to Mr. Pancake."

Everyone at the table chuckled.

"Can we get her on the national anthem for our next game?" Theo joked, nudging Levi.

"She's got better pitch than you," Levi teased, dodging a flick from Theo's spoon.

"Careful," Jenna said. "You're all gonna be working for her one day when she's famous."

Mya tilted her head. "What's famous?"

"It means you sing loud, and people clap," Owen said.

Mya beamed. "I already do that!"

After breakfast, the boys packed their gym bags while Noah and Jenna helped Mya into her pink backpack with the sparkly butterfly zippers. It was a special day, her first whole week at preschool, and although she was excited, Jenna could see the slight nervous flutter in her daughter's eyes.

"You're going to do great," she whispered, buckling Mya into the car seat. "Just be yourself and remember, use your words."

"Can I use my singing words too?" Mya asked with a grin.

"Especially those," Jenna replied, kissing her on the forehead.

At drop-off, preschool was alive with colorful cubbies, squeals of laughter, and the faint smell of graham crackers. Mya clung to her mom's hand for a moment, wide-eyed as she took in the classroom full of new faces, blocks, books, and singing animals on the rug.

A warm voice greeted them at the door. "Good morning! And you must be Mya."

The woman was tall, with silver streaks in her curly hair and a smile that made Mya's shoulders drop slightly. Her name tag read Ms. Talbot.

"She's a little shy at first," Jenna said.

"Aren't we all?" Ms. Talbot replied. "But she'll warm up in no time."

Before Jenna could say another word, Mya's eyes landed on a basket of toy microphones sitting on a nearby shelf. Her grip loosened.

"I can sing with those?" she asked.

"Absolutely," Ms. Talbot said with a twinkle in her eye. "Those are our 'Big Voice' tools. Would you like to try?"

Mya nodded quickly and released her mother's hand, toddling toward the basket as though it had been calling her name.

Jenna watched for another few moments, heart swelling and tightening all at once. Then she turned and walked out, whispering a silent prayer as she always did when leaving her babies somewhere new.

By mid-morning, Mya had claimed her spot near the reading carpet and was already making her mark.

While other children fumbled with puzzles or built towers with blocks, Mya hummed her way through every activity, building, painting, and even snack time. It wasn't loud or distracting. It was just... constant. And in tune.

Ms. Talbot smiled to herself as she sat beside Mya during a coloring activity. "You know, Miss Mya, you're going to be a singer one day."

Mya didn't answer, just kept coloring a purple lion with a perfectly content look on her face. She had no clue what Ms. Talbot meant. Her three-year-old world didn't include ambition or careers. To her, singing was just how she breathed.

But the words stuck in the air, almost like a prophecy.

After circle time, while other children were rubbing their eyes and settling down on mats, Mya sang softly to her stuffed bunny as she lay him on a pretend pillow.

"Shhh... bunny's sleeping... go to sleep..."

Ms. Talbot quietly scribbled a note in her journal: Mya hums melodies during nearly every task, strong tonal memory. Encouragement may help with vocal confidence.

When Jenna returned that afternoon, Mya ran to her with wide arms.

"Mommy! We made paper cats and sang about the moon!"

"You sang about the moon?" Mom smiled as she scooped her up.

"I made the cat purple. Ms. Talbot says I'm gonna be a singer!"

Jenna's brow lifted as she looked toward Ms. Talbot.

"She's got a natural ear," the teacher said warmly. "She doesn't miss a note."

Jenna glanced down at her daughter, who was now humming a tune that sounded suspiciously like a familiar song, but with made-up lyrics about pancakes and bunnies.

"Well," Jenna whispered, pressing her cheek to Mya's curls, "sounds like someone's finding her voice."

As the garage door opened and the SUV eased into the driveway, Mya was already unbuckling her seatbelt and chattering away from the back seat.

"Mommy, Ms. Talbot said I'm gonna be a singer!" she announced again, clutching a paper cat covered in glitter.

Jenna smiled and glanced in the rearview mirror. "She sure did. She said, "You have a strong voice, and you sing through everything.""

They walked into the house, the smell of spaghetti and garlic bread greeting them from the kitchen. Noah stood at the stove, stirring sauce while the boys sat around the table, thumbing through their playbooks and elbowing each other.

Jenna placed her purse on the counter and looked toward her husband. "You'll never believe what Ms. Talbot said today."

Noah raised an eyebrow. "She says Mya was trying to direct the preschool choir?"

"Close," Jenna laughed. "She said she's going to be a singer one day. Said she's never seen a child with such natural pitch and tone."

Noah looked down at Mya, who twirled in the middle of the living room like a ballerina, humming the same tune she'd made up at school. He chuckled. "She does hum everywhere we go."

Levi scoffed at the table. "She can't sing. She's only three."

"Levi," Jenna said firmly, turning toward him. "Be kind."

"But it's true!" Levi shrugged. "She's just a baby."

Noah set the spoon down and leaned on the counter. "So were you when you started throwing a football, son. Just because she's young doesn't mean it's not real."

Theo looked up from his binder. "She does sing a lot. And she doesn't sound bad."

Mya climbed into her booster seat at the table and picked up her sippy cup. "I like singing. It makes my belly feel happy."

Noah grinned. "That's how I feel watching you kids do anything you love."

That Saturday, the family filled two rows of the Chelseaville Junior High Academy stadium bleachers. The sun beamed high above the field, where Theo and Levi stood in formation, shoulder pads wide and helmets gleaming. The crowd buzzed with energy…parents chatting, cheerleaders chanting, little siblings tugging at snow cone wrappers.

Jenna sat beside Noah in the second row, with Mya perched on her lap, wearing her mini pom-poms and glittery sneakers.

"I hope Levi remembered to stretch," Jenna said, shielding her eyes from the sun.

"He'll be fine," Noah replied. "He was doing jumping jacks before we even left the house."

When the announcer's voice came over the loudspeaker, the stadium quieted.

"Ladies and gentlemen, please rise for the singing of our national anthem."

The opening notes rang through the speakers, bold and familiar.

Mya sat up straight, her little lips parting. Then, soft and sure, she began to hum perfectly in sync with the melody. Her small voice followed every note, not missing a single shift in tone or timing. She clutched her stuffed bunny in one arm, the other waving a pom-pom in rhythm.

A woman sitting behind them leaned forward and whispered, "She's going to be a natural. You hear that pitch?"

Jenna turned to look at Noah.

He was already looking at her.

Their eyes met, and in that split second, neither spoke, but the message was clear.

They heard it too.

Not just the sweetness of her humming, but the control. The instinct. The music is living inside her.

After the anthem ended and the crowd erupted in cheers, Mya clapped along and giggled.

"She's not just humming," Jenna said quietly. "She's connecting to it. Feeling it."

Noah nodded slowly, emotion building behind his calm exterior. "It's in her, just like the game is in the boys. It's not something you teach. It's given."

Jenna looked out at the field, watching their sons line up for the kickoff. "The boys are natural athletes. They move like they were born in a field. But Mya... Mya's different."

"She's gifted with sound," Noah said softly. "And with heart."

He reached for Jenna's hand and gave it a gentle squeeze.

Then he spoke aloud, not just to his wife, but as if he were anchoring the moment in faith.

"But unto every one of us is given grace according to the measure of the gift of Christ."

Ephesians 4:7 KJV

Jenna exhaled, her heart full.

She glanced down at Mya, who was now swinging her legs and singing a song in a new, made-up rhythm, utterly unaware of how she was already changing the atmosphere around her.

Jenna rested her head lightly against Noah's shoulder.

"She's going to move mountains one day," she whispered.

Noah smiled. "One note at a time." That evening, after a long day filled with sports, sunshine, and one unforgettable rendition of the national anthem, the Carter house settled into its familiar nighttime rhythm.

The boys were upstairs winding down, though "winding down" in the Carter household usually meant stomping around in sock slides, tossing footballs into laundry baskets, and arguing over who got the last chocolate chip cookie. But down the hall, in the smallest bedroom with lavender curtains and glow-in-the-dark stars on the ceiling, the mood was much softer.

Jenna sat on the edge of Mya's bed, smoothing the covers around her little frame. Mya held her plush bunny tight, her eyes heavy but still bright.

"Can I sing you a song, Mommy?" she asked.

Mom smiled, brushing a curl from Mya's forehead. "Of course, baby. Sing me something sweet."

Mya sat up just enough to rest her back against the pillow. Her tiny voice filled the room like a gentle breeze. She sang a familiar tune with perfect pitch.

Her pitch was tender and unshaken, her tempo steady and sincere. There was no performance in her voice, love, a lullaby wrapped in faith and innocence.

Mom's eyes welled with tears as she listened, her heart caught somewhere between wonder and worship.

When Mya reached the final note, she whispered, "Amen," and lay back down.

Mom leaned over and kissed her cheek. "That was the most beautiful thing I've ever heard."

From the hallway, a quiet voice interrupted.

"I guess... she can sing a little bit."

Mom turned her head and saw Levi standing just outside the doorway, arms crossed and trying not to look too impressed.

"Just a little bit, huh?" she teased.

Levi shrugged, stepping into the room. "I mean, for a three-year-old."

Mom smiled. "Thank you for saying that."

Levi walked over and gently placed Mya's bunny closer to her face. "Goodnight, Mini Popstar."

Mya giggled sleepily. "Night, Levi."

As he left the room, Mom whispered a prayer under her breath, pulling the covers snug around Mya one last time.

"Thank You, Lord, for her voice... and the heart You've put behind it."

She turned off the lamp, leaving only the soft glow of the ceiling stars and the warmth of a melody still lingering in the quiet.

Mya drifted to sleep humming the same song, notes like petals, falling gently into the night.

Chapter 4
Candles and Consequences

The smell of frosted cupcakes and barbecue chicken wings drifted through the Carter house like a holiday morning. Pink and lavender streamers hung from every corner, and a giant glittery banner stretched across the dining room: "Happy 5th Birthday, Mya!" Sparkling balloons floated near the ceiling, and a table near the window overflowed with wrapped presents in colorful paper and curly ribbons.

Mya sat on a princess-themed cushion in the middle of it all, her pink party dress poofed around her like a cupcake liner, and a small paper crown sliding down one side of her curls. She didn't say much, just smiled politely every time someone handed her a gift or complimented her curls.

"She's so sweet," Aunt Rachel said, kneeling to take a picture with Mya. "And growing like a weed!"

Mya gave a soft smile but leaned shyly into her mom's side.

"She still doesn't love being the center of attention," Jenna said warmly. "But she's been humming since breakfast."

Noah chuckled from the grill outside. "That's how you know she's happy."

Inside, cousins ran wild through the hallway, chasing balloons and spilling chips across the floor. Theo and Levi had retreated to the backyard with a football, while Owen, who was now ten and fiercely competitive, was trying to impress his cousin Michael with his miniature golf swing in the living room.

"Watch this, Michael. It's all in the wrist," Owen said, holding the kid-sized club like a pro.

Dad appeared in the doorway just as the club whooshed inches from a lamp. "Owen," he said, stern but calm, "put the golf club away. This is not the place for that."

"I'm just showing him how to grip it, Dad," Owen replied, twisting the club backward.

"You've been told twice," Dad warned. "Please. Put it. Away.

Owen groaned and nodded, but instead of putting it back in the closet, he kept twirling it like a baton.

Then it happened.

With a sharp swing and a loud crack, the plastic club smacked Michael square across the nose. The room fell silent as Michael stumbled back, both hands covering his face.

Blood started dripping between his fingers.

"Ow! You hit me!" Michael cried.

Owen froze, panic spreading across his face. "I didn't mean to! I swear!"

Mom rushed in with a wad of paper towels while Aunt Rachel pulled Michael gently to the kitchen sink.

Dad stepped forward with the slow, deliberate calm that came only when he was mad.

"I asked you three times."

"I didn't think I was swinging that hard," Owen said, his voice breaking.

"That's the problem, you weren't thinking."

Owen's eyes filled with tears as he looked down at the club in his hand. "I didn't mean to hurt him."

Dad reached for the club and gently pulled it from Owen's grip. "It doesn't matter. You did. And when we don't listen, people get hurt. Now sit in the living room. You're done playing for the day."

"But it's Mya's birthday…"

"You can join the party again after we sing to your sister. Right now, I need you to sit and think about what just happened."

Owen sulked into the living room, flopping onto the couch with his arms crossed. He could still hear the party laughter from the kitchen, the ripping of wrapping paper, and Mya's quiet thank-yous.

Back at the center of it all, Mya picked at the hem of her dress. Despite the loud cousins and camera flashes, she hadn't said much. That was just her way. Even at five, she was more of an observer than a performer.

But she had her moments, especially when the music was on, or when Mom or Dad leaned in and whispered, "You don't have to be loud to be strong."

She perked up when her brothers returned to the kitchen, followed by Dad carrying the birthday cake, a vanilla round with strawberry filling and tiny pink flowers. Five candles flickered on top, casting a golden glow across the frosting.

"Alright, everyone!" Jenna called. "Time to sing to the birthday girl!"

Everyone gathered around the kitchen table as Mya climbed onto the chair reserved just for her. She looked up at the flames, nervous, a little bashful, but smiling.

"Come on in, Owen," Dad called from the kitchen doorway.

Owen appeared slowly, hands in his pockets, his face still blotchy. He walked over and stood beside the table, eyes on the cake, then on Mya.

"I'm sorry I missed everything," he said softly.

"You can sing now," Mya whispered.

Then the room erupted into a warm chorus of "Happy Birthday to you…"

Mya swayed gently as they sang, her fingers curling around the edge of the table. When it was done, she took a breath and blew out all five candles without hesitation.

Cheers filled the room. Someone clapped. Another cousin yelled, "Cake time!"

Levi leaned over to Theo and whispered, "Okay... so maybe she can sing a little bit."

"Dude, she didn't even sing," Theo smirked.

Levi shrugged. "She hummed. And she looked cute while doing it. I guess that counts."

Jenna glanced over at Noah, who was watching Mya with his arm draped around her shoulders.

"She's still shy," Jenna whispered, "but her light's getting stronger."

Noah smiled. "It's already in her. She doesn't know how bright it is yet."

As the sun dipped low over Chelseaville, casting soft gold light through the windows, the Carter home slowly quieted. The echoes of laughter and stomping feet faded, replaced by the occasional rustle of plastic wrap as leftovers were packed, balloons popped, and paper plates were stacked in the trash.

Guests began hugging each other goodbye. Aunt Rachel gently guided Michael, still sniffling but mostly recovered, toward the front door.

"It's okay," Michael said bravely to his mom. "I think I still like Owen."

Dad stood on the porch with Cousin Chris, shaking his hand again. "Man, I'm sorry about what happened. He wasn't trying to hurt anyone."

Chris nodded. "I get it. He's just got to learn when to turn it off. You know how some folks in the family get, though..."

Noah raised an eyebrow. "Yeah. I heard a few whispers."

"They're just being old-school judgmental," Chris said with a shrug. "Still, it might help to tighten things up. Kids follow energy."

"I know," Noah replied, rubbing the back of his neck. "We're working on it."

Back inside, Grandma Rose, still in her lavender Sunday cardigan and low heels, was wiping down the kitchen table with a damp cloth, humming under her breath as she moved slowly and deliberately. When she looked up and saw Owen sneaking a second cupcake, she motioned with one finger.

"Boy, come here."

Owen sighed, cupcake still in hand. "I already said I was sorry, Grandma."

"Mmm-hmm," she replied, folding the cloth and drying her hands. "And now you're going to listen."

He dragged his feet as he approached her, shoulders already sagging.

She stepped close, eye to eye with him.

"Owen Charles Carter, you are a good boy. But today you acted foolishly. When your father tells you to put something down three times, and you don't, what are you saying?"

"That I wasn't listening," he muttered.

"No. What you're saying is, 'I know better than my father.' And that is dangerous," she said, tapping her index finger on his forehead. "Especially when you're swinging a club around people's faces."

Owen looked at the floor. "I didn't want to hurt Michael."

"You didn't want to, but you did. And a real man owns what he causes, not just what he intended. Understand me?"

He nodded quietly.

She leaned in and hugged him. "You're still my sweetheart. But don't make me raise my voice next time. I've still got it."

He laughed a little. "Yes, ma'am."

Then Grandma Rose turned her attention to Mya, who was sitting on the couch with her doll, softly humming again, unaware that her voice had already made more impact than she could understand.

Grandma Rose walked over and knelt gently.

"Mya baby," she said, brushing a curl from the little girl's forehead. "That song you sang to your mama last night, it stayed in my ears all day."

Mya blinked shyly, gripping her doll tighter. "Mama told you about the song?"

"She sure did. And I think the Lord heard it too."

Mya looked confused but flattered. She tilted her head.

"I think," Grandma Rose continued, "it's time you sang at church one Sunday morning."

Mom's eyes widened from the kitchen. "Oh, Mama... she's only five."

"She's ready," Grandma Rose said firmly.

Dad walked back in from the porch. "You think so?"

"I know so. Don't be afraid just because she's small. David was small. Jeremiah was young. The Lord doesn't wait for birthdays to use somebody."

Mom sat on the edge of the couch. "She's just never sung in front of people like that before. It's a lot of pressure."

"She doesn't have to perform," Grandma Rose replied gently. "She just has to sing. There's a difference. Noah crossed his arms thoughtfully. "We don't want to push her."

"We're not pushing," Grandma Rose said with a smile. "We're planting."

Mya looked between the adults, unsure if they were still talking about her. She crawled up into her mom's lap and whispered, "Can I sing with the microphones at church?"

Mom hugged her close. "You'd like that?"

Mya nodded slowly. "Only if I can wear my shiny shoes."

Dad laughed. "Deal."

Grandma Rose stood slowly, smoothing her cardigan. "Well then, it's settled. Let the child praise Him. Let her start small and grow with her gift. Just like we all did with ours."

As the house returned to its late-evening stillness, Jenna and Noah exchanged a glance. There was nervousness in their eyes, but also a sense of peace.

Because maybe, just maybe, their little girl was starting to find her voice not just in song, but in purpose. That night, after the party quieted and Grandma Rose had gone upstairs to rest, Jenna and Noah sat on the edge of their bed, the house finally still around them.

"She's so little," Jenna whispered, toying with the hem of her pajama sleeve. "I don't want to overwhelm her."

Noah leaned back on his elbows. "But she's not scared. That counts for something."

"She doesn't even realize what she's carrying," Jenna added. "That voice... that gift... It's so big, but she's still so small."

"Exactly," Noah said with a soft smile. "Which means we don't teach her to fear it. We teach her to give it to God."

Jenna sighed, the tension finally leaving her shoulders. "Alright. Sunday it is."

Noah reached over and took her hand. "We let her sing."

Sunday morning arrived crisp and bright, sunlight pouring through the stained-glass windows of Red Riverstone Baptist Church. The sanctuary buzzed with greetings and rustling bulletins. The choir stood in their maroon robes, swaying lightly as the organ warmed up. Pastor Shaw sat in the pulpit chair with his holy scriptures resting across his lap.

Mya stood at the front, dressed in a white dress with tiny gold shoes, her curls pinned back with a pearl clip. She stood just behind the microphone, not fidgeting, just waiting. Grandma Rose sat proudly on the front pew, hands folded tightly, eyes glistening before a note had even been sung.

"Before the Word comes forth this morning," the choir director announced, "we have a very special soloist. Please welcome Miss Mya Carter, age five."

Whispers floated through the congregation, and a few raised eyebrows. But the room quieted as Mya stepped forward. The pianist played the opening chords of "Amazing Grace."

Her voice started soft. Pure. Steady.

"How sweet the sound..."

And then it grew richer, rounder, deeper than anyone expected. With every line, her tone carried not just melody but emotion well beyond her years. She wasn't performing. She was testifying. The notes filled the sanctuary like a prayer wrapped in velvet.

By the time she sang the final line:

"But now I see…"

There were sniffles and tears across the pews.

One deacon pulled a handkerchief from his jacket. A woman near the back rocked slightly, hands raised in silent worship. Even Pastor Shaw was visibly moved.

The moment Mya finished, the choir director gently stepped forward, touched her back, and directed her toward the pew where her family waited.

She padded down the steps, smiling shyly as the congregation gave a warm, stunned round of applause, not the loud clapping of a performance, but the reverent sound of hearts being touched.

She slid in between her mother and Grandma Rose and immediately rested her head on Grandma's shoulder. Grandma kissed her crown and whispered, "That's my girl."

Jenna wiped her eyes and whispered, "You were amazing."

Down the row, her brothers stared at her as they'd never seen her before.

Theo, now sixteen, leaned forward. "That was… wow."

Levi, fifteen, nodded slowly. "She really can sing."

Owen, twelve, grinned. "Okay. She's not just a singer. She's got power."

For once, they didn't tease. They didn't joke. They just sat in awe of their little sister, who had just turned five, and moved the congregation to tears.

After Pastor Shaw delivered his sermon, still visibly stirred, church members lined up to speak with the Carter family.

"Mya blessed my whole spirit," said one older woman, taking her mother's hand. "That child has an anointing."

"She's a worshipper," added another. "Don't ever let anyone dim that light."

Others turned to Noah. "You must be so proud. Are the boys into music too?"

"No," he chuckled, glancing at his sons, who stood proudly behind them. "They're more into touchdowns and tournaments."

"They're bright, respectful young men," said Deacon Howard, shaking each boy's hand. "Strong minds and strong gifts."

Jenna looked over at Noah, both of them glowing, not just with pride, but with something more profound. Gratitude.

But no one beamed brighter than Grandma Rose.

She sat nearby with her hands folded on her purse, watching every compliment like it confirmed what she already knew.

After all, she had believed in Mya's gift long before anyone else heard it.

"She's gonna do something mighty," Grandma whispered to herself.

And as Mya giggled beside her, climbing into her lap and hugging her neck, it was already beginning.

Chapter 5
A Light That Travels

The crayons were neatly lined up on Mya Carter's desk: blue, pink, yellow, and orange, and she was currently using the purple one to draw a picture of a big stage with sparkles floating in the air. In the center of the stage was a girl with a microphone and shiny shoes.

Ms. Mason walked around the kindergarten classroom with her usual gentle energy, but today, she kept glancing at Mya.

Yesterday at Red Riverstone Church, she had witnessed something she would never forget: Mya, tiny and delicate, singing a solo that left grown men in tears. The little girl didn't just sing. She ministered. Her voice was clear and powerful, but it was her spirit that moved the room.

That morning, in the teacher's lounge, the buzz was still alive.

"That Carter girl in Ms. Mason's class? Whew!" said Mrs. Douglas, the 3rd-grade teacher. "I nearly ruined my makeup."

"She's what, five?" asked the school counselor. "That voice belongs to someone twice her size."

"She sang like she's been here before," Ms. Mason said with a proud grin. "I want her in the school play."

Back in the classroom, Ms. Mason walked over to Mya's desk and knelt beside her.

"Mya," she said softly.

Mya looked up, her eyes wide. "Yes, Ms. Mason?"

"I was at church yesterday."

Mya blinked. "You were?"

"I was," Ms. Mason smiled. "And I heard your beautiful voice. I'm so proud of you."

Mya looked down shyly and colored the microphone on her picture gold.

"You have a gift, sweetheart. And I'd love for you to be in the school play in the spring."

Mya looked up again. "But that's for the big kids."

"I know," Ms. Mason said gently. "But this year, the sixth graders are doing Kinderella, and I spoke with the drama teacher. We'd like you to be the Fairy Godmother."

Mya gasped. "Do I get wings?"

Ms. Mason chuckled. "Yes. And a wand. And you get to sing a song on stage."

Mya clapped her hands quietly. "I know songs, and I love to sing!"

"I thought you might."

Ms. Mason stood up, her heart full. There was something special about this little girl. The special that didn't need attention, it just drew it, naturally.

Meanwhile, across town at Chelseaville Academy, each of Mya's older brothers was deep in the rhythm of their school day.

Theo Carter, now sixteen and in the 10th grade, walked through the tall double doors of Chelseaville Academy with his backpack slung over one shoulder and a football playbook sticking out of the side. He was smart, tall, and grounded, with a calm presence that earned him his teachers' trust and his teammates' respect.

During first-period honors literature, he found himself locked in a heated debate over a historical novel of dreams, destiny, and brotherhood clashing across the table like fire and flint. His insights were sharp and thoughtful; his teacher had even pulled him aside the previous week to suggest that he join the honors society.

At lunch, he sat at a corner table with his best friend, Jaylen, and two of the team's linemen, talking about Friday night's game.

"We gotta lock in," Theo said between bites of chicken nuggets. "Coach is watching film clips from the second quarter, and we missed at least three open routes."

Jaylen nodded. "Yeah, but you carried that final drive, bro. You're the only one who stays calm under pressure."

Theo shrugged, brushing it off. "I just do my job."

But when someone at the table asked, "Hey, wasn't your little sister the one who sang at Red Riverstone Church yesterday?" Theo grinned and nodded proudly.

"Yep. That was Mya."

Levi, now fifteen, was a freshman but already built like a junior. Fast, bold, and bursting with energy, he was the Carter child who thrived in motion. In Algebra, he tapped his pencil to a beat only he could hear. In Spanish, he cracked jokes with his partner while still getting every answer right.

He wasn't always the quietest in class, but he was sharp.

During gym, Levi led his team to victory in a fast-paced flag football scrimmage. Afterward, the coach pulled him aside.

"Have you ever considered track, Levi? With that speed, you could clean up in the 100-meter."

Levi just grinned. "Can I do both?"

He was the type who wanted it all. And somehow, he usually managed to make it work.

Later that day in homeroom, a classmate mentioned Mya's church solo.

"My mom said she sang better than half the people on those singing competitions," the boy said.

Levi grinned and nodded coolly. "That's my sister."

Owen, at twelve and in the 7th grade, was the quiet thinker. Always in a hoodie, always sketching in the corners of his notebooks when he wasn't practicing his golf swing. Academically, he was ahead, especially in science and math. His teacher had already recommended him for advanced placement courses in the spring.

During lunch, he sat under the bleachers with a few of his golf teammates, analyzing swings from the last tournament.

But that afternoon in his social studies class, his teacher paused to say, "Owen, is your sister Mya? Someone sent me a clip from church yesterday."

Owen's eyes widened. "Wait?"

"She's got something special."

Owen smiled faintly. "Yeah, we're just now figuring that out."

Back at Chelseaville Elementary, Mya's day ended with finger painting, snack time, and one final song as the class cleaned up.

"Who wants to lead the goodbye song?" Ms. Mason asked.

A few hands shot up.

But then, slowly, Mya raised hers.

"Go ahead, Mya."

And in her sweet, clear voice, Mya began:

Goodbye, goodbye, we'll see you soon...

The class joined in, swaying and singing.

But no one could deny it; her voice stood out.

Even at five, Mya Carter was a light that traveled from the kitchen to the church, to the classroom.

And now... to the stage.

As the final school bell rang, Ms. Mason wiped her hands on a tissue, smoothed the corner of her desk, and picked up her phone. She had been meaning to make this call all day.

She dialed the number from the emergency contact list and waited.

"Hello?" Jenna Carter answered, her voice warm and upbeat.

"Hi, Mrs. Carter. This is Ms. Mason, Mya's kindergarten teacher."

"Oh! Hello, Ms. Mason! Is everything alright?"

"Yes, everything's fine. Actually... better than fine," she chuckled. "I'm calling to talk to you about something exciting."

Jenna sat down at her drafting table, balancing the phone on her shoulder. "Go on."

"Well, as you know, Mya's voice left quite an impression on Sunday morning at church. It's been the talk of the teachers' lounge. We're doing a school-wide production of Kinderella this spring, six months from now, and we'd love to invite Mya to play the Fairy Godmother. She'd get a solo part to sing songs as the fairy godmother, and we'd work closely with her to help her feel comfortable."

Jenna raised her eyebrows and smiled softly. "Wow... that's quite the opportunity."

"I understand she's young, but we'll make accommodations. She wouldn't be overworked, just supported."

"Well, thank you for thinking of her. She'll be so excited," Jenna said. "I'd like to talk to her dad first before giving a definite answer. But we're honored you asked."

"Of course. Let me know when you've had a chance to discuss."

"Will do. Thank you again, Ms. Mason."

Jenna hung up. An hour later, she heard the front door swing open.

Noah's voice boomed from the hallway, "Everybody inside! Shoes off!"

The sound of backpacks hitting the floor, sneakers squeaking, and laughter filled the house again. Mya's small feet scurried across the hardwood as she burst into the living room.

"Mommy! Mommy! Ms. Mason wants me to be the Fairy Godmother in the school play!"

Jenna smiled knowingly. "Oh really?"

"I get wings and a wand! And a sparkly dress! And I get to sing!" Mya twirled around, arms stretched wide.

Noah stepped in from the hallway, keys in hand. "Wait, what? A play?"

Jenna stood up and gently filled him in on the details of the call. "They're doing Kinderella. Sixth grade leads. Ms. Mason wants to make an exception for Mya."

Noah blinked, clearly caught off guard. "Sixth grade? She's in kindergarten."

"She'd sing one song," Jenna added. "Ms. Mason promised it wouldn't be too much."

Before Noah could respond, Mya tugged on his sleeve with both hands. "Please, Daddy? Please, please, please? I wanna wear wings and sing at the show!"

He crouched to her level and kissed her forehead. "It's not a 'no,' sweetheart. But Mommy and I need to talk about it. That kind of thing is a big deal."

"But I already practiced the song!" she squealed.

Jenna and Noah exchanged a look that said everything: We need to think this through.

The evening progressed at its usual pace. The boys knocked out their homework at the kitchen table while half-watching sports clips on their tablets. Later, they tossed a football around in the yard and played video games once the sun dipped behind the trees.

Dinner consisted of Alfredo penne noodles with chicken, broccoli, spinach, and tomatoes, garlic toast, and a large salad. They all gathered around the table, laughing about Levi's bad Spanish accent and Theo's failed attempt at baking cookies in Home Economics.

"So," Dad said between bites, "I hear Mya's already in show business now."

The boys looked up, mildly amused.

"She gets to be the fairy godmother," Owen said. "She's got the big voice for it."

"She's gonna make the other kids sound like backup singers," Levi added.

"I think it's kinda cool," Theo said. "She's already doing what she loves."

Mya smiled proudly, Alfredo sauce on her cheek.

After dinner, the house began to quiet. Homework was done. Lunches packed. Teeth brushed. The older kids retreated to their rooms, and Mya was tucked into bed with her bunny and glittery dreams.

Later that night, Jenna and Noah lay in bed, just like always, side by side, finally breathing in the peace that came only after the house slowed down.

"I know she wants this," Jenna said softly, "but I'm still nervous. She's only five."

"I am, too," Noah replied, folding his arms under his head. "I don't want to say yes just because it feels good in the moment. We have to think long-term. We don't want her to feel like she has to perform just to be accepted."

"Exactly," Jenna whispered. "I want her to enjoy being a kid... and not feel pressure."

They sat in silence for a moment before Noah added, "But... It's a school play. It's fun. And Ms. Mason seems thoughtful about the whole thing."

"And she'd love it," Jenna said with a small smile. "She really would."

"I say we pray on it tonight and give Ms. Mason our answer tomorrow," Noah said.

Jenna nodded. "That sounds right."

And as they turned off the light, the sound of Mya's faint humming drifted from her room down the hallway, a tiny melody echoing in the night.

A sign that her gift wasn't going anywhere... and maybe, it was time to let it grow. The sun had barely stretched over the rooftops of Chelseaville when Jenna stood in the kitchen, coffee in hand, watching the light slip across the hardwood floor. The morning calm wrapped itself around her like a warm shawl.

She pulled out her phone and tapped the number saved under Ms. Mason, Mya's kindergarten teacher.

"Good morning!" Ms. Mason answered cheerfully.

"Good morning, Ms. Mason. This is Jenna Carter."

"Oh! Hello, Mrs. Carter!"

"I wanted to let you know that we talked about it as a family," Jenna said, her voice warm but steady. "And we'd be honored to let Mya participate in the Kinderella play this spring."

There was a delighted pause. "Oh, that's wonderful news! Thank you so much, Mrs. Carter. She's going to be a perfect Fairy Godmother."

"We trust you'll take care of her and keep things balanced," Jenna added. "She's still our baby."

"Absolutely," Ms. Mason assured her. "We'll make this a joyful experience for her."

After they hung up, Jenna turned and smiled to herself. But she wasn't finished.

She poured a second cup of coffee and stepped into the quiet dining room to make one more call, the one her spirit insisted on.

"Hey, Mama," she said as Grandma Rose picked up on the first ring.

"I figured you'd be calling me first thing," her mother said. "My spirit told me this morning."

"She's doing it," Jenna said softly. "The school play. We're letting her sing."

There was no pause. No hesitation.

"Then you thank the Lord with everything in you," Grandma Rose said. "Don't wait until opening night. Don't wait until the applause. You give Him thanks now."

Jenna closed her eyes, emotion swelling in her chest.

"Yes, ma'am."

Then Grandma Rose's voice, consistently strong but wrapped in velvet, began to quote the Word:

"O give thanks unto the Lord, for He is good:

For His mercy endureth forever."

Psalm 107:1 KJV

Jenna whispered, "Amen."

And in that sacred morning stillness, the Carter family's next chapter quietly began not just with a role or a song, but with gratitude for the gift, the journey, and the God who gave both.

Chapter 6
Wings and Words

Every Saturday morning for the past three weeks, Mya Carter had traded her cartoons and cereal for stage lights and script pages.

While most five-year-olds were still rubbing sleep from their eyes, Mya was lacing up her glittery ballet flats and pulling on a soft lavender practice dress, her rehearsal outfit for the role of the Fairy Godmother in the spring production of Kinderella.

The older kids from sixth grade had welcomed her shyly at first, unsure how a kindergartner would fit in. But once Mya opened her mouth to sing, all hesitation vanished. Her version of each fairy godmother song floated through the elementary school auditorium like sunlight through stained glass, sweet, warm, and captivating.

"Let's take it from the top," the drama teacher, Ms. Perry, called out, standing near the footlights. "Mya, remember to stretch your arms like you're sprinkling magic, not swatting flies."

Mya nodded thoughtfully, lifting her imaginary wand with both hands.

One of the sixth-grade girls leaned over and whispered, "She's kind of amazing."

By the end of rehearsal, Mya's cheeks were flushed, her crown slightly askew, but she was glowing from the inside out.

When Dad picked her up from rehearsal, she climbed into the back seat still humming. Her wings were drooping a little, and glitter clung to her forehead, but she was proud. Her bag of snacks sat beside her, untouched.

"You have fun, fairy girl?" he asked with a grin.

"I made a wish and turned Melissa's dress into sparkles!" Mya said, waving her wand.

He chuckled. "You turned the whole room into sparkles, baby."

Back at home, the boys were already gathered in the living room. Theo had just finished a biology project on the computer, and Owen was organizing his golf gear in the corner. Levi, the ever-vocal jokester, was stretched out on the couch with a sports drink in hand.

When Mya walked in with her wings still strapped on and her lavender rehearsal dress a bit wrinkled, Levi raised an eyebrow and smirked.

"What in the world are you wearing?" he asked, half-laughing.

"It's my costume," Mya said proudly. "I'm the Fairy Godmother."

Levi sat up dramatically. "You look more like a... flying mosquito."

Theo let out a low "bruh."

Mya's smile faltered. She looked down at her dress, tugging at the frilly hem.

Before she could say anything, Dad stepped into the room, face firm and tone sharp.

"Levi."

Levi's grin faded. "What? I was kidding."

Dad didn't raise his voice, but every word was heavy with meaning. "We don't tear down our family, especially not with jokes dressed up as compliments."

"I didn't mean it like that," Levi said quickly.

"I don't care how you meant it. What matters is how it landed. Look at your sister."

Levi turned. Mya was still holding her wand, eyes now lowered to the floor.

"Levi," Dad said again, softer this time, "we protect her. We cheer her on. That's what big brothers do. If you can't say something that lifts her, keep it to yourself."

There was a long pause.

Then Levi stood and walked over to Mya.

"Sorry, Peanut," he said. "You don't look like a mosquito. You look like... like you flew in from a sparkly cloud or something."

Mya blinked at him, then gave a slow smile.

"Okay," she said. "But I'm not a peanut. I'm a fairy."

Dad chuckled, finally easing. "That's better."

As the room returned to its usual rhythm, Theo reached over and plucked some glitter off Mya's wing. "Just don't fly into my room. I need peace in there."

Mya giggled, lifted her wand, and tapped him lightly on the shoulder. "Back off, brothers."

Everyone laughed, even Levi.

And in that small but significant moment, the Carter family took one more step in learning how to honor the light within each of them.

The Carter family had arrived at Grandma Rose's house like they always did on the first Sunday of the month, arms full of Tupperware, banana pudding, and sleepy smiles. The scent of roasted chicken, collard greens, and sweet cornbread filled every corner of the house. Gospel music played low in the background as laughter and footsteps echoed through the hallway.

The dining table, covered in a lace cloth with matching floral napkins, was nearly too full for plates. Grandma Rose always cooked as though she expected ten extra guests.

As the family gathered around the table, Mya sat proudly between Mom and Grandma Rose, still humming bits of the musical under her breath.

Her sparkly wand rested in her purse; even though they weren't at rehearsal, she never went anywhere without it now.

Grandma Rose scooped some macaroni onto Mya's plate and leaned in with a warm smile. "Alright now, baby girl, how's my star doing?"

Mya beamed. "I love rehearsal, Grandma! We practice every Saturday, and Ms. Perry says I know all my lines already!"

"She does," Jenna added. "And she hasn't missed a single Saturday."

"Three months straight," Noah said proudly. "And she still wakes up before the alarm."

Grandma Rose reached for her sweet tea and raised an eyebrow at Levi across the table. "And how are we doing? Still behaving like a proper big brother?"

Levi smiled sheepishly. "Yes, ma'am. No more mosquito jokes."

Theo chuckled into his water glass.

"She's working hard," Grandma said, turning back to Mya. "But more importantly, she's doing it with joy. That's how you know it's from the Lord."

"I feel happy when I sing," Mya said, chewing on a buttered roll. "Even if I mess up."

"You won't mess up," Grandma Rose said gently. "And even if you do, He'll use it. That voice is wrapped in purpose."

Owen looked up from his plate. "Do we get to miss school on the day of the play?"

"No," Mom said, without missing a beat. "Nice try."

"But we are all going," Dad added. "Whole row reserved. I already talked to Principal Johnson."

"Ms. Perry said they might let Mya close the first act," Mom said. "She's never had a kindergartner open a scene before."

"Don't that beat all," Grandma Rose said, shaking her head in awe. "Five years old and already walking in her calling."

Then she grew quiet, her eyes gently fixed on her granddaughter.

"You just stay close to Jesus, baby girl. You keep singing for Him first. Not for applause. Not for praise. But for Him."

"I will," Mya nodded, picking up her plastic wand and tapping it on her cornbread. "This is for Jesus."

Everyone laughed.

After dinner, the family moved to the living room, where Grandma insisted on taking "practice pictures" for the play, lining everyone up like it was already opening night. The boys groaned but smiled anyway.

Dad looked around the room and saw his family: strong sons, a glowing wife, a faithful mother-in-law, and a five-year-old girl with a calling far bigger than her age.

Three months to go.

But her story had already started.

And the whole family was beginning to realize... they weren't just watching her shine. They were part of the light. The Carter house had settled into its usual calm after Sunday dinner, after leaving Grandma's house. The boys were upstairs: Theo finishing last-minute touch-ups on a science paper due on Monday, Levi watching football highlights on his tablet, and Owen sprawled across his bed, sketching swing angles from the last golf meet. Mya had already fallen asleep on the couch with her wand clutched in her hand and glitter on her cheek.

Mom and Dad sat in the living room, the soft glow of the lamp casting golden light around them. Noah's arm rested behind Jenna on the back of the couch, and they were mid-conversation about the school play when Jenna's phone buzzed.

She glanced at the screen and raised an eyebrow.

"It's Ms. Mason," she said, sitting up a little straighter.

"On a Sunday night?" Noah asked.

She answered. "Hello?"

"Hi, Mrs. Carter, sorry to call so late. I hope I'm not interrupting anything."

"No, not at all," Jenna replied. "Everything okay?"

"Yes. There's a community event happening this Saturday evening at the Falling Rock Community Center, a mid-size gathering for senior residents and volunteers. Just a couple of hours long, nothing too fancy. One of the performers had to cancel, and we were wondering... would Mya be willing to sing a short solo?"

Jenna blinked. "This Saturday?"

"Yes. I know it's last-minute, but it would be a wonderful opportunity, low pressure, local crowd. I was thinking of Amazing Grace. She's already familiar with it, and I believe her voice would truly move the crowd."

Jenna glanced at Mya, who stirred briefly on the couch but didn't wake.

"She's never sung in front of seniors before," Jenna said. "But... it could be good prep for the play."

"She doesn't have to wear a fancy dress or anything, just be herself."

Jenna nodded slowly. "Okay. I'll talk to my husband now, but I think we're on board."

Ms. Mason sighed with relief. "Thank you so much. I'll email you the details tonight."

Jenna ended the call and set the phone down.

Noah looked at her. "What was that about?"

She smiled softly. "Ms. Mason wants Mya to sing Amazing Grace at a community event this weekend for seniors and volunteers. One of the performers canceled, and they need someone to fill in."

"Wow," Noah said, letting the words settle in the room. "That's soon."

"She said it's a mid-size event. Nothing high pressure."

"She's five," he reminded gently.

"I know," Jenna replied. "But this isn't the first time she's sung in front of people. And it's not about impressing anyone. It's about preparing her. Trusting the gift."

Noah looked at Mya, sleeping peacefully with her tiny hand still resting over her chest.

"You think she's ready?" he asked.

"I think... she wants to be."

Noah nodded. "Then let's give her a chance."

Jenna leaned her head on his shoulder. "She's going to be okay, right?"

"She's going to be more than okay," he said. "She's walking in what she was born with."

They sat in silence for a few moments, just listening to the soft hum of the house.

And then Jenna whispered, almost to herself, "Amazing grace, how sweet the sound..."

Mya didn't stir, but a faint smile appeared on her face.

It was settled. The week had been long, heavy, and packed to the brim for the Carter household.

Noah had just wrapped up a demanding stretch at the bank, processing multiple loan applications for small businesses while juggling staff training and back-to-back client meetings. He hadn't even eaten lunch on Thursday, and by Friday afternoon, his shirt collar felt like it was made of sandpaper.

Jenna, on the other hand, had just submitted the final rendering for her latest project with Blue Meber and Red Meber Design Studio, a full redesign for the local mall renovation, complete with skylights, green space, and a sleek, modern layout that took nearly four weeks of revisions to perfect.

By the time the last school bell rang that Friday, the Carter kids burst out of their classrooms with more energy than their parents combined.

"School's out!" Levi shouted as he climbed into the backseat of the SUV.

"Forever!" Owen added dramatically, even though he knew it was only for the weekend.

Theo, still in his football hoodie and always the most composed, chuckled and plugged in his headphones as he slid into the passenger seat. "I'm just glad I don't have to write another essay for at least 48 hours."

In the far back seat, Mya bounced with excitement, legs swinging in her pink leggings. "Guess what, guess what, guess what?" she sang.

Mom glanced at her through the rearview mirror. "You're singing at the community center tomorrow?"

"Yes!" Mya squealed. "And I practiced it all week! Listen... 'Amaaaaazing graaaace...'"

The boys glanced at one another silently, their faces saying what their mouths didn't.

They'd heard Amazing Grace approximately forty-three times that week. At breakfast. In the car. During homework. Once, even in the hallway at 6:30 a.m.

But they said nothing.

Because Dad's words still echoed in their minds: "We encourage each other in this house. Even when we're tired, even when it's not our thing, we support our family."

And so, they nodded, smiled, and let Mya finish the first verse, again.

As they pulled into the driveway, Jenna turned and said, "I don't know about y'all, but I am not cooking tonight."

"I second that," Dad mumbled, loosening his tie.

"Let's get pizza from the local place around the corner," Theo offered.

"Oh yeah!" Owen agreed. "They make the crust from scratch."

"Sold," Jenna said, already dialing. "Three large pizzas, thirty BBQ wings, and two orders of breadsticks from the pizza shop, it is."

By 6:15 PM, the Carter family was gathered around the coffee table, passing plates and licking fingers as the smell of homemade garlic crust and bubbling cheese filled the living room.

Never disappointed.

They had barely finished eating when Mom flipped on the family movie night pick, an animated comedy about a talking horse and his dream to be a football player, which seemed fitting.

Mya cuddled between Mom and Grandma Rose, who'd stopped by after holy scriptures study just in time for dessert.

"Your voice ready for tomorrow?" Grandma asked, handing her a juice pouch.

"I've been practicing all week, Grandma," Mya said with sleepy confidence.

"I know, baby. I've heard it through the phone, three nights in a row," Grandma chuckled.

Noah rested his feet on the ottoman and wrapped his arm around Jenna's shoulder. "I think she's more prepared than any of us ever were for anything."

"Except maybe Levi," Jenna teased. "He's always prepared to eat."

"I am," Levi said proudly, reaching for a leftover chicken wing.

The room filled with laughter, warmth, and the kind of peace that only comes from simply being together.

And as the night wore on, the movie flickered across the screen, Mya fell asleep against her mother's side, her little voice mumbling one final time before drifting off.

And not a single boy rolled his eyes.

Because tomorrow, she wouldn't just be singing at the Falling Rock Community Center.

She'd be singing with purpose. With family. And with grace. As Saturday evening settled over the community center, the building buzzed with warm conversations, folding chairs shifting on the hardwood floor, and the scent of potluck dishes lingering from earlier in the day. Seniors and volunteers filled the room, many holding paper cups of sweet tea or lemonade, eager for the night's final performance. A quiet hush fell as Ms. Mason stepped to the podium.

"Tonight," she said with a gentle smile, "we have a very special young lady who's going to close out our event. Her name is Mya Carter, and I believe, no, I know, her voice is a gift from God."

The audience clapped politely, turning their attention to the stage.

Mya stood near the microphone, her hands folded neatly in front of her. She glanced toward the back of the room where her family sat, her mother giving her an encouraging nod, her father with his arm draped around her shoulder, and her brothers, surprisingly quiet, watching closely.

She took a breath. Then another.

And then, she sang.

"Amazing grace, how sweet the sound…"

Her voice rang out clear, deep, and unshakably rich. For a moment, time felt suspended. There was something sacred about the way she carried each note, letting the song rise and fall like waves rolling over the souls in the room. It wasn't just a performance. It was a testimony, a release.

The elders leaned forward. Several women wiped their eyes. Even the men, some with arms crossed and expressions set in stone, softened under the power of her voice. The weight of her words reached into memories and stirred something eternal. It wasn't just about how beautifully she sang; it was what she sang through.

Tears rolled down Ms. Shirley's cheek as she whispered, "That child has an anointing."

As Mya reached the final verse, her eyes lifted to the ceiling.

Her voice soared, unafraid, unwavering. It filled the room like a holy wind.

The last note lingered, then faded into a reverent silence.

And then, a thunderous applause erupted. The crowd stood. Some clapped. Some shouted "Hallelujah!" Others placed a hand over their chest, too moved to speak.

Jenna clutched Noah's hand, her eyes glistening. "She did it," she whispered.

He nodded, smiling widely. "She didn't just sing. She ministered."

Mya stepped down from the stage, cheeks flushed, a soft smile on her face. She didn't need to say a word.

Tonight, the little girl who once hid behind self-doubt stood tall, her voice not only heard but felt.

And in the hearts of everyone present, something shifted.

Because grace didn't just sound sweet tonight...

It sang.

Chapter 7
A Song That Stays

The air outside the community center was crisp with the gentle breeze of early spring, but inside the Carter family's car, it was warm, filled with joy, laughter, and proud smiles.

"Did you hear how clear her voice was?" Jenna beamed, glancing at Noah in the driver's seat.

"I'm still hearing it," he chuckled, looking at Mya through the rearview mirror. She was humming the last few notes of Amazing Grace, swinging her legs with delight in her booster seat.

Theo leaned toward her and gave a playful nudge. "You sounded like a real grown-up singer up there, Mya."

"I'm not a grown-up," she replied thoughtfully. "I'm just me."

"That's all you needed to be," Grandma Rose chimed in from the backseat. "And you sang from your heart, just like I told you."

By the time they pulled into the driveway, it was nearly bedtime, but the night wasn't over yet.

Inside the house, the smell of late-night Swedish meatballs filled the kitchen. Jenna tossed the noodles while Noah warmed the garlic bread. Everyone changed into comfy clothes and gathered around the table.

Mya sat at the head of the table with her hair still in bows from the performance. She looked sleepy but happy.

As they passed plates around, Levi stretched and groaned dramatically. "Do we still have to hear her sing now that the concert's over?"

Everyone chuckled.

But before anyone could say a word, Mya stood up in her chair and put her hands on her hips.

"If you don't want to hear it," she declared, "then close your ears. Because I'm not going to stop singing, it brings me joy, and I am singing to the Lord… That's what Grandma Rose tells me."

The room went quiet for a beat, then Grandma Rose let out a proud laugh.

"Well," she said, dabbing her eyes, "I guess that settles that."

Jenna smiled and kissed Mya's forehead. "Amen to that, baby."

Levi raised his hands in surrender. "Okay, okay! I was playing. You can sing all you want."

"No takebacks," Mya said, grinning.

That night, after dishes were done and everyone was tucked into bed, Mya sat quietly at her window, looking up at the stars.

"Thank You, God," she whispered. "I'm glad I sang tonight. I hope you liked it."

Then, in the stillness of her room, she began to sing again…softly, sweetly, just for Him.

The Spring Play had finally arrived at Chelseaville Elementary… "Kinderella: A Modern Lemon Twist!" The auditorium buzzed with energy as families, students, and community members filled every seat. Children dressed in pastel outfits raced up and down the aisles, while teachers ushered parents toward their assigned rows.

Jenna Carter clutched her program as if it were a golden ticket. She nudged Levi and Theo forward as Grandma Rose shuffled behind, along with Owen, holding a bouquet of lavender tulips wrapped in sparkly foil.

"Please find a place near the center; we have reserved seats," Jenna said quietly. "Here are our seats, so Mya will be able to see us."

But one person wasn't there yet.

"Noah!" she said aloud, rechecking her phone. "Why is he not picking up?"

Across town…

Noah gripped the steering wheel, frustration tightening in his chest as brake lights stretched endlessly ahead. A delivery truck was blocking two lanes. He tried to remain calm, but the dashboard clock glared at 6:24 p.m.

"Come on, come on…" he muttered. The play started at 6:30 p.m. sharp.

His phone buzzed with Jenna's name.

"I'm almost there," he said quickly. "Tell Mya I'll be there. I promise."

"She's going on right after intermission, please don't miss it," Jenna pleaded. "She's been waiting six months for this."

Noah made a sharp turn down a side street, parked three blocks away, and ran.

Backstage…

Mya stood still while Ms. Perry, the drama teacher, adjusted the sparkly silver shawl on her shoulders. Her light blue dress glittered under the backstage lights, and a gold plastic wand rested in her small hands.

"You ready, Fairy Godmother?" Ms. Perry asked.

"Ready," Mya said, smiling. "I've been practicing in the mirror every night."

"You've also been singing to the mirror every night," Ms. Mason said with a chuckle as she added a swirl of glitter to Mya's cheek. "But you know what? Tonight, you're not pretending. You are the Fairy Godmother."

"I know," Mya said seriously. "Because Grandma Rose said when you believe in yourself, anything is possible."

Ms. Mason winked. "Then go show them."

In the auditorium…

The lights dimmed. Jenna looked behind her in panic, but there was no sign of Noah.

Then, just as the principal walked on stage to give opening remarks, Noah slipped into his seat beside her, panting and out of breath.

"I made it," he whispered.

Jenna grabbed his arm. "You'd better not blink, or you'll miss her."

The play began.

Laughter echoed as Kinderella's stepsisters danced awkwardly across the stage in neon tutus. The audience clapped as Prince Jaden announced the royal ball, and Kinderella, played by Melissa, wearing sneakers and a glitter hoodie, sighed dramatically about not having a dress.

Then came the moment.

Smoke rolled across the stage floor.

The lights turned a shimmering white.

A small figure stepped into the glow.

Mya.

The Fairy Godmother had arrived.

She twirled onto the stage with a glowing wand, silver wings, a bright yellow costume shaped like a lemon, and a broad smile that could melt even the grumpiest heart.

"Well, well, well," she said, her voice loud and clear. "You didn't think I'd let you stay home on the fanciest night of the year, did you?"

The crowd roared with laughter and delight.

Then Mya lifted her wand, and in a beautiful, sing-song voice, began her solo:

"When you are told no, and your heart says whoa...

Just believe in God who made your heart."

Her voice rang purely and confidently.

The audience leaned in, mesmerized by the smallest cast member owning the most significant moment. Even the older kids on stage stopped to watch her, their faces lit with admiration.

"A lot of faith, a lot of joy,

And soon that pickle turns out to be just tickles.

You are blessed, strong, and sweet...

Now go, dear sweetie, and dance on your feet... go dance!"

With a wave of her wand, confetti sparkled in the air. The crowd gasped, then broke into thunderous applause.

Backstage, Ms. Perry whispered, "That girl was born for this."

After the final curtain call, Mya joined the cast for bows. When it was her turn, the spotlight shone on her, and she curtsied low, her wand held high like a queen.

Dad stood and clapped the loudest. "That's my girl!"

At home later that night...

The family crowded around bowls of buttery popcorn and leftover baked chicken. Everyone was talking over each other.

"I loved the part when you said, 'dance on feet!'" Owen said, trying to imitate her voice.

"Yeah," Levi added with a grin, "do we still have to hear her sing now that the play's over?"

Mya stood tall on the couch cushion, hands on her hips.

"If you don't want to hear it," she said proudly again, "then close your ears, again! Because I'm not going to stop singing. It brings me joy, and I am singing to the Lord. That's what Grandma Rose tells me all the time."

The room fell silent, then burst into laughter and applause.

Grandma Rose dabbed her eyes with a napkin. "And I meant every word of it.

That night, as the house grew quiet, Mya whispered a prayer from her bed.

"Thank You, God. I love being your gift."

And before falling asleep, she hummed the melody of her song, soft, sweet, and full of joy.

The next morning, the house was still glowing from the afterglow of Mya's performance. Her costume wings lay draped over the back of a chair, and her wand now had a special spot on her nightstand. Even Levi had stopped teasing her for now.

As Jenna washed dishes after breakfast, her phone buzzed. It was Ms. Mason.

"Good morning, Ms. Mason!" Jenna answered cheerfully.

"Jenna," Ms. Mason said, her voice filled with warmth. "I just wanted to thank you again for allowing Mya to be part of the Kinderella production. Having her on that stage... it was like watching a little miracle unfold. She lit up that room."

Jenna smiled, glancing at Mya in the other room, twirling slowly in her pajamas, still singing softly to herself. "She loved it. It did something to her confidence."

"I could see that," Ms. Mason continued. "Which is precisely why I'm calling. I want to recommend something.

Jenna stood still. "I'm listening.

"There's a school, not just any school, it's called Chelseaville Performing Arts Center. It's a place where young children like Mya can thrive. Acting, ballet, and vocal development are all there. And they're gentle with the kids. They bring out what's already inside of them."

Jenna's heart stirred.

"I spoke with the director this morning," Ms. Mason added. "They'd love to offer Mya a spot in their beginner's program. It's a year-long program, every Wednesday evening and Saturday morning."

"Oh wow..." Jenna said softly. "That sounds amazing."

"It is," Ms. Mason agreed. "The cost is about $3,500 for the year, which I know is an investment. But Jenna, she's worth every penny. I'm not trying to sell you on it; I just wanted to make sure you knew what was available. You don't have to make a decision now. Maybe just let her try a trial class."

Jenna nodded slowly, even though Ms. Mason couldn't see her.

"Thank you, Ms. Mason. That means so much."

That evening, Jenna brought it up while folding laundry in the living room with Noah.

"She was so proud last night," she said, smiling as she folded Mya's blue dress and set it in a keepsake box.

Noah glanced up. "She had every reason to be."

Jenna hesitated, then said, "Ms. Mason called today. She thinks we should consider enrolling Mya in Chelseaville Performing Arts Center."

Noah raised his eyebrows. "Performing arts?"

"She'd be doing ballet, acting, voice training, and real development stuff. They only take a few kids her age. Ms. Mason said they saw something in Mya."

"Well, that's easy to see," Noah replied.

"It's $3,500 for the year. Two days a week. Wednesdays and Saturdays."

Noah sat back and exhaled. "It's not a small number."

"I know," Jenna said. "But it's a seed."

They sat in thoughtful silence.

"I'm not saying yes right now," Jenna added quickly. "I told her I wanted to talk with you first. But I'd like to let at least Mya try it. See how she feels."

Noah nodded. "Let's look at the budget this weekend. Maybe we can adjust a few things and make it happen."

Jenna smiled.

The next day, Jenna called Ms. Mason back.

"Hi, it's Jenna. We're interested. We want Mya to try the first class, see how she does."

"I'm so glad to hear that," Ms. Mason replied. "She belongs there."

Later that next evening, Jenna stepped out onto the back porch, phone in hand, the spring air wrapping gently around her like a blanket. The kids were inside watching a cartoon while Noah finished up dinner prep. She took a deep breath and dialed Ms. Mason back.

"Hi, Ms. Mason, it's Jenna," she said warmly.

"Oh, Jenna! I was thinking about you."

"I wanted to say thank you again. For believing in Mya and giving her that stage."

"Mya gave us the moment," Ms. Mason said with a soft chuckle. "That child has something rare, Jenna. Not just talent, but presence. And I've only seen that a few times in all my years."

"Well," Jenna replied cautiously, "I did talk to Noah about the Chelseaville Performing Arts Center. We wanted to get more information about the center. But with the cost, I think we'd feel more comfortable letting her try it out first before committing to the full program."

"That's completely fine," Ms. Mason said quickly. "They do offer a trial class. There's no pressure. Just let her walk into the space, see how she responds."

Jenna let out a breath of relief. "That would be perfect."

"And Jenna..." Ms. Mason's voice lowered with intention. "This school is the real deal. I've had students go on to perform on major opera stages, act in major film productions, and even open for gospel artists. The dance studio isn't just a hobby; it sets the stage for careers. But even more than that, it gives children a safe place to blossom. And your daughter, she could bloom in ways you can't even imagine yet."

Jenna was quiet for a moment, her heart full. "Thank you for sharing this with us. I know how much Mya loves performing... but she also needs people who will speak life into her. And you've done that."

"I see her, Jenna. She reminds me of why I started teaching in the first place."

After hanging up, Jenna sat on the porch swing, dialed another number, and waited.

"Hey, baby girl," Grandma Rose answered on the second ring.

"Hi, Mama," Jenna said, her voice lighter. "You got a minute?"

"For you? Always."

"I just got off the phone with Ms. Mason. She thinks Mya should try out for the Chelseaville Performing Arts Center at this school. It's for kids who want to sing, act, dance... all of it."

"Oh?" Grandma Rose's voice perked up. "And they'll take her at five?"

"They said she could try a trial class. It's pricey for the full year, but Mama... they've had kids go on to real stages. The big stage, even. Ms. Mason said Mya has that 'presence.'"

"She's always had something special," Grandma Rose replied gently. "Even when she was just humming in her crib. That girl's been singing to the Lord since before she could talk."

Jenna smiled, eyes misty. "I just don't want to push her too fast. But I also don't want to hold her back."

"You won't," Grandma Rose said confidently. "God opens doors in His timing. This might be one of them."

That night, Jenna peeked in on Mya before bed. She was curled up, clutching her wand, her soft snores barely heard over the sound of her humming in her sleep.

Jenna whispered, "Okay, baby. We'll let you try it."

And just like that, another door quietly opened.

Chapter 8
The First Step

Saturday morning came quickly.

The sky was bright, the air smelled like fresh lilacs, and butterflies danced in the breeze as Jenna pulled into the small parking lot of the Chelseaville Performing Arts Center. The building was nestled between a quiet café and a bookstore, with tall windows and colorful banners that read: "Awaken the Dancer, Singer, and Much More."

Mya sat in the back seat, her legs swinging, wearing her brand-new pink leotard under a navy hoodie. Her hair was pulled into a neat curly bun, and her little ballet slippers were tucked inside a drawstring bag on her lap.

"You are sure you're ready?" Jenna asked, turning around to look at her.

Mya grinned. "I was born ready. Right, Grandma Rose?"

"That's right, baby girl," Grandma Rose said from the passenger seat. "Now go in there and shine like I know you will."

Inside the studio, soft classical music floated through the air. The front lobby was buzzing with parents checking in, children skipping around in tights, and teachers calling roll from clipboards.

A young woman, wearing a headset and smiling brightly, approached them.

"Hi! You must be Mya Carter?" she said.

"Yes, ma'am," Mya answered confidently.

"I'm Miss Elise, dance instructor. I'll be leading the beginner's ballet and creative stage movement class today." "You all will meet Ms. Carmen soon. She is the vocal coach."

Jenna crouched down beside Mya. "You got this, baby. I'll be right out here with Grandma Rose."

Mya nodded, gave her a quick hug, and followed Miss Elise into the bright hallway lined with mirrors, posters of past shows, and framed photos of former students. Some of them looked like stars.

One in particular caught Mya's eye, a girl in a glittering gown holding a Broadway playbill with her name in lights.

Mya whispered under her breath, "Maybe one day that'll be me."

Inside Studio Room B, the air was filled with giggles, tapping feet, and a few squeals of excitement. Twelve kids were scattered around, stretching and twirling. Some were older, a few her age, but Mya was the only one standing with both hands clasped in front of her, still and poised.

Miss Elise clapped her hands. "Let's start with our warm-ups and introductions! Who's new today?"

Mya raised her hand.

"Welcome, Mya! Tell us one thing you love to do."

"I love to sing to the Lord," she said proudly.

Some of the kids tilted their heads. A few smiled.

"Beautiful," Miss Elise said. "That's what the arts are about...expression from the heart."

As the class went on, Mya twirled, stretched, balanced on tiptoe, and mimicked dance movements with careful attention. Then came "Stage Presence Time," a chance for students to act out scenes and sing character lines.

Miss Elise handed Mya a scarf and said, "I want you to pretend this scarf is magic. You're the fairy godmother. Use your voice. Demonstrate your abilities to illustrate your skills."

Without hesitation, Mya stepped forward.

She waved the scarf high and declared with bright, glowing eyes:

"Your thoughts don't just stay in your head. You have to speak them, dance them, and sing them! That's what Grandma Rose tells me!"

The class clapped.

Miss Elise crouched beside her and whispered, "You are made for this, sweetheart."

After class, Mya came bouncing out of the studio, her face flushed with excitement.

"Well?" Jenna asked as Mya ran up and hugged her.

"I love it!" she beamed. "Can I come back next week?"

Jenna looked down at her daughter's glowing face. Then at Grandma Rose.

They both smiled

"Yes, baby," Jenna said. "We'll find a way to make it work."

Later that night, Mya stood at her bedroom window, holding her wand as if it were a microphone.

"Thank You, God," she whispered. "I took the first step today. Please help me keep going forward."

Then she sang softly to the stars:

"I believe in what You gave me,

Even if I'm small.

Because when I walk with you,

I know I'll never fall."

Next Wednesday came too soon....

Inside the Center, Ms. Elise welcomed the children with a joyful clap of her hands.

"Alright, young stars, today we're warming up our voices, learning some dance basics, and trying our stage presence games!"

Among the group was a confident, polished seven-year-old girl named Brittany Abraham, dressed in a designer leotard and a glittering hair bow that sparkled with every turn of her head. She had poise, control, and a practiced smile. Everyone in the room seemed to know her name.

"Hi, Brittany!" some girls called out.

"My mom said Brittany's been in commercials," whispered another girl near Mya.

Mya just nodded politely and kept stretching.

When it came time for voice warm-ups, each child had a chance to sing a short solo. Brittany stepped forward with a polished performance of a well-known Broadway tune, complete with big hand gestures and a dramatic bow.

The room clapped until Mya was called.

She stepped forward, her hands clasped, and began singing softly as she made up her lyrics:

"God is good, and I love him..."

Her voice was pure, potent, and undeniably moving; even the teachers paused in their work. It wasn't rehearsed or polished; it was anointed power.

When she finished, the room was silent for a moment, then she erupted in surprised applause.

But Brittany's smile faded.

She crossed her arms and turned away.

After class, as the students gathered their bags, Brittany approached Mya in the hallway.

She looked her up and down.

"You think you're special because you can sing loudly?" she said sharply.

Mya blinked, unsure how to respond.

"I've been acting since I was four. This is my place. You're not going to take my spotlight."

Then, without warning, Brittany shoved her. Mya stumbled and fell to the floor, scraping her hand on the tile.

Before anyone else could see, Brittany was already gone.

Mya's lip trembled as she stood, brushed herself off, and hurried outside, eyes filled with tears.

Grandma Rose was waiting at the curb, car door open and arms out.

Mya burst into tears the moment she climbed inside.

"What happened?" Grandma asked gently, pulling her close in the back seat.

"She... she pushed me. Brittany. She said I was trying to take her spotlight. I didn't mean to. I just sang the song. I was just being me..."

Grandma Rose held her tighter. "Oh, baby."

"I don't want to go back," Mya sniffled. "Maybe I don't belong there."

Grandma Rose gently lifted Mya's chin.

"Look at me, sugar. Don't you ever let someone else's fear steal your gift."

Mya looked up, eyes glistening.

"Sometimes," Grandma said, "when someone stands out or draws attention, others might feel overshadowed. That's not your responsibility, and you shouldn't feel obligated to diminish yourself. You should continue to do your best not for recognition, but because it's the right thing to do."

Mya's lip quivered. "But what if people don't like me?"

"They didn't like Jesus either," Grandma said gently. "But he kept walking. He kept healing. He kept loving others. And so will you."

Mya let out a shaky breath. "Okay."

"And next time someone tells you, you don't belong," Grandma Rose added, "you just smile and say: 'God made room for me before I ever walked in the door.'"

Mya smiled, her spirit slowly lifting. "Can I still sing in the car?"

"You better," Grandma said, buckling her in. "You've got work to do."

As they pulled off, Mya began humming softly again, her voice rising stronger with each note.

And just like that, the enemy's lie was drowned out by the truth of her purpose.

It has now been two weeks since Mya Carter began her time at the Chelseaville Performing Arts Center, and she has already made a lasting impression.

Every Wednesday evening and Saturday morning, she entered the studio with her tiny ballet bag, a gentle smile, and a voice that could stir the room into silence.

It wasn't just her sound, it was her spirit. Even at five years old, Mya carried something that couldn't be taught.

By the end of the first week, the teachers had begun whispering during snack breaks.

"She doesn't just sing, she ministers," Miss Elise said to Ms. Carmen, the vocal coach.

"Her tone is clear, but it's her intent that carries it. We need to push her in a good way. Help her grow."

"She's young," Ms. Carmen agreed. "But she's teachable. I say we build her up, give her confidence and energy to match that gift."

That Saturday, they introduced a new vocal exercise that required the kids to perform a short solo and use movement with the music.

Most children giggled or stumbled. But when Mya sang, her body naturally flowed with the rhythm of hand motions, a gentle spin, and even a confident step forward on the last note.

"She's got stage instincts," Ms. Carmen whispered to Ms. Elise.

"She's a natural-born lead."

But not everyone was cheering.

Brittany Abraham, now watching Mya rise faster than she had in three years of training, couldn't hide the fire building in her chest.

"She only knows one church song," Brittany scoffed to a group of girls during break. "She's not even that good. She sings loudly."

One girl frowned. "But she sounds like the girl from that princess movie."

"She does not," Brittany snapped. "She sounds like a crying baby."

A few giggled, unsure how to respond.

Brittany wasn't finished.

"She's a show-off. And she thinks just because she prays before she sings, she's better than everybody."

Mya heard these things.

Not all at once, but piece by piece. Whispers. Giggles. Eyes glancing her way, then quickly looking down.

Her stomach twisted. She didn't tell her mom or Grandma Rose. Instead, she stayed quiet, hoping it would go away.

But it didn't.

The following Wednesday, the class was asked to sing a song that made them feel brave. Ms. Carmen gave them all the choice to sing solo or in a small group.

Brittany immediately paired up with two girls, leaving Mya alone.

She hesitated.

Ms. Carmen knelt. "Would you like to sing by yourself or wait for a group, sweetheart?"

Mya looked at the ground. Then up again. "I'll sing by myself."

As the piano played, she stepped forward and sang:

Stay strong and protect your gift, protect your heart,

For the Lord will help you, and I know he will. . ."

Ms. Carmen wiped a tear from her cheek. "That's it," she whispered. "That's the courage I want every student to find."

The class clapped, but Brittany rolled her eyes.

Later, as the students lined up for dismissal, Brittany walked past and mumbled, "Little church girl. Think you're special."

That was the final straw.

Outside, Grandma Rose waited by the car.

Mya walked out slowly, eyes downcast.

"Baby girl," Grandma said. "What's on your heart?"

Mya looked up. Her voice trembled, but this time, she didn't hide. "Grandma, Brittany's been mean to me. She tells the other kids not to talk to me. She says I don't belong here… just because I sing about God."

Grandma Rose's eyes softened. "Have you told your teacher?"

Mya shook her head.

"Well," Grandma said gently, "You've been brave on stage, now it's time to be brave off stage too. Speaking the truth in love doesn't make you weak; it makes you strong."

The following practice day, before warm-ups began, Mya tugged gently on Ms. Carmen's sleeve.

"Can I talk to you?"

Ms. Carmen knelt beside her, surprised by the quiet seriousness in Mya's eyes.

"I just wanted to say… Brittany keeps telling the other kids mean things about me. She says I'm a show-off. That I don't belong, and she pushes them not to be my friend."

Ms. Carmen's face grew firm, but calm. "Thank you for telling me, Mya. I'm proud of you for using your voice in the right way."

"I don't want to get her in trouble," Mya whispered.

Ms. Carmen nodded. "You didn't. You did the right thing."

That afternoon, Brittany was pulled aside after class.

In a quiet, respectful tone, Ms. Carmen spoke clearly and distinctly.

"Brittany, I want you to be honest. Have you been saying unkind things to the other students about Mya?"

Brittany looked away, shoulders tense. "I just… I've been here longer. She's new. And everyone's paying attention to her."

"I understand you feel that way," Ms. Carmen said gently. "But tearing someone down will never make your light shine brighter. It only makes it darker."

Brittany's eyes filled with frustrated tears. "I used to be the best one."

"You still can be amazing," Ms. Carmen said. "But you'll never grow if you let jealousy get in the way of kindness. You're better than that."

Brittany didn't respond, but her face began to soften.

Outside, when Mya reached the car, Grandma Rose noticed the change in her eyes.

"Well?" she asked.

"I told the teacher," Mya said quietly. "And she said she was proud of me."

"You should be proud of yourself, too."

Mya looked out the window as they drove away, her heart lighter.

This time, she didn't hum to herself.

She sang.

Softly, but boldly.

Because she knew her voice wasn't strong.

It was brave.

Chapter 9
The Spotlight Divides

Six months had gone by like a blur. Mya Carter had blossomed. Her shoulders no longer slouched with insecurity, and her voice no longer quivered when she sang. At the performing arts school, Mya had found her rhythm, literally and figuratively.

Dance had become her second language, and vocals her first love. She still had moments where doubt crept in, but Grandma Rose's morning prayers and nightly affirmations echoed louder than the old whispers of unworthiness.

It was now mid-season at the school, and that meant one thing: the Spring Performance Showcase. The hallways buzzed with excitement. Flyers were taped to lockers and bulletin boards. Parents and guardians had received their invitations, and students had two weeks to rehearse their solo or duo routines before the big night.

Mya stood near the audition board posted outside the main auditorium. Two clipboards were taped beside it, one labeled VOCALS, the other DANCE DUOS.

Ms. Elise, the upbeat vocal coach with wild curls and fiery encouragement, managed the vocal sheet. Ms. Carmen, sleek and stylish in her leotard, managed the dance sign-up.

Mya's eyes scanned the sheet. The slots were filling quickly. She glanced at Brittany's name and saw it, Brittany Abraham & Maria Santos, Dance Duo.

It didn't surprise her. Brittany had a way of commanding the room even when she wasn't trying. She had been acting professionally since the age of four, and it showed in the way she walked, performed, and carried herself. But behind the poise, Mya had sensed a quiet resentment brewing, especially since the day she sang "Amazing Grace" and had the entire community center on its feet.

Mya hesitated before signing her name. Then she took a breath and wrote in firm strokes:

Mya Carter, Solo Vocal: "Go Tell It on the Mountain"

Ms. Elise peeked over her shoulder and smiled. "Excellent choice, Mya. That song fits your voice and your spirit."

"Thanks," Mya said, feeling a warm glow of affirmation rise in her chest.

Down the hall, Brittany saw her write her name and leaned into Maria. "Of course she's singing solo," she muttered. "She always needs the spotlight."

Maria looked uncomfortable but didn't respond. The truth was, Maria liked Mya. She thought Mya was kind and brave. But she also didn't want to get on Brittany's bad side, especially not before their duo performance.

Back in the rehearsal studio, the atmosphere was electric. Kids were practicing in every corner: tap shoes clicked, vocal runs filled the room, and laughter echoed through the space.

Ms. Carmen called out, "Duos, over here! Solos, vocal warm-ups with Ms. Elise!"

Mya moved confidently to her corner, humming her melody under her breath. Across the room, Brittany twirled effortlessly in front of the mirror, her gaze occasionally flicking to Mya's reflection. There was something in her eyes, a fire, a challenge, and perhaps, a fear.

As rehearsal continued, Ms. Elise pulled Mya aside. "Let's work on your breath control at the bridge 'Go Tell It on the Mountain.' You're hitting the high notes beautifully, but remember, that's the moment where your heart has to lead the way."

Mya nodded. "I've been practicing it every night. I want it to be perfect."

"It doesn't have to be perfect," Ms. Elise said gently. "It just has to be honest. That's what moves people."

Meanwhile, across the studio, Brittany whispered something to Maria, then cast another look toward Mya. Maria followed her gaze and sighed. She wished Brittany would just let it go.

But jealousy has a way of tightening its grip when the spotlight feels threatened.

As the afternoon sun filtered through the high windows, the students continued to rehearse. Some were laughing, others were sweating with determination. For Mya, this performance wasn't just a showcase. It was a statement.

A quiet declaration:

I belong here. I was born for this.

The following week, rehearsals intensified. Each day after school, Mya changed into her soft pink dance shoes and warm-up hoodie, then met Ms. Elise in the studio for vocal training before heading over to the main stage for full-cast choreography.

Ms. Elise was pushing her harder now, not because Mya was falling behind, but because she believed in her. "Control your breath, Mya," she'd say, tapping gently on her diaphragm. "Let the note rise from here, not your throat. You're not just singing words. You're telling a story."

Mya nodded, sweat already glistening on her forehead. "Yes, ma'am."

But not every corner of the room felt so encouraging.

Brittany had perfected the art of smiling in front of the teachers and sneering when their backs were turned. She never said much, just enough to sting.

"Powerhouse girls here," Brittany whispered to two other girls as Mya walked by with her music binder.

"She's always trying too hard."

"I heard she used to be fat," one of the girls added, snickering.

Mya's hands tightened on her folder, but she kept walking. She knew what Grandma Rose would say: "People only talk down to you when they're already standing beneath what you carry."

Still, it hurt.

During dance warm-ups, Brittany bumped into her on the mat during stretching and didn't bother to apologize.

"Oops," she said flatly, rolling her eyes.

Maria noticed but stayed quiet. Brittany had been moodier than usual, snapping even at her. The pressure of the performance was getting to everyone.

Later that afternoon, while waiting for her car, Mya stood by the main gate alone, clutching her water bottle. Brittany strutted by with her tiny dance bag and whispered just loud enough to be heard, "Don't choke next week. I'd hate to see your big moment turn into a big flop."

Mya turned around, her lips parted, ready to say something, but then the car horn beeped. Grandma Rose waved from the passenger seat, smiling warmly.

"Coming!" Mya called, choosing peace over confrontation.

In the car, Grandma Rose noticed her silence.

"Tough day?" she asked gently.

Mya nodded, staring out the window. "Some people just don't want to see others do well."

"Jealousy can have negative effects," Grandma remarked. "Don't let it tangle around your gift. You've got something in you that can't be copied. That voice, your voice, was given by God. And no one can take that."

Mya blinked hard, her throat tightening. "It just... hurts sometimes."

"I know," Grandma Rose said, reaching over to pat her hand. "But you're not fighting alone. I'll be praying for you through every rehearsal, every note, and every step."

The next day, on Saturday's rehearsal, Mya walked in with her chin slightly higher. She still heard the whispers. Still saw Brittany's sidelong glances. But she focused on the music. On her breath. On the words that lifted her spirit:

"Over the hills and everywhere...."

When she finished her run-through, Ms. Elise clapped her hands together. "That's it, Mya! You brought it to life. The judges will remember that.

Across the room, Brittany scowled and turned away.

"One more week until the Mid-Performance Showcase," shouted Ms. Carmen.

And Mya was ready to rise.

The final week of rehearsals buzzed with nervous energy. The stage was set, the lighting crew ran technical cues, and students practiced in full costume. Every hallway was filled with music, and every studio echoed with last-minute corrections.

Mya arrived early each morning, standing center stage with her eyes closed, whispering the lyrics of "Go Tell It on the Mountain" to herself before anyone else arrived. It wasn't just a song; it had become her anthem. Her declaration. Her reminder.

Ms. Elise adjusted her mic and whispered, "You ready to change some lives?"

Mya smiled and nodded. "I think so."

But behind the curtain, Brittany watched. And fumed.

Even though her duo with Maria had been going well, Brittany couldn't shake the feeling that Mya was stealing the spotlight. Every compliment Ms. Elise gave Mya felt like a dagger. And even Maria had begun complimenting Mya openly after rehearsal.

"She's excellent, Brittany," Maria said once. "You should hear how the teachers talk about her when she's not around."

That was the last straw.

Performance night arrived too soon.

Parents filled the auditorium, cameras clicked, and a low hum of anticipation filled the air. The program booklet listed each act, and right after Act 5: Brittany & Maria – Dance Duo, was Act 6: Mya Carter – Solo Vocal.

Backstage was buzzing. Mya stood behind the curtain in her elegant navy-blue dress, mic in hand, taking deep breaths.

Brittany and Maria had just finished their dance. The audience clapped politely as they exited the stage. But as Brittany rounded the corner behind the curtain, she saw Mya standing near the edge, nervous, focused, alone.

With one glance to make sure no adult was looking, Brittany stuck out her foot as she walked past.

Mya didn't see it. She stumbled hard, her foot twisting, causing her to pitch forward toward the edge of the stage.

A collective gasp came from the wings.

Before she could hit the ground, a pair of strong arms caught her from behind.

It was Tyler Benson, a tall and confident eleventh-grader and student volunteer, who was helping with sound. He had been standing just offstage, ready to hand off the mic pack.

"Whoa, got you," he said, steadying her. "You good?"

Mya blinked in shock, her heart pounding. "Y-yeah. Thank you."

Behind them, Ms. Elise and Ms. Carmen came rushing over, both having witnessed everything from the side. Ms. Elise's jaw was tight. Ms. Carmen folded her arms.

"Brittany Abraham," Ms. Carmen said sternly, "what exactly was that?"

Brittany tried to feign innocence. "I...I didn't see her. She was standing in the way."

"We saw you," Ms. Elise said sharply. "Both of us. That behavior is unacceptable."

"We'll deal with this after the performance," Ms. Carmen added. "But trust that this will not be swept under the rug."

Brittany's eyes filled with tears, more from being caught than from guilt.

Tyler helped Mya to her spot, and Ms. Elise knelt beside her, checking her ankle.

"You okay to stand?"

Mya nodded. "Yes. I can do it."

Ms. Elise smiled gently. "Then go do it. Don't let this moment be stolen. Not by anyone."

As the curtains opened and the soft instrumental of "Go Tell It on the Mountain" began to play, Mya stepped forward into the spotlight.

Her voice, clear and rich, rose through the auditorium like a wave. People leaned in. The room fell silent.

"That Jesus Christ is born…"

Tears welled in the eyes of several parents in the front row.

"… That Jesus Christ is born."

By the time the final note rang out, the audience had leapt to their feet in applause.

Backstage, Brittany sat alone, arms crossed, while her parents stood off to the side, waiting to speak with Ms. Elise and Ms. Carmen, who approached with serious expressions.

It was time for a conversation long overdue

But onstage, Mya took a bow, strong, unshaken, and no longer hidden.

That same night, on Brittany's ride home, the Abraham family drove home in silence.

Brittany sat in the back seat, arms folded, staring out the window. Her sequin dance dress still shimmered under the soft interior lights, but the shine had long faded from the evening.

Her mother finally broke the silence. "Do you realize how embarrassed we were?"

Brittany didn't answer.

Her father glanced at her through the rearview mirror. "You purposely tripped another student. At a live performance. In front of teachers, staff, and guests."

"She was standing in the way," Brittany mumbled. "She thinks she's better than everyone."

"She doesn't act like it. But maybe you do," her mom snapped. "We didn't raise you to treat others like that."

"I work hard too! I've been acting since I was four, and now everyone is talking about her..."

"That's not an excuse to sabotage someone else," her father interrupted firmly. "You're grounded for the next month. No rehearsals. No auditions. No phone."

Brittany's eyes widened. "You can't..."

"We just did," her mom said. "And Ms. Carmen and Ms. Elise said they expect you and us to meet again next week to discuss whether you'll remain in the program."

Brittany felt her throat tighten. It wasn't supposed to go this far. She hadn't meant to ruin her future; she'd just wanted Mya out of the way.

But consequences don't care about intentions.

Back at the Carter home, soft jazz played in the kitchen, and laughter filled the air. For the first time in a long while, Mya sat between her mom and dad, just the three of them sharing stories over root beer floats and warm chicken sliders.

"You were amazing, baby," her mom said, placing a gentle hand on her back. "I had chills. That voice, Mya, you're something special."

Her dad nodded proudly. "I watched you walk out there like you owned the stage. And when you hit that high note, I swear the roof almost lifted."

Mya blushed. "I was nervous. But then I remembered what Grandma Rose always says... God didn't give me this gift to hide it."

Her mom leaned in and kissed her cheek. "We're so proud of you. Not just for singing, but for standing tall even when others tried to knock you down."

Mya's eyes glistened. "Thanks. I almost fell... but someone caught me."

Her dad smiled. "And you caught every single person in that audience."

For the first time in what felt like forever, Mya didn't feel like the quiet girl in the corner. She felt like a star who had finally come into her own, and her parents saw it too.

By Wednesday evening, the excitement from the Mid-Performance Showcase had settled, but the impact still lingered.

Ms. Elise posted a "Performance Highlights" board near the main entrance. Photos of each act were pinned with handwritten compliments. Under Mya's picture, she had written:

"Mya Carter: A voice of strength. A spirit of grace. A moment we won't forget."

Students huddled near the board, reading and pointing

Brittany was noticeably absent from rehearsal that day. A quiet buzz went through the room: some students whispered about what had happened, others avoided the topic altogether.

Maria sat beside Mya during vocal warm-ups and gently nudged her. "Hey... I'm sorry. I should've said something earlier. Brittany's been acting weird for weeks."

Mya smiled faintly. "It's okay. I'm just glad it's over."

Ms. Elise called everyone together for announcements. "Next month, we'll begin prep for our summer spotlight series. I'll be selecting a few students for one-on-one coaching sessions."

She paused, eyes scanning the room. "And I'm happy to announce that Mya Carter will be one of our featured soloists."

A soft round of applause followed. Some students clapped genuinely, while others followed politely; however, Mya remained humble, her smile small but steady.

She had walked through rejection, whispers, and sabotage, and still, she stood.

The girl who once hid in her room was now rising in her purpose. And this was only the beginning.

Chapter 10
A Year Later

A whole year had passed since the night of the Mid-Performance Showcase, when Mya's powerful voice soared across the stage, and Brittany's jealousy came crashing down quite literally. Now six years old, Mya had bloomed beautifully, her voice more confident, her posture more graceful, and her faith planted deeper than ever.

At home, the Carter household was still loud and full of energy. Theo and Levi were busy with high school sports and video games, and Owen, now thirteen, had entered the realm of teen moods and one-word answers. He still had a soft spot for his baby sister, though he'd never admit it out loud.

One sunny Saturday morning, Mya walked into the kitchen wearing a sparkly pink tutu over her leggings and a bright yellow feather boa around her neck. She held a plastic microphone and belted out the chorus of her newest favorite song, twirling for added flair.

Owen snorted from the kitchen table, where he was pouring cereal. "You look like a walking circus."

Mya's eyes dropped, her shoulders sinking ever so slightly. She mumbled, "It's for my performance next week…"

Before she could finish, their father stepped into the room holding his coffee mug. His eyes narrowed. "Owen."

"What?" Owen shrugged, spoon in his mouth.

"You know what. We don't tear each other down in this house. I don't care if you're thirteen or thirty, nobody's too old to be corrected."

Owen grumbled, "Sorry, Mya," though his eyes stayed locked on the cereal bowl.

Mya offered a small smile and quietly resumed her twirls. Dad leaned down and kissed the top of her head. "Shine bright, baby girl. God gave you that sparkle for a reason."

That simple reassurance lifted her spirit again.

Back at Chelsaville Performing Arts School, the hallways buzzed with the start of a new season. Posters lined the walls, announcing the Winter Showcase and the return of several students. Among them, unexpectedly, was Brittany Abraham.

Brittany had been away for a year after her family temporarily relocated for her father's job. Now eight years old, she had grown taller and more composed, or so it seemed. Her curls were tighter, her dresses fancier, and her smile sweeter, but those who remembered last year's drama knew better than to assume all was well underneath.

Mya spotted her by the lockers during the Monday morning rush. For a split second, their eyes met. Brittany's smile was faint, unreadable. Mya didn't smile back, just blinked slowly, and walked past. She had grown too.

She knew now that her worth didn't hinge on someone else's opinion or their jealousy.

Later that week, in the Advanced Vocal Expression class, Mya stood at her usual place in front of the room, humming the warm-up scale under her breath. Ms. Elise tapped her baton lightly on the edge of the piano as she called for attention.

"Everyone, welcome back, Brittany Abraham. Let's be kind and gracious, we're a family here."

Polite claps echoed around the room. Brittany gave a humble nod and took a seat in the second row, right behind Mya.

As the warm-ups began, Brittany's voice stood out—a touch deeper, more mature. She hadn't lost her talent, that was clear. But Mya didn't flinch. She held her note steadily, clear as glass, and more decisive than it had been the year before.

After the session, Ms. Elise divided the students into trios to rehearse harmony-building. Mya, Brittany, and a quiet girl named

Mariah ended up in the same group. An awkward silence hovered between Mya and Brittany until Brittany finally broke it.

"I heard you got a solo last year," she said, avoiding eye contact.

Mya nodded. "I did. It was 'How Great Thou Art.'"

Brittany fiddled with the sheet music. "That's a big song."

"It was," Mya replied, calm but not boastful. "God helped me through it."

For a second, Brittany said nothing. Then: "Good for you."

Mya didn't know how to respond, so she didn't. She just turned to Mariah and asked, "Ready to rehearse the chorus?"

They sang together, and though Brittany sang well, it was Mya's voice, pure, potent, and spirit-led, that carried through the walls. There was no competition, only calling.

Back at home that evening, Jenna prepared lasagna while Noah helped Owen review a science worksheet. Mya sat at the counter, scribbling in her notebook, humming the song they'd practiced that day.

Jenna smiled from the stove. "You've been singing more, sweetie."

"I like this new song," Mya said, flipping her braid back. "It talks about finding knowledge when people try to keep you in the dark."

Jenna paused for a moment, then walked over and kissed Mya's forehead. "You're growing into a bright, brave girl. And we're so proud of you."

Dad chimed in from the table, glancing at Owen. "Especially when you rise above the noise."

Owen groaned. "I said sorry already."

Mya giggled. For now, peace filled their home.

Friday was coming fast, and the buzz around the Carter household was all about Friday Night Lights. Under the glow of the stadium lights at Chelseaville Academy, Mya stood proudly on the 50-yard line. The air buzzed with excitement as students, families, and alums filled the bleachers for the semi-final championship game.

Her brothers, Theo, a 17-year-old junior, and Levi, a 16-year-old sophomore, stood tall with their team, hands over their hearts, pads rustling under their jerseys. They are both first-line linebackers on defense.

Dad waved from the stands, arm draped around Jenna. Grandma Rose pressed her hand over her heart, already misty-eyed.

The stadium fell silent. Mya took a deep breath and raised the microphone to sing the National Anthem.

Her voice rang out with clarity and conviction, her tone unwavering. She sang not to impress, but to honor. Her petite frame stood steady as each note wrapped the audience in a sacred stillness. A wave of pride and awe swept over the crowd. Even the referee was seen blinking back emotion.

When she hit the final line, the stadium erupted. People stood proudly, clapping, whistling, and cheering. Theo and Levi beamed from the sidelines, each giving her a proud nod.

Mya beamed, her cheeks flushed with joy. She glanced off toward the fence and caught a glimpse of Brittany again, standing near the concession stand with her parents. Her arms were folded, eyes shadowed, lips pressed in a tight line. No mockery this time. No whispering. Just silence.

That night, after the game, the family went out for frozen yogurt to celebrate.

"You did amazing, sweetheart!" Jenna said, giving Mya a big hug outside the shop.

"Seriously," Theo added, his football jersey slung over one shoulder. "You got a better reaction than our whole second quarter."

"Yeah," Levi said, elbowing her gently. "You've got stadium lungs."

Mya giggled. "Thanks, guys."

Noah handed out cups of yogurt. "I've said it before, and I'll repeat it: when God gives you a gift, you don't hide it. You honor Him with it. And tonight, that's exactly what you did."

Grandma Rose added, "You made a lot of people feel something good tonight, baby. That's not just talent. That's anointing.

Mya's heart swelled. She didn't need trophies. This moment was enough.

Back at Brittany's house, there were no celebrations.

Her mom was in the den, wine glass in hand, pretending to read a magazine. Her father sat in the kitchen scrolling through his phone, ignoring her entirely.

The silence was worse than the yelling.

Earlier, Brittany had tried to tell her mom she didn't want to do voice lessons on Saturday. "I just want one day off," she had said quietly.

"You're not serious," her mom had snapped. "You've already missed a year. You're lucky you even got back into that school."

Brittany didn't argue. She just nodded and retreated to her room. Again.

She sat on the edge of her canopy bed, staring at her untouched dinner tray. Her throat ached. Not from singing, but from holding in everything she wished she could say.

She thought about Mya, how free she looked when she sang. How supported she seemed. How loved.

For a moment, Brittany wished she could trade places with someone else, just for one day.

But instead, she curled up under her covers and whispered into the darkness, "I'm fine," though she knew she wasn't.

The car ride home from the stadium felt more like a celebration parade than a Friday night drive.

Theo sat in the backseat, practically bouncing with energy. "Did you see that sack in the third quarter? Straight through the line!"

"No, no," Levi interrupted, tossing a pretzel at him. "Mine was better. I had two tackles in a row, back-to-back. Coach said I was 'on fire.'"

"I'm pretty sure I'm the one who got the game ball," Theo grinned, stretching his arms behind his head.

"You both did great," Dad rasped from the driver's seat, his voice barely more than a whisper. "But your old man needs some tea, too much yelling."

Mom laughed softly, turning from the passenger seat. "You were louder than the cheerleaders."

"I couldn't help it," Dad whispered. "My daughter nailed the anthem, and my boys lit up the scoreboard. What else is a father supposed to do?"

Mya sat in the middle, smiling widely, her little legs swinging. "We should celebrate every game like this."

Grandma Rose chimed in from the back row, "Long as there's no yelling in the car. And someone better roll down a window...these boys smell like football and French fries."

Everyone laughed. The car was filled with light, joy, and the feeling that no matter what tomorrow held, tonight was golden.

But Wednesday evening at the performing arts center, it was far from joyful for Brittany.

She hadn't slept well all weekend. Her parents barely spoke during breakfast, and when her father left the house Sunday night without saying goodbye, her stomach hadn't settled since.

Now, as she walked down the hallway, her eyes darted toward Mya, who was laughing with Mariah and another student. Brittany looked away quickly. Her throat tightened. Her head pounded.

She had almost made it through vocal warm-ups when Ms. Carmen stopped mid-song.

"Brittany, are you okay? You're a little off pitch today."

Brittany nodded quickly. "Just tired."

"Okay. Let's pause there. Everyone take five."

As the other students headed toward the water fountains, Brittany stayed frozen in place. She didn't know why her legs wouldn't move. Her chest felt like a rubber band stretched too tight.

Ms. Carmen approached gently. "Hey," she said softly. "Walk with me?"

Brittany hesitated, then followed her out into the hallway.

They strolled past the bulletin board. Ms. Carmen didn't speak right away.

Finally, Brittany said quietly, "I think my parents are getting a divorce."

Ms. Carmen looked over, surprised but calm. "Oh, sweetheart."

"They don't say it, but... they fight all the time. Or they don't talk at all. It's like... like I'm invisible."

Ms. Carmen stopped and turned to face her. "You are not invisible, Brittany. Not here. And not to me."

Brittany's lip quivered. "I feel like... like I have to be perfect just to make them stay."

Tears filled her eyes. She wiped them fast, ashamed.

Ms. Carmen knelt slightly so they were eye to eye. "You don't have to be perfect to be loved. You're allowed to feel. You're allowed to be honest. And you are not alone."

Brittany nodded, biting her lip, finally allowing the tears to fall.

Ms. Carmen wrapped her arms around her. "Let's get you some help, not just here at school, but someone you can talk to regularly. Will you let me help you?"

A pause.

Then a quiet, "Okay."

Later that evening, after dance class concluded, many performers promptly left for their respective vehicles. Most students spilled out the doors, laughing and chattering, with performance bags bouncing, and headed for home. But Brittany sat quietly on the bench near the front office, her hands folded tightly in her lap.

She had just finished her private check-in with the dance counselor, and now she waited for her mother, dreading every second that passed.

Ms. Elise and Ms. Carmen stood near the reception desk, exchanging quiet words as they saw a sleek black SUV pull up to the curb.

"Here she comes," Ms. Elise whispered.

The passenger door swung open, and Brittany's mother, elegantly dressed in a fitted coat and high heels, stepped through the glass doors. Her eyes immediately found Brittany, then flicked to the two teachers.

Ms. Carmen stepped forward with a soft smile. "Hi, Mrs. Abraham. Thank you for coming. We just wanted to follow up…

Mrs. Abraham cut her off with a forced, clipped tone. "I'm very busy, ladies. My assistant mentioned your message. Something about Brittany's 'confiding' in you during dance hours?"

Ms. Elise nodded gently. "Yes, she expressed some concerns about things going on at home. We take those kinds of things very seriously, and we wanted to offer resources."

Ms. Carmen handed her a small packet. "There's a licensed adolescent therapist who works with families in transition. Brittany wouldn't need to miss any school."

Mrs. Abraham barely glanced at the paper before folding it tightly in half. "She doesn't need a therapist. She needs to focus. Brittany knows better than to talk about personal matters in public. Especially to teachers."

Her voice sharpened as she turned to Brittany. "Get your things."

Brittany stood slowly, her face pale.

"But…" Ms. Carmen started, stepping forward.

"I said she's fine." Mrs. Abraham's voice rang louder now. "Whatever she said was probably exaggerated. She's always been dramatic."

The air thickened.

Brittany lowered her head, shoulders drooping, and walked toward the door without saying a word.

But just before they stepped outside, her mother spun back around.

"I can't believe you said something to them," she snapped. "Why would you embarrass this family like that?"

The glass door slammed behind them.

Ms. Carmen and Ms. Elise stood frozen.

Inside the car, Brittany sat in silence as the engine roared. She stared straight ahead, her face expressionless, hands gripping the seatbelt across her chest.

Her mother didn't speak another word the whole ride home.

Something inside Brittany went cold and numb.

She swallowed the lump in her throat, closed the door to her feelings, and locked it. If vulnerability made her a burden, she would bury it. If honesty made her "dramatic," then silence would be her strategy.

From that day forward, Brittany vowed to keep it together. To appear flawless. Composed. Brilliant. No matter what it costs.

Even if it meant tearing others down to stay afloat.

Even if it meant hurting Mya, again.

Chapter 11
A Season to Remember

The sun poured across the grand lawn of Chelseaville
Academy, where rows of white folding chairs stretched toward a
wide stage draped in blue and gold. Graduation banners fluttered
in the breeze, and parents buzzed with excitement as they searched
for the perfect seats to catch a glimpse of their sons and daughters
taking their first steps into adulthood.

Among them, Noah and Jenna Carter stood tall and proud,
phones in hand, beaming with emotion. Levi, now 17 and a junior,
stood beside them in a fitted button-down and tie, while Mya,
seven years old, twirled in a soft lavender dress with white sandals
and a glittery headband. Owen, 14 years old and an 8th grader,
stood next to Grandma Rose, Uncle Leroy, and Uncle Joe, along
with a host of cousins and friends.

Today was not about her. It was about her big brother, Theo
Carter, 18, standing confidently in his cap and gown, surrounded
by classmates in navy robes and golden stoles. The Class of 2015
had arrived.

The ceremony began with the school choir singing a stirring
rendition of the school's alma mater. Tears shimmered in Jenna's
eyes. Mya clutched her father's hand tightly. The school principal
spoke about perseverance, growth, and the unique challenges the
graduates had overcome. Then came the valedictorian speech, full
of humor and heart.

Finally, the moment came.

"Theodore James Carter," the announcer read proudly.

Theo walked across the stage, his smile wide and easy. Cheers
erupted from the Carter section of the crowd, Dad's voice hoarse

but unmistakable, and Mya's high-pitched, "That's my brother!" echoing down the aisle.

Theo accepted his diploma, shook hands with the faculty, and raised it proudly before tossing his cap high with the rest of his classmates in a joyful, fluttering storm of navy and gold.

The graduation party, held later that evening, was a lively, love-filled celebration hosted at the family's home. Strings of lights were hung across the backyard, casting a soft golden glow over picnic tables, folding chairs, and platters of barbecue, pasta salad, and peach cobbler. A Bluetooth speaker played everything from R&B to old school rap, while laughter filled the air.

Levi took control of the grill with Dad's supervision, flipping burgers and calling out orders. Jenna moved through the yard with bowls of fruit and bottles of sparkling lemonade, hugging every guest who arrived.

Inside the house, a photo slideshow played on the living room TV, pictures of Theo from preschool to prom, from scraped knees to football touchdowns. Guests paused to laugh at baby photos and hugged him with congratulations.

Mya ran through the yard barefoot, dancing between cousins and grabbing second helpings of honeydew slices. She was beaming all day, but especially when Noah called for everyone's attention and tapped a spoon to his glass.

"We are so proud of Theo," he said, voice still scratchy but full of joy. "You've made us proud every step of the way, and now you're stepping into the world with courage, kindness, and purpose."

"Speech! Speech!" Levi called out, nudging Theo forward.

Theo smiled, rubbing the back of his neck. "Thank you, guys. I couldn't have asked for a better family. I'm excited about what's next: college, independence, and maybe sleeping past 6 a.m."

Everyone laughed.

Then Mya raised her hand shyly.

"Can I say something too?"

The crowd hushed.

Dad waved her forward. "Of course, baby girl."

Mya stood on the wooden steps of the back porch and looked out at the crowd with both hands held behind her back.

"I just wanted to say…" She paused, glancing at her mom and grandma for courage. "I finished my second year at Chelseaville Performing Arts Center! And I was just asked to sing a solo in the upcoming spring performance in two weeks!"

The crowd clapped and cheered. Jenna covered her mouth, emotionally.

Grandma Rose clapped her hands. "You go, baby! Keep praising Him with that voice!"

Mya blushed but smiled widely, soaking in the encouragement.

She didn't know that none of them knew that a painful disruption would soon follow this perfect night. A sudden, unexpected tragedy would leave the Carter family once again leaning on faith, love, and the strength they had built together.

But for now, they danced under string lights. For now, laughter echoed through the yard. For now, joy filled the night.

Saturday morning sunlight streamed through the blinds as birds chirped in the distance. Mya stretched in bed, her voice already humming the first few notes of her solo. Her pink backpack sat by the door, packed neatly with her sheet music, a water bottle, and her favorite honey lemon throat drops.

Downstairs, Jenna flipped pancakes on the griddle while Noah stirred a fresh pot of coffee. Theo, Levi, and Owen were still asleep, recovering from last night's graduation party, but Mya was wide awake, dressed, and ready for rehearsal.

"You nervous, baby girl?" Dad asked as he kissed her forehead goodbye.

"A little," she said honestly, tugging on the sleeves of her denim jacket. "But it's the good kind."

Mom added, "You've worked hard for this part. Go in there and show them what you're made of light, strength, and grace."

Chelsaville Performing Arts Center was already alive with movement when Mya arrived. The stage crew was adjusting lights, Ms. Elise was organizing costume pieces, and the piano accompanist ran scales in the background. Students stretched, whispered lines, or sipped from water bottles, prepping for a long day of full-dress rehearsal for the Spring Showcase titled "Spring Forward to a New Day."

Mya moved with confidence through the backstage hallway, her little sneakers squeaking on the tile. She knew her part well... "Grace and Sing," the closing solo of the performance, and had spent the last two weeks perfecting it with Ms. Carmen.

But one thing felt... off.

Brittany had been unusually quiet. Ever since class resumed after spring break, she hadn't spoken a word to Mya. Not a whisper. Not a snide remark. Not even a passing glance.

It was strange.

Mya had expected the usual eyerolls, maybe a sarcastic comment about pitch or costumes, but instead there was... silence. Brittany stayed to herself in rehearsals, took notes without making a sound, and kept her head down during vocal warm-ups.

Now, as Mya entered the auditorium, she spotted Brittany seated on the edge of the stage, her chin resting on her knees, arms wrapped tightly around herself.

"Good morning, Brittany," Mya offered gently as she passed.

No response.

Mya paused, hesitated, then walked past and joined the other students in the front row. She kept glancing toward Brittany between stretches and vocal warmups. Something was wrong. She could feel it.

Ms. Carmen clapped her hands together at the front. "Okay, everyone! We're going to run Act II straight through. Soloists, be ready backstage when called. Let's keep the energy up today!"

The piano began to play softly, and Mya turned her focus to the music, but in the back of her mind, Brittany's silence echoed louder than anything on stage.

Something was bothering her.

Something big.

And Mya didn't know it yet, but what Brittany was holding in, the truth, the fear, the pressure...

The day had finally come: Mya Carter's second Spring Showcase at Chelseaville Performing Arts Center. The sun beamed through the trees, catching on wind chimes and casting playful shadows on the walls of the Carter home. It was the first official week of summer break, and Mya had been counting down the days to this performance for months.

Jenna had taken the day off from work, determined to make it memorable for her daughter. "Today is about pampering and purpose," she'd declared.

So that morning, Jenna, Mya, and Grandma Rose headed to the local spa in downtown, a peaceful retreat tucked into a small plaza. The ladies laughed together as they picked nail colors. Mya chose lavender with glitter tips, Grandma Rose opted for rose gold, and Jenna went with a soft, neutral peach.

They soaked their feet, sipped cucumber water, and let the day's calm wash over them. For a moment, everything felt perfect. Mya felt cherished, supported, and excited. She even hummed a few bars of her solo during the pedicure, prompting the nail technician to ask, "Is that what you're singing tonight?"

"Yep," Mya smiled. "It's called Grace and Sing. I'm closing the show."

After their spa day, they returned home just in time for Mya to change into her dress, a flowing white and lilac gown with satin ballet flats. Her curls were freshly styled, pinned delicately with rhinestone clips.

Meanwhile, Theo and Levi were finishing up their shift at the local ice cream parlor, about fifteen minutes away. They had promised to meet everyone at the performance by 5:30 p.m. to save seats. Owen had just left for his one-week golf summer camp the day before, and Jenna reminded herself to text the camp director with updates.

Noah, unfortunately, couldn't be home early. He had a crucial board meeting at the local financial firm about a possible merger with another mid-region banking company, a meeting he couldn't afford to miss.

But he had made a promise: "I'll be there before the curtain rises. I won't miss her song."

At 5:30 p.m., the meeting was still dragging on.

Noah kept checking his phone. His chair shifted restlessly as he glanced between the PowerPoint presentation and the time on his watch. Finally, at 5:38 p.m., he stood up.

"Apologies, I've got to step out," he said, already gathering his things. "My daughter's performing tonight. I won't miss it."

He jogged toward the garage, jumped into his midnight blue SUV, and headed for the freeway entrance.

"Why every time baby girl has a big performance, I'm running late," he thought with a frustrated sigh, gripping the wheel.

Just as he neared the freeway ramp, a silver sedan ran a red light and slammed into the side of Noah's SUV with terrifying force.

The vehicle spun out of control, violently flipping three times into oncoming traffic. Tires screeched. Horns blared. Glass shattered across the road.

A bystander called 911 immediately.

Paramedics arrived within minutes and began stabilizing Noah as he drifted in and out of consciousness. He was bleeding heavily from a head trauma, with multiple fractures and internal injuries. He was rushed to the nearest emergency room in critical condition.

Meanwhile, at Chelseaville Performing Arts Center, the auditorium buzzed with excitement.

The clock read 6:15 p.m.

The audience had filled every seat. Theo and Levi stood near the back, peering through the crowd, looking for their parents. Mya waited backstage, her hands pressed together, trying to remain calm.

But Jenna wasn't smiling.

She was in the lobby, frantically redialing Noah's number for the fourth time. The call connected, but it wasn't Noah's voice on the other end.

"Hello, is this Mrs. Carter?" a firm voice asked.

"Yes, who is this?" Jenna's voice trembled.

"This is Officer Reynolds from the local police department. I am answering your husband's phone call. He has been in a car accident…"

Jenna froze. "Is he okay?"

Your husband, Noah, was taken to Chelseaville Memorial Hospital. That is all I can say right now, ma'am. I do not want to alarm you, but I suggest you head there as soon as possible."

Tears welled in Jenna's eyes. Her body felt both frozen and electric at once. She and Grandma Rose promptly walked from the lobby to the backstage area. She told the boys to get in the car. We need to get to the hospital, it's your dad. Without hesitation, they left the building and proceeded to the parking lot.

They made their way backstage to get Mya, who was smiling brightly while conversing with Ms. Carmen.

She walked quickly toward. Our daughter, tears now streaking her cheeks.

"Mya," she said, voice tight. "We need to go. Your father's been in an accident."

Ms. Carmen and Ms. Elise both stepped forward in shock.

"What? Is he okay?" Ms. Elise asked.

"I don't know," Jenna said, trying to steady herself. "I just know it is serious. I am sorry, Mya can't perform tonight."

Mya's face fell. "What happened?"

"We'll talk in the car," Jenna said, gently but firmly. "We have to go now."

Ms. Carmen leaned down and hugged Mya tightly. "Sweetheart, you have already made us so proud. Go be with your dad."

Ms. Elise placed a hand on Jenna's shoulder. "Please call us when you know more. We will pray. We will all pray."

As Jenna and Mya rushed out of the building, the curtain rose behind them.

But for the Carter family, the spotlight had just shifted.

And their hearts now wait in the shadows of a hospital room, desperate for a miracle.

Chapter 12
Racing Toward the Unknown

Just minutes earlier, Jenna had sprinted out of the auditorium lobby into the parking lot, her face pale, and her eyes wide.

"We need to get to the hospital now," she said to Theo, who had been waiting by the car. "Leave your car. Ride with me. I need everyone together." Theo didn't argue. One look at his mother's face told him everything he needed to know. Jenna blinked back tears as she sped down the street towards the freeway, gripping the steering wheel like it was the only thing keeping her upright.

The city lights blurred as Jenna gripped the steering wheel even tighter, her knuckles white, her heart pounding louder than the tires on the pavement. Her mind raced faster than the car.

Next to her in the front passenger seat, Theo sat silently, jaw clenched, his graduation ring glinting in the fading daylight. In the backseat, Levi stared blankly out the window, trying to process the words car accident and critical condition. Beside him, Mya clung tightly to Grandma Rose's hand, her lavender dress wrinkled, and her sparkling shoes forgotten beneath the seat. She hadn't spoken a word since they left Chelseaville Performing Arts Center.

The silence in the car was thick, heavy with fear, questions, and the unspoken "what ifs" clawing at everyone's chest.

"I.... I don't know anything yet," she finally said, her voice cracking as she glanced at Theo. "The officer just said it was serious. He was rushed to Chelseaville Memorial Hospital."

"Did he say if he's awake?" Levi asked from the back; his voice was smaller than usual.

"No," Jenna whispered. "He wouldn't tell me."

Mya looked up suddenly, her voice breaking like glass. "Is Daddy going to die?"

"No, baby," Jenna said quickly, her voice sharper than she meant. "No. We are not going to think like that. We're going to get there, and we're going to pray, and your father is going to fight. He's strong."

Grandma Rose reached over and gently rested a hand on Jenna's arm. "Eyes on the road, baby. I've got the prayers covered."

Theo finally spoke. "What happened?"

Jenna shook her head. "Someone ran a red light. Hit him near the freeway ramp. The SUV flipped... they said three times."

Levi let out a low breath, leaning forward to rest his elbows on his knees.

Mya covered her ears. "I don't want to hear it. I want him to be okay."

"I know, sweetheart," Jenna said, her voice trembling. "Me too."

As the car weaved through traffic, the setting sun dipped below the skyline, casting everything in a golden-orange haze. The world outside kept moving families out for dinner, joggers on sidewalks, lights flickering on in quiet homes. But inside the Carter SUV, time seemed to stand still. Every second stretched long and uncertain.

Finally, they reached the emergency entrance of the medical center. Jenna pulled into the red zone, threw the car in park, and barely turned off the engine before rushing out.

"Everyone, stay close. Do not wander," she said firmly, grabbing Mya's hand and motioning the boys to follow.

They pushed through the automatic glass doors and were met with cold, sterile air and the sharp scent of antiseptic. Nurses rushed by with clipboards, phones rang in the distance, and the low murmur of pain and urgency filled the waiting room.

"I'm looking for my husband," Jenna said to the front desk nurse, her voice rising with desperation. "His name is Noah Carter.

There was an accident. He was brought in not long ago. Please, I need to see him."

The nurse's face softened. "One moment, ma'am. Let me page the trauma doctor."

Jenna turned back to her children, her face full of fear, and she was trying desperately to hide.

Theo stepped closer and wrapped his arm around her shoulders. "We are here, Mom. We are together. No matter what happens, we will be okay."

Jenna nodded, clutching Mya's hand tighter as a young doctor in blue scrubs walked briskly toward them.

And in that moment, all they could do was hold onto each other... and brace for whatever was coming next.

The young doctor approached swiftly, his name badge slightly tilted, and a tablet clutched tightly in his hand. His expression was calm, but Jenna could read beneath the surface. There was something heavy there, something no family ever wants to see.

"Mrs. Carter?" he asked gently.

Jenna stepped forward, her voice caught in her throat. "Yes. That is me. These are my children, Theo, Levi, and Mya. And my mother, Rose."

"I'm Dr. Leemondson, the trauma physician overseeing your husband's care." He took a breath before continuing. "Your husband was brought in approximately twenty-five minutes ago with significant injuries from a severe collision. He is stabilized now, but..." He paused, as if searching for the right words. "He's in a medically induced coma."

Jenna blinked. "A coma?"

"Yes," he said softly. "The impact caused a traumatic brain injury. His SUV flipped several times, and we believe he struck his head during the rollover. He also has multiple fractures to his left lower three ribs, a broken clavicle, and a partially collapsed lung. But the most concerning injury is to his brain. There's swelling... and we're doing everything we can to control it."

Jenna's legs buckled slightly. Theo grabbed her elbow to steady her.

"Is he going to wake up?" Levi asked, his voice shaking.

Dr. Leemondson looked at each of them carefully. "We just do not know yet. The next 48 to 72 hours are critical. We will closely monitor his neurological activity. Right now, we are keeping him sedated to prevent further damage."

"But he's alive?" Mya asked, eyes wide, barely above a whisper.

"Yes," Dr. Leemondson nodded. "He's alive, little ma'am."

Jenna felt like the floor had vanished beneath her. She wanted to scream, to cry, to demand answers, but she knew that wouldn't change anything. Her husband, her partner, her best friend, was fighting for his life in a sterile room just down the hall.

"Can we see him?" she asked, voice trembling.

"One at a time for now," the doctor said. "Just for a few minutes. He won't be responsive, but it may help. I'll have a nurse escort you in."

As he walked away, Jenna turned to her children. Theo's eyes were glossy but unblinking. Levi looked like he was swallowing a lump the size of a brick. Mya was still holding Grandma Rose's hand, trembling.

Jenna knelt in front of her daughter and tucked a curl behind her ear. "Daddy's in a deep sleep, honey. But he's strong. You know that, right?"

Mya nodded, barely.

"We're going to believe God for healing," Grandma Rose added, stepping in. "That is what we do. We stand together. We pray. And we trust Him."

Jenna wiped her tears and stood tall. "Theo, I am going in first. Stay with Grandma and the kids. Okay?"

Theo nodded, swallowing hard.

Jenna followed the nurse down the hallway, her heels clicking softly against the tile. With every step, her breath grew shorter, as if the weight of what she was walking toward was pressing on her chest.

And then she saw him.

Noah lay still beneath crisp white sheets, machines softly beeping, an oxygen tube at his nose, and a bandage across the side of his forehead. He looked... nothing like the man who had kissed her goodbye that morning.

Tears streamed down Jenna's face as she walked to his bedside.

She reached for his hand, warm but unmoving.

"Baby," she whispered, her voice cracking. "It is me. I'm here."

She sat down and gently laid her head against his arm.

And for the first time all day, Jenna let the full weight of her fear fall.

After what felt like both a minute and a lifetime, Jenna stepped out of Noah's room. Her cheeks were still damp, but her posture was steady, anchored by love, even in the storm.

She looked at her oldest son. "Theo, it's your turn."

Theo nodded and silently followed the nurse down the hallway. The automatic door eased shut behind him with a quiet hiss.

Theo stood at the threshold of his father's hospital room, frozen for a moment. The man in the bed was the same one who had taught him how to drive, how to shave, how to shake a man's hand and look him in the eye. But right now, that man looked... small. Still. Helpless.

He moved toward the bedside slowly, then pulled up the chair and sat beside him.

"Dad," he said, clearing his throat. "It's Theo. You already knew that. I, uh... I don't know what to say, but I love you. You should have left the meeting early."

His voice cracked.

"Remember when we talked about my major? And you said I could do anything as long as I did it with integrity?" He chuckled. "I chose finance because I wanted to be like you. I haven't told you that yet. I wanted it to be a surprise."

He reached for his father's hand, gripping it with both of his.

"I know you can't hear me... but I'm going to keep showing up, Dad. For Mom. For Mya. For Levi. For Owen. For all of us. But I need you to wake up, okay? Not just for us, but for you."

He blinked rapidly, wiped his face, and stood.

"I love you."

Theo walked out and looked at Levi, who gave a silent nod. He stayed seated. He whispered to his mother, I cannot go," said Levi. "It's ok, baby, just stay here with me."

Jenna looked at Grandma Rose. "Would you take Mya in next? I'll stay out here with the boys."

Grandma Rose nodded gently. "Come on, baby girl.

Mya held Grandma's hand tightly as they entered the dim hospital room. The beeping machines were louder now that the room was quiet. Mya hesitated as they approached her son-in-law's bedside.

"He doesn't look like Daddy," she whispered.

"No," Grandma said softly. "But that is still him. His spirit is still in there. His body needs rest right now."

Mya climbed up gently into the chair beside the bed. Her eyes filled with tears as she looked at the bandages and wires. She reached for her father's hand and held it close to her cheek.

"Daddy, it's Mya," she said, her voice breaking. "I wore my pretty dress, the one you picked out. And I was ready to sing. I was."

She sniffled. "But then Mommy said we had to come here. And I did not get to sing. But that is okay. I'll sing when you're awake, okay? I will sing for you."

Her voice cracked into a soft hum. Then she sang gently, in a whisper:

I love you, Daddy…I love you, Daddy…please wake up, please don't leave me! I need to sing to you…..Mya wiped her tears and fell into her grandma's side.

Grandma Rose placed a hand over her heart and closed her eyes.

When Mya finished the verse, she leaned forward and kissed her father's arm. "Please wake up soon, Daddy. I miss your jokes. And your pancakes."

When Mya stepped out of the room, Grandma Rose took a deep breath and walked over to the bed. She had prayed for many people over the years, in hospital rooms, at nursing homes, and in living rooms, but this one cut deep.

She placed her hand on Noah's chest and whispered:

"Father God, you know this man better than any of us. You gave him breath. You gave him purpose. And you can give him healing. We know the doctors see a coma, but you see a soul. You see destiny."

Tears slipped down her cheek as she continued.

"Cover his mind. Shrink the swelling. Mend every break. Strengthen his lungs. Lord, we are not asking for what we deserve, but for what You can do. Touch him right now, in the name of Jesus."

She paused, placed a kiss on Noah's forehead, and whispered, "I love you like a son."

Then she turned and walked out, her shoulders strong, but her heart was heavy.

In the waiting room, Jenna, Theo, Levi, and Mya sat in silence together. A nurse brought them warm blankets and a tray of juice boxes and crackers. Outside, the sky had turned black.

But inside the hospital, the Carter family waited in faith and fear for dawn, for healing, for a miracle they refused to stop believing in. After everyone had visited with their father, husband, and son-in-law, the nurse entered the room to monitor his condition.

Inside Noah's deep thought of consciousness. He floated in a weightless calm. There were no machines, no pain, no chaos. Just warmth. Just stillness. Just memory.

He stood on a dusty football field beneath a fall sky, shoulder to shoulder with his sons, Theo and Levi, laughing, blocking, running. The cheers from the sidelines faded into the sound of waves, and suddenly he was with Owen, standing at the edge of a bright green course, watching his youngest son line up a perfect putt during their first father-son golf tournament.

Noah smiled.

Then the scene shifted again.

This time, he was sitting in the front row of Chelseaville Performing Arts Center, watching Mya, his baby girl, sing beneath the glow of the spotlight. Her voice filled the air with light. He rose to his feet, clapping, heart swelling with pride.

The lights dimmed.

And then, in a soft moment, he lay in bed beside Jenna, her head nestled against his shoulder, their legs tangled beneath the blanket. They whispered about nothing and everything about the kids, retirement plans, dreams, and the silly things that made them laugh after 22 years of marriage.

Noah closed his eyes in that memory, just as Jenna had in real life, resting, safe, whole.

But then… the warmth changed.

The light around him began to shift into something more golden, unseen yet deeply familiar. A quiet voice, deep and steady, began to echo.

"A time to be born, and a time to die…"

Noah turned toward the voice, stepping into a meadow filled with light he could not explain. It was not sunlight; it was something more profound. It shimmered from within.

"A time to plant, and a time to pluck up that which is planted…"

He looked around and finally asked, "Who's there?"

Silence for a moment.

Then the voice spoke again, calm but final.

"Your time is drawing near."

Noah shook his head. "Please. I need more time. My kids...they are still growing. Mya... she needs her daddy. Jenna and I still have more stories. His voice dropped to a broken whisper. *"I'm not finished."*

The voice did not reply.

Noah took another step forward. "Please. Just give me more time. I'm not ready to leave them yet."

Stillness. Then... one small word whispered into the atmosphere.

"No."

A single tear slipped down Noah's cheek.

In the hospital room, Nurse Danielle sat monitoring Noah's vitals. Her eyes flicked up to the screen. His blood pressure had spiked.

"Doctor!" she called out. "You need to see this."

Dr. Leemondson walked in quickly, eyes scanning the monitors.

More tears.

"Wait...look," Nurse Danielle pointed. "Tears. He's crying."

The doctor stepped closer, stunned. "That's... unusual. He's still completely unresponsive."

"Then why is he crying?" she asked, her voice barely above a whisper.

He had no answer.

Just then, the monitor's beeping changed.

A sudden, high-pitched tone.

The ECG line straightened.

Flatline.

"No... no, no, no," Danielle said, pressing the code button. "He was stable!"

The doctor sprang into action, calling for a crash cart.

But in Noah's world, the light began to fade.

The memories stilled.

And for a moment, all was quiet.

The sound of alarms echoed down the corridor.

Red lights blinked above ICU Room 4, and medical staff flooded through the door.

In the waiting area, Jenna stood up instinctively, eyes locked on the hallway. A nurse came running.

"Mrs. Carter… It's your husband. You need to come now."

Her blood went cold.

"What happened?" she whispered, already walking.

"His heart… it stopped."

Jenna didn't wait for permission. She sprinted past the nurse, her heels clicking like gunshots against the tile. Theo, Levi, Mya, and Grandma Rose followed behind her, their legs and lungs burning with dread.

When they reached the door, no one stopped them.

They burst into the room, and what they saw broke them.

Noah lay still, pale, the monitors screaming flatline. His chest was exposed, wires clinging to his skin. A nurse stood beside him, her hands pressed down rhythmically, pumping his chest with desperate precision. Dr. Leemondson stood at his side, calling out vitals as another nurse loaded a second syringe.

"Epinephrine in," someone said. "Charging paddles, clear!"

Jenna froze in the doorway, her body paralyzed. Then the sob burst from her throat like a thunderclap.

"No, Noah! No! Please, God!"

She ran to his side, falling against his chest, the nurses stepping back just enough to let her touch him.

"Noah, please… stay. Stay with me," she wept. "You promised me forever!"

Theo stood motionless, his face twisted in silent agony. Then he dropped to his knees at the foot of the bed, sobbing uncontrollably. His strong frame shook with every breath.

Levi clenched his fists, punching the side of the wall, his teeth gritted against the scream he refused to let out.

Mya, sweet little Mya, stared, frozen in place. Her voice trembled.

"Daddy… wake up."

She took a small step forward, and Grandma Rose gently knelt beside her, wrapping her arms around the little girl.

"Why won't he wake up?" Mya whispered, over and over, as her tears soaked her grandmother's blouse.

Jenna cradled Noah's face with both hands, rubbing his forehead. His eyes remained closed, lips slightly parted.

"I need you," she cried. "You can't leave us. Please don't leave us…"

The monitor still read flatline.

One long, piercing tone filled the room.

Grandma Rose stood and placed her hand over Noah's chest.

With trembling lips, she began to pray.

"God of life and mercy… breathe again into Your servant. If there is one more breath in his lungs, call it forth, Lord. Not by our will, but by Yours. Let Your glory be known in this room."

The nurses stepped back. Even the doctor paused, heart caught in the sacred silence.

And still… no movement.

Jenna clung tighter.

Theo wept harder.

Mya whispered, "Please, Jesus…"

The monitor did not change.

Time slowed. Grief wrapped itself around the Carter family like an unrelenting fog.

It was a room full of people, but one soul was missing.

And for the first time since they'd walked in, hope felt like it was slipping through their fingers.

Chapter 13
A House Without His Voice

They had turned the machines off.

The room, once filled with urgent shouts and mechanical beeping, was now still, eerily still.

Noah lay in the center of the room, peaceful at last. His face no longer strained, the lines of pain erased. But his stillness cut deeper than any visible wound.

The family stayed.

No one wanted to be the first to let go.

Jenna sat in the chair beside the bed, her head resting gently on Noah's chest, her tears soaking into the fabric of his gown. She didn't care who watched. This wasn't for them. This was for him.

"This isn't how we were supposed to end," she whispered. "You were just late... that's all."

Theo stood behind her, his hand resting on her shoulder as silent tears ran down his face. He had seen pain before. He had seen people cry. But he had never seen his mother like this. It shattered him.

Levi had taken a seat by the window, hands over his face, staring blankly out into the orange glow of the rising sun. His body felt heavy, like lead had filled every bone.

Mya curled into Grandma Rose's lap on the small sofa against the wall. Her voice was barely audible as she repeated, "He was supposed to hear me sing."

Grandma held her tighter, whispering, "He did, baby. He did. Your daddy heard it."

No one spoke much more. They just stayed. Each minute passed like a sigh.

Eventually, a nurse kindly stepped in. "Take your time, but let us know when you're ready."

Jenna nodded, brushing Noah's forehead with one last kiss.

One by one, they said their goodbyes. Soft hands held his, soft words clung to the air. The pain was raw. Real. Relentless.

The ride home was silent.

Theo drove his mom's car. The only sound was the low hum of the tires against the road and the occasional sniffle from the backseat.

Mya sat between Jenna and Grandma Rose, clutching her dad's jacket, which still smelled faintly of his cologne. Levi leaned against the window, earbuds in, but the music was turned off.

No one had the energy to speak.

Even the city felt quieter, as if the world had taken notice of what was lost.

As they pulled into their driveway, Jenna stared blankly ahead. Porch lights flickered on automatically. A sprinkler turned in slow circles across the lawn.

And then her heart dropped.

"Oh God... Owen," she gasped.

Everyone looked at her.

"I...I forgot about Owen. He's still at camp. He doesn't even know."

Jenna buried her face in her hands, fresh sobs overtaking her.

Theo turned off the ignition and placed a steady hand on her back. "We'll call them. We'll bring him home."

Jenna shook her head, devastated. "He should've been here... He should've had the chance to say goodbye."

Grandma Rose spoke gently, "He'll still get to grieve. In his way. The Lord will meet him there, just like He's meeting all of us."

Jenna wiped her eyes and opened the car door, stepping into a world that looked the same, but felt utterly changed.

Noah wouldn't be opening the door tonight; there was no laughter from the kitchen.

No teasing from the hallway. Just echoes...just grief.

Just an empty spot at the head of the table.

The house felt too quiet. Too cold. Even with all the lights on, it felt dark.

After they arrived home, Jenna gently asked Theo and Levi if they could retrieve the car they'd left behind at Chelseaville Performing Arts Center. Neither of them hesitated. They needed to move. To breathe. To feel anything but the grief suffocating their home.

Theo grabbed the spare keys, and the two brothers climbed into the second car, pulling out of the driveway into the still summer night.

For a while, they drove in silence.

Then Levi spoke.

"He didn't get to hear her sing."

Theo didn't answer right away. His hands tightened on the steering wheel.

"I mean," Levi continued, voice raw, "we were there. We were all there. And he was trying to get there too. And now he's just... gone."

Theo exhaled slowly. "He was always running to be there for us. Even when it cost him something."

Levi wiped his face. "I don't know how to do this without him."

Theo's voice cracked. "I don't either, man."

They pulled into the empty school lot. The exact spot they had stood in just hours earlier, full of anticipation and excitement. The building stood silent now, still dressed in showcase banners and glowing marquee lights that read: "Spring Showcase – Spring Forward to A New Day."

Levi leaned his head back against the headrest. "I didn't say goodbye."

Theo looked at him. "Neither did I."

A beat of silence.

"But we can still live like he's watching," Theo added. "We can carry him with us. Every day."

Levi nodded slowly, eyes wet. "Yeah."

They didn't move for a moment, just sat there, letting their pain exist without rushing to fix it. Then Theo reached for his phone.

"I have to call the camp. Owen needs to know."

Back in the driver's seat, Theo searched through his contacts and found the number for Chelseaville Junior Golf Camp. He pressed call.

After a few rings, a cheerful voice answered.

"Junior golf camp," Coach Ryan said."

"Hi, this is Theo Carter. I'm calling about Owen Carter, my little brother. He's at your camp."

"Ah, yeah, Owen! Great swing on that kid. Just hit a straight shot across the eighth hole today."

Theo's voice caught. "I need to bring him home."

A pause. "Is everything okay?

Theo closed his eyes. "Our dad… he passed away. Just a few hours ago. It was a car accident. We haven't told Owen yet."

The coach was silent for a beat. "I'm so sorry, Theo. Truly. I can be ready to release him whenever you are."

"I'll be there first thing in the morning."

"Of course. We'll keep him comfortable tonight. We won't say anything until you get here."

"Thank you," Theo whispered.

After the call ended, he sat still, his phone resting on his knee.

"You think he'll understand?" Levi asked quietly.

Theo shook his head, tears returning to his eyes. "No. But I'll be there when he does."

He turned the key and started the engine. The two brothers left the empty parking lot behind, returning not just with a car but with a deeper bond. A silent vow between them to protect what was left, no matter how broken they felt inside.

The next morning, sunlight crept into the Carter home, but it brought no warmth, only light that felt intrusive, unwelcome, foreign in a house now hollow with grief.

Jenna hadn't left the bedroom.

Last night, she had paced the floor, barefoot, wearing the same clothes from the day before. She walked in circles around the bed, through the bathroom, past the closet, over and over, until her heels felt swollen and raw. Her heartbeat was fast, but her mind moved slowly, like someone underwater.

She had opened Noah's dresser, then his closet. She ran her fingers across the jackets he wore on Sundays, the shirt he wore to Mya's last recital. The pants had his favorite leather belt still looped inside. His laundry bag sat against the corner wall, full of clothes he hadn't yet washed.

She knelt beside it slowly. Opened it.

And then the scent hit her, his smell, a faint cologne, mixed with detergent and sweat, and something warm and familiar.

Jenna fell to the floor, clutching handfuls of his worn t-shirts to her chest. She curled into them like a child. Her tears soaked the fabric.

Eventually, her body gave out from exhaustion.

She fell asleep inside the closet, cocooned in grief, cradled in his scent. Not the bed they shared. Not the room they built together. But among the evidence that he had been.

Downstairs, Grandma Rose had stayed the night, unpacking spare blankets, fluffing pillows, doing what mothers and grandmothers do when everything falls apart. She had stayed up late in the guest room holding Mya, who had cried silently until her little chest heaved from sobbing. Eventually, Mya curled into Grandma's arms and drifted into a restless sleep.

The next morning, Grandma tiptoed through the kitchen, brewing tea instead of coffee. She wanted calm, not energy.

She looked toward the hallway where Mya was still asleep. She turned to the stairs, where Jenna had not yet emerged. Then her eyes drifted toward the front window.

The driveway was empty.

Because Theo and Levi had left before sunrise.

Neither boy had truly slept.

After returning from the school parking lot the night before, they had stayed up in Theo's room, talking. Not long conversations. Just scattered memories and sudden bursts of weeping that neither of them apologized for.

"How do we live without him?" Levi had asked sometime around 3 a.m.

"I don't know," Theo had answered. "But we will."

And now, in the gray-blue light of dawn, they were on the road to Chelseaville Junior Golf Camp, hearts heavy and unsure how to deliver the worst kind of news to a little brother who hadn't even unpacked his golf shoes yet.

Chapter 14
Family Emotions

The drive to the golf camp was quiet, just like the drive home had been the night before. But this silence wasn't empty; it was loaded with fear, with the burden of being the bearer of sorrow.

Theo and Levi parked near the camp lodge. Birds chirped somewhere in the trees, and kids laughed in the distance near the putting green. The world here hadn't changed yet.

But it was about to.

Coach Ryan met them at the gravel path and pulled them aside with a firm handshake and a somber nod. "He's inside the lounge area watching a golf tutorial. He doesn't suspect anything."

Theo nodded. "Thank you for keeping him calm."

Ryan glanced toward the building. "You sure you don't want me to talk with him first?"

"No," Theo said softly. "He needs to hear it from me. From us."

Inside the lodge, Owen sat cross-legged on a couch, munching on pretzels and watching a video of pro golfers breaking down their swings. He turned around the moment the door opened.

"Hey!" he grinned. "What are you guys doing here? Wait, is Mya's performance today?! Did I miss it?"

Theo's smile faltered.

Levi stepped forward, swallowing hard. "Hey, bud."

Owen tilted his head. "What's going on?"

Theo crouched in front of him, gently taking Owen's hands. "Owen… we need to talk to you, okay?"

Owen looked between his brothers.

Theo's voice broke. "Something happened… to Dad."

Owen's smile faded. "Is he okay?"

Theo could barely say the words. "No, buddy. He was in a car accident the other day."

Owen sat up straighter, heart pounding. "Is he in the hospital?"

Theo's lips trembled. "He didn't make it, Owen. He…he's gone."

Owen blinked once.

Then twice.

Then his body swayed.

"No…" he whispered. "No, no, no…"

Before Levi could react, Owen collapsed, fainting in place.

Levi lunged, arms out, but didn't catch him in time.

"Owen!" Theo cried, dropping to his knees beside his brother.

Coach Ryan rushed in. "Sarah! First aid, now!"

Owen lay unconscious for a moment, his small chest rising and falling fast. Levi propped his head up gently. Coach Ryan handed them a cool towel while Sarah grabbed a flashlight to check his pupils.

"Owen, come on, buddy," Theo whispered. "Come back."

Slowly, Owen's eyelids fluttered.

He blinked against the light.

Then, realization hit.

And he screamed.

"No! No! You're lying! YOU'RE LYING!"

He thrashed, trying to get up. "Take it back! Tell me you're joking!"

Theo tried to hold him. "Owen…"

"DON'T TOUCH ME!" he screamed, eyes wild. "Where's Daddy?! Where is he?!"

Coach Ryan grabbed him from behind, trying to restrain him gently. "Easy, son. Easy."

Owen kicked and swung, trying to fight his way loose. "I HATE YOU! You're lying! YOU'RE LYING! I want my dad!"

Levi backed away in tears. Theo stayed still, letting Owen scream it out, even when it broke him in half.

Coach Ryan held Owen close, rocking him as the boy cried out in deep, uncontrollable grief. "It's not fair... It's not fair... he was going to hear her sing... he said he'd be there."

The room felt sacred in its pain.

No one spoke.

Even the staff stood in quiet reverence as Owen sobbed into Coach Ryan's chest, shaking.

And Theo, crouched on the floor, whispered the only words he could manage through his sobs:

"I'm so sorry, Owen. I'm so, so sorry."

"Let me speak with Owen alone while you all gather his things," said Ryan.

The door to Owen's small cabin creaked open as Theo, Levi, and Sarah quietly stepped inside. The morning sun filtered through the blinds, casting a warm, dusty glow over the twin bed covered in golf polos, a half-packed duffel bag, and Owen's golf glove tucked under a notebook.

The silence was heavy.

Theo walked over and began folding Owen's clothes, careful not to disrupt anything more than necessary. Levi picked up the boy's golf cleats, brushing a speck of dirt from the toe before gently placing them in the side compartment of the bag.

Sarah crept with them, placing Owen's toiletries into a zip pouch. "He was excited to be here," she said softly. "Talked about his dad nonstop."

Theo paused, his eyes stinging again.

"He was supposed to be here," he whispered.

Levi zipped up the bag. "He was always supposed to be there."

They worked quietly and carefully until every item was packed and ready to return home.

Across the campus, in a small, shaded corner by the equipment shed, Coach Ryan sat on a bench beside Owen, who leaned forward with his arms on his knees and his head down. His face was pale and puffy from crying. The wind ruffled his hair gently, but he didn't move.

Coach Ryan didn't rush.

He just sat beside him, hands clasped, waiting until the boy spoke first.

Finally, Owen whispered, "I don't want to go home."

"I know," Ryan said quietly.

"I didn't even get to say goodbye."

Ryan nodded slowly. "I didn't either. When I lost my dad, I was twenty-one. It's been ten years… and it still hurts."

Owen looked up at him, surprised. "You too?"

Coach Ryan gave a small, broken smile. "Yeah. Big, strong coaches cry, too, kid. Especially when they love big."

Owen swallowed hard. "How long did it take to stop hurting?"

Ryan leaned back against the bench, staring out at the trees. "It doesn't ever stop hurting. However, it does become lighter, like carrying a backpack full of rocks. Every day, you get a little stronger… or maybe the rocks get a little smaller. You keep walking anyway."

Owen's eyes filled again.

"I'm scared to go home."

Ryan turned toward him, voice gentle but sure. "Home is where healing starts. Where you cried with your family, and you remember every good thing your dad was. Where you talk about him until the silence starts to feel like a story instead of a punishment."

Then he reached for a folded paper in his pocket. "I keep this with me. Want to hear it?"

Owen nodded slowly.

Ryan unfolded the paper, edges worn and softened over time. He read softly:

"A time to weep, and a time to laugh;

A time to mourn, and a time to dance."

Ecclesiastes 3:4 KJV

"Right now, Owen... this is your time to weep. And that's okay. It's holy. It's honest. But I promise, one day, you'll laugh again. Not because you forgot him... but because you'll carry him with you."

Owen wiped his eyes.

Coach Ryan wrapped an arm around his shoulders. "You're not alone. Not now. Not ever."

From a short distance away, Theo and Levi stood by the car, watching. Theo whispered, "He's in good hands."

Levi nodded. "Dad would've liked him."

A few minutes later, Coach Ryan walked Owen over to his brothers. The duffel was packed, and the ride home was waiting.

Owen didn't say much; he didn't need to.

He just hugged Coach Ryan tightly, holding on longer than expected. And Ryan whispered, "You're brave, Owen. Keep walking."

As the car doors closed and the Carter brothers pulled away, the sun shone gently on the winding road ahead.

The journey back home had begun.

And with it, the journey through grief, together.

The house still didn't feel right.

Back at home, it had been nearly 48 hours since they returned from the hospital, and yet every room felt suspended in time like the very walls knew that something, someone, was missing.

Jenna stood at the kitchen counter, staring down at a half-filled glass of orange juice. Her hand rested on the rim, but she hadn't taken a sip. She had showered that morning out of habit, but the water felt cold, no matter how hot it ran.

She was physically present. Emotionally, somewhere between yesterday and forever.

Across the kitchen, Mya sat cross-legged on one of the stools, clutching a small drawing she'd made for Owen. It was crayon-colored: a house, a tree, and stick figures labeled "Owen," "Mya,"

"Theo," "Levi," "Mom," and "Dad." She'd added angel wings to the one that said "Dad."

"Will Owen cry, Mommy?" she asked quietly.

Jenna turned toward her slowly. Her voice was soft, almost cracked. "He might. He probably will."

Mya frowned, lowering her head. "Can I give him this when he gets home?"

Jenna nodded, her lips trembling. "Yes, baby. I think he'll need that."

She walked over and placed a hand on Mya's back, gently rubbing in circles the way Noah used to do when the kids were sick or sad.

Then she turned her gaze toward the staircase.

"I need to get his room ready."

Mya perked up. "Can I help?"

"Yes," Mom said, with the faintest shadow of a smile. "Let's do it together."

Owen's room smelled faintly of cologne and bubblegum, the two things he always kept in his backpack. His clothes were still in piles from packing for camp. His comic books were stacked high on the nightstand, and his favorite Tigers baseball cap still hung from the corner of the bedpost.

Jenna took a deep breath and began straightening things. Mya fluffed the pillows while her mother folded the extra blankets at the foot of the bed.

"I think he'll be mad," Mya whispered.

"Maybe," Jenna said gently, smoothing out the comforter. "But that's okay. We all feel a lot of things right now. Mad. Sad. Confused."

"I was mad last night," Mya admitted, sitting on the edge of the bed. "I prayed that God would make Daddy wake up. But he didn't."

Jenna knelt in front of her, cupping Mya's face. "It's okay to feel that way. God can handle our madness. He's still listening."

Mya blinked back tears. "Do you think Owen will stop talking like Brittany did?"

Jenna wrapped her arms around her daughter. "No. He's hurting, but he won't stay silent. We're going to love him through it. Just like we're doing for each other."

Downstairs, Grandma Rose placed a fresh pitcher of lemonade on the table and laid out sandwiches for the boys, because grief didn't stop stomachs from growling.

She paused at the kitchen window, watching the driveway.

"They will be here soon," said Grandma Rose.

Then the sound of tires rolling across the driveway sent a jolt through the house.

Jenna froze at the foot of the stairs, Mya clutched her mother's hand tightly, and Grandma Rose stepped from the kitchen, drying her hands with a dish towel, heart bracing for what was about to unfold.

The car door shut.

Then another. Then another.

The front door opened slowly.

Owen stepped inside first, his small frame tense, eyes red-rimmed, shoulders sagging beneath the weight of what he now knew.

Behind him came Theo, his protective hand resting lightly on his brother's back. Levi entered last, silent, expression unreadable, but his chest moved quickly, rising and falling like waves against rocks.

Jenna knelt on the floor before Owen could take another step.

Her arms opened wide.

And Owen ran.

He collided with her so hard that they both fell to their knees. Jenna wrapped her arms around her son, holding him like she had when he was a baby, when a scraped knee was the worst pain he knew.

"Mommy…" he whimpered into her neck. "He's gone."

"I know, baby," she whispered, rocking him gently. "I know."

Mya stepped forward timidly, holding the drawing close to her chest.

"Owen…" she said softly.

He turned toward her slowly, his eyes heavy.

She held out the crayon picture, trembling. "I made this for you."

He looked at it, at the wings she'd drawn on their father, and a sob escaped his throat. He dropped to his knees and hugged Mya so tight she could hardly breathe.

"I miss him already," he cried.

"I do too," she said, rubbing his back. "So much."

Theo knelt beside them, placing one arm around Owen and one around Mya. His eyes flooded again.

Then Levi stood frozen, fists clenched, lips trembling. His breath was short.

Theo looked up. "Levi…

And that's when it happened.

Levi fell to his knees, covered his face, and let out a broken, guttural cry, louder than he meant, deeper than he realized.

"I can't do this… I can't, he's supposed to be here!

He sobbed into his palms, shoulders shaking uncontrollably.

Grandma Rose dropped the towel and knelt beside her grandsons.

And there, in the middle of the living room, on the carpet worn by memories and movie nights, the Carter family collapsed into each other.

Theo, Levi, Owen, Mya, Jenna, and Grandma Rose, arms tangled, foreheads pressed together, tears flowing freely.

There were no speeches. No reassurances.

Just the sound of grief shared in a sacred circle.

The pain was real.

But so was the love.

And somehow, in that small moment, through all the breakdown, they still had each other. The tears still flowed.

They had huddled together for what felt like forever, crying, clinging, breathing in each other's pain as if holding one another could somehow shield them from what was now real.

Eventually, the sobs softened into silence.

And it was Grandma Rose who broke it, her voice cracking but full of conviction.

"Let's pray," she whispered, lifting her head slightly from the circle.

No one moved or argued.

They just leaned in closer.

Grandma Rose reached out her hands, calloused from years of caregiving and prayer, and took hold of Jenna and Theo's hands, completing the circle.

She closed her eyes, swallowed the lump in her throat, and began.

"Father God... we don't understand."

Her voice trembled.

"We don't understand why you took Noah. He was a husband. A father. A covering. A protector. He was ours."

Tears spilled down her cheeks.

"But Lord, we come to You anyway. Because we know you're the same yesterday, today, and forever. Even in the valley. Even in the pain."

Mya's head rested on Owen's shoulder, their eyes closed tightly as Grandma continued.

"God, we're broken. We're hurting. But You said in Your Word that You are near to the brokenhearted. So be near to us now, Lord. Provide us with a sense of peace that is not easily explained."

Theo squeezed Levi's shoulder gently as Grandma Rose's voice deepened.

"Help us remember Noah's love, not just in photographs, but in how we treat each other. Let his strength live through his sons. Let his tenderness echo in Mya's voice. And give Jenna the strength to keep leading this family even when she feels empty."

Jenna wept silently, her head bowed low, one hand covering her face.

"Lord, I don't ask You to take away our sorrow... I ask you to walk with us through it. Carry us when we can't carry ourselves."

She paused, voice thick with emotion.

"And Father... if there's ever been a moment You've listened in from heaven, it's now. Hear these tears. Hear these hearts. And hold Noah close. Tell him we love him. Tell him we'll never forget him."

A long silence followed.

Then Grandma Rose whispered one final word, steady and sacred.

"Amen."

And in that moment, although nothing was fixed and the pain still lingered, the room felt held.

The grief didn't disappear.

But neither did the presence of God.

Chapter 15
The Hardest Goodbye

Two days had passed since the world stopped spinning for the Carter family.

The air in the house was thick, still, and unmoving, as if even time itself were grieving.

Outside, the sky was gray, overcast, with low-hanging clouds casting long shadows across the lawn. Inside, the house remained dim, with curtains drawn and lights off.

Jenna stood at the front door, dressed in black slacks and a soft gray blouse, her eyes hollow but steady. In her hand, she held a notepad filled with questions she didn't want to ask and decisions she didn't want to make. Funeral arrangements. Obituary draft. Casket choice. Worship song selections. Reception food. Burial or cremation.

All things a wife should never have to decide while still smelling her husband's scent on his side of the bed.

Grandma Rose stood beside her, car keys in hand, purse looped over her arm. She wore navy blue and her church shoes...the ones she reserved for weddings and funerals.

She glanced back down the hallway.

"The kids still in bed?" she asked gently.

Jenna nodded. "I didn't wake them. None of them ate much yesterday."

Grandma Rose gave a small sigh. "Grief makes time move strangely. Sometimes slow. Sometimes not at all."

Jenna looked up toward the ceiling and exhaled. "I still keep expecting him to walk down the stairs and say something ridiculous just to make me smile."

A long silence passed between them.

Then Jenna straightened her shoulders.

"Let's get this over with."

They stepped outside, locking the door behind them.

Inside, the house remained quiet.

Upstairs, Theo lay wide awake, staring at the ceiling with his hands folded across his chest. He hadn't slept much, not since the hospital. His room still smelled faintly of the cologne his dad had given him the previous Christmas. It sat unopened on the dresser. He couldn't bring himself to use it yet.

Levi was curled under his blanket, earbuds in, though no music played. He stared at the window, watching the branches outside sway in the wind. He hadn't cried again since the living room breakdown, but his silence was loud, almost deafening.

In the guest room, Mya lay beside Owen, both still tucked beneath the quilt Grandma Rose had laid over them the night before. Mya's arm rested over her brother's chest, her breathing soft and shallow. Owen clung to the drawing she had given him…the one with angel wings drawn over their father.

The children didn't speak.

They didn't play.

They didn't move.

And in the stillness of the home, it was clear that grief had settled in not as a visitor, but as a presence that now shared their space. Jenna and Grandma Rose left the house without drawing attention, allowing the children to spend several hours on their own. Mom told Theo to keep a close eye on Mya.

The car ride to Chelseaville Chapel & Funeral Services was quiet.

Jenna kept her gaze fixed on the road ahead, though her hands trembled softly on her lap. She hadn't spoken much since they left the house, and Grandma Rose respected the silence. Some things were too sacred for words. Too painful to fill with small talk.

As they turned into the curved stone driveway, Jenna whispered, "I can't believe we're planning Noah's funeral."

Grandma reached across the seat and gently squeezed her hand. "Neither can I, baby. But we'll get through this. One breath at a time."

The chapel stood in solemn elegance, draped in ivy and framed by low white columns. A gold plaque by the glass door read:

Providing services to families since 1939 with Grace, Dignity, and Love.

Jenna stared at the words as if they were written in a foreign language. Grace and dignity felt miles away from what she was carrying inside.

As they entered the front lobby, the scent of soft flowers and polished wood filled the air. A woman in a gray dress suit stood at the reception desk. Her eyes were kind. Her smile was careful.

"Mrs. Carter?" she asked softly.

Jenna nodded.

"I'm Andrea. We spoke on the phone yesterday. I'll be helping you with the arrangements."

Jenna tried to return the smile but couldn't quite manage it.

"Right this way," Andrea said, leading them into a quiet consultation room filled with books, samples, and forms.

Jenna sat slowly, her hands clasped so tightly her knuckles turned white.

Andrea opened a folder gently. "I know this isn't easy. So, we're going to take our time, okay? We'll walk through everything together."

Jenna gave a slow nod. "I want it to be simple... but meaningful. He wasn't flashy. But he was... everything to us."

Grandma Rose dabbed at her eyes with a tissue and placed a steady hand on Jenna's back.

Andrea spoke gently. "Let's start with the service itself. Were you thinking a traditional church funeral or a chapel memorial here?"

"Church," Jenna said immediately. "That was his home. He was baptized there. He... sang in the choir."

Andrea made a note. "And the date?"

Jenna paused. "Saturday. That gives us four more days."

Andrea nodded. "Will there be a viewing?"

Jenna hesitated. Her voice cracked. "Yes. Just for the family. Friday evening. I...I don't know if I can see him like that, but the kids may need it."

"And the burial?"

"At Chelseaville Memorial Park. He said he wanted to be next to his parents."

Andrea turned to the next page. "Do you have a pastor in mind?"

Grandma Rose finally spoke. "Pastor Shaw prayed with us when we lost my husband. He'll know what to say."

They went through casket choices next, Jenna choosing a rich mahogany with soft ivory lining.

"He hated anything too fancy," she said with a weak smile. "But he deserved something strong."

When it came to selecting the music, Jenna paused the longest. She flipped through the hymn options until her finger stopped on one:

"It Is Well With My Soul."

Her voice broke. "That one."

Grandma Rose let out a soft breath and closed her eyes.

After nearly an hour and a half, the arrangements were completed on paper, at least for now.

But in Jenna's heart, nothing felt finished. Nothing felt real.

As they stood to leave, Andrea placed a hand on Jenna's shoulder. "You're doing beautifully. You're honoring him well."

Jenna didn't respond. She couldn't.

She just nodded and strolled toward the door, carrying not just papers and pamphlets, but the unimaginable weight of preparing the world to say goodbye to her husband.

The scent of warm garlic and sesame oil filled the Carter home that evening, not because someone had cooked, but because Jenna didn't have the energy to stand in front of a stove.

She and Grandma Rose returned home just after six, carrying large brown takeout bags from their favorite Chinese restaurant on the edge of town.

"I didn't feel like cooking," Jenna said softly, setting the food on the kitchen counter. "But we still needed to eat."

"No one's expecting you to do it all," Grandma said gently, unpacking containers. "Not tonight. Not for a while."

She opened the boxes: chicken lo mein, beef and broccoli, shrimp fried rice, steamed dumplings, and crispy spring rolls, Noah's favorite. There was enough for everyone to take a little of everything.

Jenna called upstairs.

"Dinner's here!"

One by one, the kids emerged.

Theo and Levi came down first, quiet but alert. Mya held Owen's hand as they entered the dining room together.

The table had been cleared, and candles lit softly in the center. Not to make things fancy, but to bring warmth to a house still wrapped in shadows.

Plates were passed, chopsticks and forks scraped gently against the containers, and for a few quiet minutes, they ate…because grief demanded it, and love required it.

But as Owen stared at the two golden spring rolls on his plate, his shoulders fell.

He pushed them aside.

Grandma Rose noticed. "You okay, baby?"

Owen looked up, his voice flat. "Those were Dad's favorites."

Everyone paused.

"I don't think I can eat them anymore," he said quietly, his eyes wet. "It just… doesn't feel right."

The room went still.

Then Grandma Rose reached across the table and touched his hand.

"Owen," she said softly, "we all need to be strong. But I don't think your daddy would want you to give up something you love…especially not something that reminded you of him."

Owen blinked.

"He wouldn't want food to hurt you," she added. "He'd want it to make you smile."

Theo nodded slowly. "Dad used to sneak those into his lunch when Mom told him he needed to eat healthy."

Jenna cracked a faint smile. "He'd pretend like he didn't know how they got in there."

Everyone chuckled, just a little.

It wasn't much. But it was something.

After a few more bites, Jenna set down her fork and took a deep breath. The service is set for Saturday. Pastor Shaw will lead it. We'll have time for each of you to share something… if you want."

Theo wiped his mouth and nodded. "I do."

Jenna looked at him gently. "You've decided what to say?"

Theo cleared his throat, eyes on the table. "I'm going to talk about the time Dad taught me how to change a tire in the rain. I was mad at first, but he made it fun. He always found a way to teach without making you feel dumb."

Levi added quietly, "I want to share about our late-night talks. When he'd knock on my door after everyone went to bed, he'd sit at the edge of my bed and ask how my heart was doing, not just school, not just football, but my heart. Loving myself"

Mya straightened in her seat. "I'm going to sing a special song."

Owen looked up, surprised.

"You sure?" Jenna asked.

Mya nodded. "He didn't get to hear it that night… but maybe he will now."

Everyone looked toward Owen, giving him space.

He stared down at his plate, then whispered, "I want to read something."

"What kind of something?" Grandma asked gently.

"I don't know yet," he said, his voice fragile. "Maybe a letter."

"That's perfect," Jenna said, wiping her eye. "Whatever's in your heart."

They sat there together, the scent of soy sauce and sesame still lingering in the air, the spring rolls slowly growing cold—but the memories? Warm.

And through the heaviness, one truth gently rose among them:

Noah Carter was gone.

But his presence?

It hadn't been left.

Not really.

Not with this kind of love around the table. The night before the funeral at the Carter home, it was dimly lit; the hush of preparation and remembrance had replaced the living room's usual warmth. A stillness hung in the air, not the kind that comes from peace, but the kind that sits beside grief, whispering that morning is coming, and with it, the hardest goodbye.

Jenna sat alone at the edge of the bed, her hands folded in her lap. Noah's sweater, his favorite one, navy with frayed cuffs, was wrapped around her shoulders like armor.

She stared at the floor, speaking softly to herself.

"I won't speak tomorrow," she whispered. "I can't."

She had written notes earlier in the week and crossed out paragraphs. Tried to form sentences that could capture him. But every time she wanted to read them out loud, her voice collapsed into sobs. So, she stopped trying.

"I'll let the kids speak," she whispered again. "That'll be enough."

But the ache in her chest screamed louder than words ever could.

Across the hallway, Owen stood in front of the mirror in his room, his voice shaking as he practiced.

He held a small piece of lined paper in both hands.

"I wrote this for you, Daddy," he read aloud. "Even though I can't see you anymore, I know you're still watching. I miss your pancakes, your silly dance moves, and how you made me feel brave, even when I was scared."

His bottom lip quivered. He paused, then tried again, repeating the last line slower.

"I miss your pancakes... your silly dance moves... and how you made me feel brave..."

From the hallway, Levi leaned against the doorframe. "That's perfect, O. You're doing great."

Owen turned. "I keep messing it up."

Levi walked over and knelt beside him. "Mess it up a hundred times. It's still the truth. And that's what matters."

Then he entered Theo's room. Theo sat on the edge of his bed with Levi, reading over the note cards they had written earlier.

"I'm going to talk about the day he taught me to change that tire," Theo said, gripping the card tightly. "It was pouring. I was frustrated. But Dad didn't let the rain ruin it. He turned it into a joke. He repeatedly stated, "A man learns best when his socks are soaked." Theo responded with a slight smile. "I didn't get it then. But I do now."

Levi read his card quietly. "Mine's about the night before my science fair... when I couldn't figure out my project and wanted to quit. Dad stayed up with me 'til 2 a.m. I just sat on the floor and asked myself what I cared about. Said I could talk about fish tanks or stars or anything, as long as I spoke with heart."

Theo nodded. "That's who he was. Always pointing us back to what mattered."

Downstairs, in the soft glow of a single lamp, Grandma Rose sat on the couch with her holy scriptures open across her lap. Her fingers gently traced a verse she had marked with a ribbon earlier that day.

"Blessed are they that mourn: for they shall be comforted."
Matthew 5:4 KJV

She read it again and again, whispering it softly. Then she closed her eyes and prayed silently for strength, for peace, and for God to hold her babies in the hours to come.

In the next room, Mya sat in the corner with a stuffed bunny tucked under her arm. She hummed softly, just the melody of the song she had chosen.

She stood quietly by the window, softly humming "Amazing Grace."

The same song she had heard her father singing in the kitchen once, when he thought no one was listening. The song she knew would make everyone cry.

But she was going to sing it anyway.

Because Daddy didn't get to see her sing last time.

This time, she would make sure he heard her.

Even from heaven.

The house remained quiet that night. No TVs. No phones.

Just the sound of pens scribbling, papers folding, and hearts whispering their last rehearsals for the man they loved.

Jenna sat by the window, looking out at the stars, her hand resting over her heart.

"You were the best part of me. I miss you," she whispered into the night.

And then silence returned.

Not to suffocate.

But to make room for the sacred weight of what tomorrow would bring.

Chapter 16
The Day We Let Go

The house was silent, too silent.

The kind of silence that carried weight, that wrapped itself around the walls and pressed into every heart still tucked beneath blankets upstairs.

It was the morning of the funeral. And no one wanted to move.

Not Theo, not Levi, not Mya, and certainly not Owen, who had wrapped himself into a tight ball under his sheets, as if staying still could somehow rewind time.

Even Jenna, who had always been the first one up, remained buried under the covers in the main bedroom, her eyes open, fixed on the ceiling, heart numb.

But downstairs, a soft clatter of pans could be heard.

Grandma Rose was already awake.

She moved slowly but purposefully through the kitchen, her robe tied tight, her holy scriptures resting on the counter beside a plate of biscuits. She didn't cook much, just enough to bring a little comfort. Scrambled eggs. Toast with apple butter. A fresh pot of coffee. A plate of sliced fruit for the kids, because she knew Noah would've wanted them to eat something.

She moved with quiet reverence, humming an old hymn beneath her breath.

"Great is Thy faithfulness…

Her voice trembled as she sang, but she didn't stop.

This was how she grieved with prayer in her chest and food on the table.

By 7:30 a.m., she made her way to the staircase and called gently up.

"Children, it's time to rise. There's food waiting. And we've got to get ready to honor your daddy."

No one answered right away.

But slowly, one by one, they emerged.

Theo came down first, shirt untucked, tie draped around his neck like he wasn't ready to finish dressing just yet. His eyes were swollen but steady.

Then Levi, who didn't speak, just sat at the table and reached for a slice of toast, chewing slowly, like his body needed the fuel even if his spirit resisted it.

Mya came down with her hair still in satin rollers, her hands clutching her black ballet flats. She sat quietly beside Owen, who followed last, his dress shirt wrinkled from sleeping in it, his eyes vacant, his voice gone.

They sat around the table in silence as Grandma moved gently among them, placing food before each child like a sacred offering.

"I know it's hard," she said softly, setting down a plate of fruit in front of Mya. "But you need something in your stomachs. You can't say goodbye on an empty heart and an empty belly."

Jenna finally came downstairs a few minutes later, her black dress in place, her makeup light, her eyes swollen but determined. She didn't speak. Just kissed each of her children's heads and sat beside her mother with a cup of coffee she didn't drink.

The clock on the wall ticked quietly.

Each passing minute was one step closer.

The church. The music. The casket. The memories.

Today was the day they would lay Noah Carter to rest.

But not his presence.

That, his love, his strength, his laughter, that would remain.

In Theo's leadership.

In Levi's sensitivity.

In Owen's quiet courage.

In Mya's voice.

And in the way Jenna took her next breath.

Because even though today meant letting go...

It also meant holding on to what would never die. The family arrived, and the church parking lot was already filling with cars when the Carter family van pulled up to the side entrance.

The church, Noah's second home, stood in solemn beauty under the weight of grief. The front doors were propped open, a soft breeze carrying the scent of fresh lilies and the faint sound of piano chords being played gently inside.

Theo stepped out first in a fitted black suit, adjusting his tie with trembling fingers. Levi followed, rubbing his hands together as if trying to warm his nerves. Mya held tightly to Jenna's hand, her satin dress shoes barely touching the pavement. Owen hesitated before stepping out. His feet felt heavy, like the church steps were made of stone.

Grandma Rose stood tall and steady behind them all, clutching her leather-bound holy scriptures book to her chest.

A deacon approached with a kind smile and gentle voice. "We're ready when you are, Sister Jenna. The sanctuary is open."

Jenna gave a slight nod.

As they walked through the side door into the sanctuary, the Carter family was greeted by a hush that swept through the crowd. Church members and family friends stood in silence, bowing heads and whispering prayers.

At the front of the sanctuary, beneath soft lighting and a large wooden cross, stood the casket.

Noah's casket.

Mahogany wood. Ivory lining. A floral spray of white roses and blue hydrangeas, the family's colors. A framed photograph rested beside it: Noah smiling widely, wearing a suit with Mya in his arms and Owen clinging to his leg.

The moment Owen saw it, he stopped.

His small body froze.

His eyes locked on the casket, and the reality of death, the finality of it, came crashing down like a tidal wave.

"No…" he whispered.

Then louder: "No! No, no, no…"

Jenna reached for him, but it was too late.

Owen broke down.

His knees buckled beneath him, and a gut-wrenching wail burst from his chest. "That's my dad! That's my daddy!"

Gasps echoed from a few guests, and several deacons moved quickly from the front pews. Two men gently caught Owen just before he collapsed to the floor.

"Easy, son… we've got you."

He sobbed violently into the shoulder of one of the deacons, clutching the man's lapel as if it were his father's jacket.

Theo stood behind him, fists clenched, holding back his tears. Mya cried quietly against Grandma's side, while Levi stared at the casket, frozen, his eyes blinking rapidly as if trying to make it disappear.

Jenna knelt in front of Owen, her tears streaming. "We're here, baby. We're all here."

The deacons slowly helped Owen to his seat on the front pew, just beside Grandma Rose. She held his trembling hand and whispered, "Let it out, sweetheart. Let every tear fall."

The sanctuary remained still for a moment, stilled by the rawness of a little boy's pain.

And then… a gentle hum began from the choir loft.

Soft. Slow.

"Jesus, keep me near the cross…"

The pianist played as people began to file quietly into the pews behind the family.

Owen sat with his head bowed, body still trembling, the picture of innocence shattered by loss.

The Carter family remained together in the front row, linked by grief and love, ready to say goodbye, but still praying for the strength to make it through.

And at the front of the church, Noah Carter rested peacefully.

Gone from the earth.

But not from their hearts.

The Funeral Service begins with the soft hum of the choir fading. The piano keys quieted.

The sanctuary was packed, yet the sound of sniffles echoed through the air like raindrops on a glass window. Friends, co-workers, neighbors, and church members all sat with heavy hearts, hands folded, and heads bowed. The atmosphere was sacred, fragile.

At the pulpit stood Pastor Shaw, a man with silver at his temples and fire in his spirit. He adjusted the microphone, cleared his throat, and gazed out across the crowd, pausing at the Carter family seated in the front row.

He gripped the edges of the podium as he needed it to stand.

"Church…" he began, his voice already thick with emotion. "Today we gather not because Noah Carter passed away, but because he lived. Because he loved it. Because he left behind something worth remembering."

A ripple of quiet amens filled the room.

He continued, "Noah was a man of laughter and loyalty. He was a husband who loved his wife, a father who protected and provided for his children, and a servant of God who sang when in pain and gave when he had little. He was present. That's a rare thing in this world. And that's why this hurts so deep."

He paused, his voice breaking.

"This wasn't the plan. Not for us. Not for his family. But the holy scriptures tell us in Isaiah 55 KJV that God's ways are higher than our ways. And today, in our grief, we still trust Him."

He turned slightly toward the family pew.

"The children have asked to speak now. And I believe their voices will honor their father in a way only they can."

He stepped down gently.

Theo rose first, slowly walking toward the podium, adjusting his jacket as he wiped his palms on it. His voice was steady, but barely.

"My dad was my hero," he began. "But not the kind in movies. He didn't wear a cape or fight villains. He was the kind who showed up every single time."

He took a breath, eyes welling.

"He taught me how to change a tire in the pouring rain. I was mad, soaking wet, and complaining the whole time. But he just laughed and said, 'A man learns best when his socks are soaked.' I didn't get it then. But I do now. Life isn't about comfort. It's about courage."

He choked on the last word but forced himself to finish. "And Dad… I promise to lead like you led. To love like you loved."

Applause wasn't needed. Silence was louder.

Levi came next, strolling to the mic with his hands in his pockets.

"I'm not as good with words as my brother," he said softly, eyes down. "But Dad never cared about the right words. He cared about the real ones."

He paused, steadying his voice.

"Sometimes, late at night, he'd knock on my door just to check in. He'd sit at the end of my bed and say, 'How's your heart, son?' Not my grades. Not my game. My heart."

Levi's eyes filled.

"And I wish I had one more of those nights. One more time to say, 'It's not okay, but I'm gonna be okay… because you made me strong.'"

Then he walked back to the pew, his shoulders trembling as he sat.

A moment passed.

Then Owen stood.

He strolled, clutching a folded piece of notebook paper in his hand. His voice was soft and shaky.

"I wrote a letter to my dad," he said. "I want to read it."

He unfolded it, his hands trembling.

"Dear Daddy,

I miss you more than I can put into words.

I miss your pancakes. Your silly dancing. The way you called me 'champ' even when I lost.

I wanted you to come to my tournament. I wanted to show you that I've improved.

But I know you're watching.

And I'll keep trying to make you proud.

I love you, Daddy.

Always."

Owen's voice broke on the last word.

Jenna stood and gently guided him back to the pew, wrapping her arms around him as he sobbed into her side.

Then the room stilled again.

Mya stood quietly and made her way to the front, where a microphone had been set up just beside the piano.

She nodded to the pianist.

The first notes began.

And then she sang....

"Amazing Grace..."

Her voice, small but strong, carried across the room like a breeze through stained glass. Eyes filled. Hands covered mouths. Even the stoic broke down as she poured her soul into each word.

By the final note, even the choir was crying.

And heaven, surely, was listening.

When Mya finished, she gave a slight bow and returned to her seat, where Grandma Rose took her hand.

Then, slowly, Grandma Rose got up and walked to the pulpit, her holy scriptures open and marked.

She didn't speak right away.

She read:

"Blessed are they that mourn: for they shall be comforted."
 Matthew 5:4 KJV

She looked out at the crowd, tears in her eyes but fire in her voice.

"This pain we feel... It's holy. Because it means we loved deeply. But the Word of God promises that we will be comforted. So don't you let go of hope. Don't you stop loving. And don't you forget what Noah Carter stood for. He wasn't perfect... but he was faithful."

She closed the book.

"And that kind of faith doesn't die. It lives on. Right here." She placed her hand over her heart. "In each of us."

A standing ovation would've been fitting but instead, the sanctuary filled with quiet weeping and silent nods.

The funeral wasn't over.

But the legacy of Noah Carter had already been spoken loud and clear.

Chapter 17
Earth to Earth, Ashes to Ashes

The sanctuary emptied slowly.

No one wanted to be the first to rise. The weight of grief hung heavy in the air, settling like morning fog on every shoulder and heart. Rows of friends and loved ones whispered as the family stood, Jenna, Grandma Rose, Theo, Levi, Owen, and Mya were forming a solemn line behind the casket.

Pallbearers, made up of Noah's closest friends, deacons, and cousins, took their positions beside the polished mahogany. With white gloves and heavy hearts, they lifted his body from the altar and began the slow, measured walk toward the church doors.

A solo violin played softly…"Precious Lord, Take My Hand."

Mya clung to Jenna's side, her face buried in her mother's arm. Owen walked in silence, holding Theo's hand so tightly that his knuckles turned white. Levi kept his head down, jaw clenched, willing himself not to fall apart again.

Outside, the sky was overcast, a gentle breeze rustling the edges of the tent that had been set up at the Chelseaville Memorial Park Cemetery.

Dozens of cars formed a quiet, winding procession behind the hearse, headlights glowing like candles in mourning. The family rode together, packed in silence, Grandma Rose whispering scripture softly in the back seat, barely audible over the sound of the wheels on the road.

At the cemetery, folding chairs were lined in neat rows beneath the canopy. A large floral arrangement of white lilies and hydrangeas stood beside the gravesite. The air smelled of damp soil and fresh-cut grass.

When the casket was placed above the grave, Pastor Shaw stepped forward again. His voice was softer now, steadier, like a shepherd preparing to let go of one of his own.

He looked out over the crowd and took a long, deep breath.

"Today, we commend our brother, our friend, our husband, father, and son, Noah Carter, back to the earth from which he came."

The wind brushed across the crowd like a holy hush settling over the field.

"For dust thou art,

And unto dust shalt thou return."

Genesis 3:19 KJV

"Earth to earth... ashes to ashes... dust to dust."

Jenna's lips quivered, and she clutched Mya closer.

Pastor Shaw closed his eyes, lifting his voice once more.

"We say farewell to Noah, not in despair, but with hope...hope that he has found peace, that his legacy will continue, and that his family will find comfort each day as they remember him."

A soft amen echoed through the crowd.

Then came the hardest moment of all.

The final goodbye.

Each family member rose one by one.

Jenna stepped forward first. She placed a single white rose atop the casket, her fingers lingering as she whispered, "I'll love you forever." She fell to her knees unexpectedly. Theo and Levi knelt with her to help her back up.

Theo came next, tears falling freely as he touched the wood and said, "You made me a man."

Levi placed his letter beside the rose, whispering, "I'll check on Mom every day. I promise."

Owen trembled as he approached. He pulled out a crumpled drawing from his coat pocket, the same one Mya had made for him, and placed it gently atop the rose.

Then Mya walked forward.

She didn't say a word.

She just leaned forward and kissed the corner of the casket softly, as if she were sealing her song in the very wood.

Finally, Grandma Rose stood tall.

She lifted her holy scriptures and declared, voice firm but broken:

"Weeping may endure for a night,

but joy cometh in the morning."

-Psalm 30:5 KJV

As the casket was slowly lowered into the earth, many wept openly. Some held hands. Others stood in quiet reverence.

And when the first shovel of soil dropped, its sound deep, finally, echoing, there was no turning back.

But there was still holding on.

Holding on to faith.

Holding on to one another.

And holding on to the love that death could never bury.

Later that afternoon, at the Carters' home, the house was already alive with movement.

Cars lined both sides of the street. Voices floated from the front porch. The smell of seasoned chicken, baked macaroni, and fresh rolls spilled through the open windows. Friends, neighbors, and church members had shown up with arms full of foil-wrapped trays, pies in boxes, gallon jugs of iced tea, and lemonade.

Grief had a way of drawing a crowd.

Jenna stepped out of the car slowly. She glanced toward the front steps, where two of the church mothers waited with open arms. She offered a slight nod, too tired to smile, and took Mya's hand as they walked up together.

Inside the house, warmth greeted them, not the comforting kind, but the weighty kind. Too much food. Too many voices. Too much kindness when all you wanted was quiet.

The dining table overflowed with a variety of dishes: fried catfish, collard greens, sweet potatoes, deviled eggs, meatballs, cornbread, peach cobbler, and banana pudding. Paper plates and folded napkins sat in neat stacks beside plastic forks. A framed photo of Noah, surrounded by votive candles, stood in the center of the table like an altar of remembrance.

Grandma Rose gently took over hosting, receiving guests with grace and ensuring everyone had something to eat. But her eyes never strayed far from her grandchildren.

Theo moved through the crowd like a shadow, accepting handshakes and awkward condolences with a nod, offering tight smiles, answering questions he didn't want to be asked.

Levi sat on the edge of the living room couch, plate untouched in his lap, knees bouncing restlessly. A few of his teammates came by to hug him, but he barely spoke.

Mya sat beside the window with her plate in her lap, picking at her food while watching kids her age chase each other in the yard like it was just another Saturday.

And Owen stood at the hallway entrance, holding a cup of lemonade, watching the room like it was all happening without him, like the world had moved on, and he hadn't.

From across the room, Sister Geraldine approached Jenna, gently placing a warm hand on her shoulder.

"I just wanted to say, your children spoke so beautifully today. You raised them right, honey. Noah would be proud."

Jenna nodded politely. "Thank you."

She didn't say more.

She didn't need to.

As the house buzzed with murmurs of memories and spoonfuls of sorrow, a strange sense of comfort began to settle.

Not peace. Not yet. But presence.

The presence of people who cared. Of community.

Of food and laughter and tears, all coexisting in the same space.

At one point, someone turned on soft gospel music in the background. A familiar hymn played, "Going Up Yonder." Mya hummed along under her breath, her voice delicate.

Near the end of the evening, Grandma Rose gathered the children in the kitchen. She looked each one in the eyes and said quietly, "When everyone leaves, and the house gets quiet again... remember this day, not for the pain, but for the love. This is what your daddy built. A family that's surrounded. Covered. Held."

Jenna came over and pulled them all into a group hug, arms around shoulders, hands on backs, heads leaning into one another.

And for a few seconds, the warmth felt real.

Noah was gone.

But his love had filled every room.

And for tonight, that was enough to get through. Later that night, by 8:30 p.m., the last car had pulled away.

The laughter was gone. The murmur of prayers and memories had faded. The smell of collard greens and lemon pound cake still lingered in the air, but the warmth had vanished with the guests.

Now there was only silence.

And leftovers. And grief.

Jenna stood at the kitchen sink, staring at a mountain of plates but unable to move. Her hands were resting on the edge of the counter, her wedding ring pressing into her skin. She didn't even hear Grandma Rose come up behind her.

"Leave those dishes," Grandma said gently. "Let grief have the night off."

Jenna nodded, eyes still empty. "I don't even know where to start tomorrow."

"You don't have to start tomorrow," Grandma whispered. "You just have to survive it."

They turned off the lights and left the kitchen in silence.

Upstairs, the children were retreating into their worlds.

Theo lay in bed with his arms behind his head, staring at the ceiling fan spinning slowly above him. The room still smelled like the cologne his dad used to wear. He pulled out the necktie he had worn to the funeral, still draped over his doorknob. Holding it to his chest, he let a few tears slip quietly down his face.

He had always thought he'd have more time to ask his dad how to be a man… how to choose the right job… how to propose one day. Now, all of those questions were swallowed in silence.

Levi sat at his desk, flipping through the pages of an old comic book he and his dad used to read together. His eyes scanned the images, but he couldn't process anything. His fingers trembled when he reached the back cover, where his dad had once doodled a little stick figure family labeled: Us.

Levi closed the book slowly and pressed it to his chest, rocking gently in his chair. His grief didn't roar. It whispered. Constantly.

Owen was curled up in his twin bed, staring out the window. He refused to change into pajamas, still wearing his funeral suit pants and dress socks. His favorite trophy from last summer's golf camp sat crooked on his dresser; he hadn't touched it in days.

A small flashlight rested under his pillow, the one his dad always told him to use in case of storms. Tonight, he turned it on, not for the dark, but for the memory.

"Goodnight, Daddy," he whispered into the silence. "Don't forget me."

Mya was tucked into the guest room again, choosing to sleep near Grandma Rose. She had refused her favorite blanket and instead held tightly to her dad's old hoodie. It still smelled like him, warm, musky, safe.

She hadn't said much since the repass. She just hummed softly to herself like a lullaby that might bring him back.

"Grandma," she whispered.

"Yes, baby?" Rose said gently, her holy scriptures still open beside her.

"Do you think Daddy saw me sing?"

Grandma paused, fighting tears.

"I know he did."

Mya nodded slowly and drifted off with her fingers curled into the hoodie's sleeve.

In the Main Bedroom, Jenna stood in the closet again. No lights on.

Just her silhouette in the dark, holding Noah's jacket close to her face, breathing him in, trying to remember what his presence felt like in a world that now moved without him.

She didn't cry this time. She just stood. Frozen.

Lost.

Chapter 18
The Silence After the Song

It had been six days since the funeral.

The Carter household was slowly stirring back to life, though nothing about it felt normal.

Theo and Levi had returned to their summer jobs at the local ice cream parlor, trying to fill their afternoons with blenders, orders, and cold cones that melted faster than the ache in their chests. They smiled at customers. They even joked with each other on breaks. But the laughter felt forced, like borrowed joy they hadn't earned yet.

Owen spent most of his days in his room. Occasionally, he'd come downstairs to sit beside his mother or follow Grandma Rose around the house. He hadn't spoken much, but he started journaling, scribbling thoughts and memories about his dad in the spiral notebook his coach had given him.

But for Mya, something had shifted.

This morning, she stood at the kitchen table, brushing her hair into a neat ponytail as Jenna zipped up her duffel bag.

"You are sure you're okay going to rehearsal today?" Jenna asked gently.

Mya nodded slowly. "I just want to go… and come right back."

Jenna kissed the top of her head. "Okay, baby girl."

Grandma Rose watched from across the room, her eyes cautious but hopeful.

In the early afternoon, Grandma Rose arrived at the Chelseaville Performing Arts Center with Mya.

The rehearsal room buzzed with energy as the students prepared for the summer showcase. Dance shoes tapped the floor. Vocal warmups filled the halls. Bright lights beamed across the polished stage.

But Mya stood off to the side, unusually quiet.

Ms. Elise gave her a warm smile. "Ready for your solo, Mya? Let's run it once before we break."

Mya gave a tiny nod and walked onto the stage.

The music began, her cue to sing the same song she once sang boldly in the church.

She opened her mouth.

And the words came softly, gently, almost whisper-like.

But before she could finish the first verse, Brittany Abraham, standing just offstage, leaned toward two other girls and whispered loud enough for Mya to hear:

"Why does she keep singing that song? Her dad's gone. He's never going to hear her again."

The words sliced through the air like a dagger.

Mya stopped singing.

The piano faltered.

Everyone turned toward her, confused.

Her throat closed. Her eyes were stung. She looked out into the seats of the empty theater, where her father once promised he'd always be sitting, and she saw… nothing.

She stepped down from the stage without a word.

"Mya?" Ms. Elise called gently. "Are you okay?"

But Mya kept walking, right out of the rehearsal hall.

Ten Minutes Later, she was sitting inside the front office waiting for Grandma Rose.

The double doors flew open.

Grandma Rose stepped inside with fire in her stride. She received a call from one of the assistants who had seen Mya crying in the hallway.

"Where's Ms. Elise?" she asked firmly.

Moments later, both Ms. Elise and Ms. Carmen met her in the front office.

"Something happened today," Grandma began. "My granddaughter came to the car with tears, and it wasn't from nerves. It was from cruelty. She was mocked for singing a song to her father. And I want to know what you're going to do about it."

Ms. Carmen looked stunned. "We didn't know…"

"Brittany Abraham," Grandma said bluntly. "She's been bullying my grandbaby off and on for over two years. And today, she crossed the line."

Ms. Elise nodded slowly. "We'll speak to her and her parents. We're so sorry, Mrs. Watkins."

Grandma Rose's voice softened. "Just be aware, my granddaughter is hurting, and this was the last straw. She's not coming back."

"But Mya is gifted," Ms. Carmen replied. "She belongs here."

"She belonged with her family more, who're also grieving," Grandma said. "And that stage, today, reminded her of what she lost. So, she's choosing peace over performance."

Ms. Elise wiped the corner of her eye. "We'll miss her. We really will."

That evening at home, Mya's mother sat next to her on the back porch, where Mya was hugging her knees to her chest.

"You don't want to go back?" Jenna asked quietly.

Mya shook her head.

"He's not there anymore."

Jenna brushed a strand of hair behind her daughter's ear.

"Okay," she said gently. "Then we'll find another place to let your voice grow again. On your time. When you're ready."

Mya leaned into her mother's side.

And for the first time in a long while, she didn't hum.

The music had gone quiet.

The summer was coming to an end, and the sun was already climbing high above the horizon when the Carter family's SUVs pulled into the campus lot at a college in Kentucky.

Two cars. Five family members. One mission.

Theo's transition to college marked the first time a child of the Carter family attended school.

Jenna stood beside the trunk of her SUV, carefully lifting the last plastic tote of supplies, bedding, notebooks, extension cords, and laundry detergent. Levi tossed a duffel bag over his shoulder, while Grandma Rose handed Theo a small gift bag containing a journal and a holy scriptures book.

"I wrote something on the inside cover," she whispered. "For when the noise gets too loud, and you need to hear God's voice."

Theo gave a tight smile, his eyes shimmering with emotion.

Owen stood off to the side, chewing on his lip and blinking fast. He didn't want his big brother to see him cry.

Mya clung to Theo's arm with both hands. "You said you'd teach me to ride the four-wheeler."

"I still will," Theo said, kneeling in front of her. "Just on the weekends or when I come home."

"You better," she said, trying to smile through the tears.

Once the last box was dropped off in his dorm, they all stood outside his building in a long, quiet embrace. Theo hugged his mother last; her fingers wouldn't let go.

"You got this, baby," Jenna whispered. "You hear me? You've got this."

"Only because you and Dad showed me how," he replied.

Then, as the cars pulled away, Theo waved from the front steps. Mya waved back until he disappeared behind the blue brick walls of his new life.

One week later, it was back-to-school Monday morning, and the house buzzed with the usual flurry of first-day nerves and excitement.

Levi, now a high school senior, stood tall in his varsity football hoodie. His duffel bag of gear sat by the door. He was thriving, recognized around school as a team leader and top defensive player.

"You sure you don't want to ride with us today?" Jenna asked as she sipped her coffee.

"Nah," Levi said, flashing a confident grin. "I'm good."

He gave Mya and Owen a side hug before heading out. The front door slammed behind him with the familiarity of routine, but Jenna couldn't help notice how grown he looked now.

Owen, now in 9th grade, buttoned his flannel shirt as he stared at the mirror. His backpack sagged heavily on his shoulders, but his face looked older, too, more thoughtful.

"Are you ready for school?" Jenna asked, adjusting his collar.

"I guess," he muttered. "Still feels weird without Dad here."

Jenna gave him a soft squeeze. "He's still with us. Every single step."

Mya, now a fourth grader, twirled once in her pink dress and matching backpack, unsure of how excited she was to be returning. It was her first school year without a performance calendar and without her father's encouraging notes taped to her lunchbox.

"You look beautiful," Grandma Rose said, coming into the kitchen with car keys in hand. "Y'all ready to go?"

"Yeah," Owen mumbled, grabbing his water bottle. Mya followed behind silently, her gaze lingering on a photo of her dad by the back door.

Jenna knelt in front of her before they left. "New season, baby girl. You're still allowed to grow. Even through the pain."

Mya nodded slowly. "I just don't want to sing today."

"You don't have to. Just be you."

Outside, the sun filtered softly through the trees as Grandma Rose drove Owen and Mya to school, her protective presence a daily blessing.

Jenna stood on the porch watching the car disappear, then turned, picked up her handbag, and headed to her car.

It was her first day back at work.

A different kind of classroom. A different type of grief.

But the same strength, inherited and rising again. Jenna arrived at work at 8:30 am.

The automatic glass doors slid open as Jenna stepped into the lobby, her heels echoing softly against the polished marble floor.

It felt strange being back here.

The elevator ride to the fifth floor was quiet, except for the low hum of instrumental jazz playing over the building's speakers. She clutched her leather briefcase a little tighter and stared at her reflection in the mirrored wall. Her makeup was flawless, her blouse neatly pressed. From the outside, she looked composed.

But inside, she felt like paper creased, thinned, and dangerously close to tearing.

When the elevator dinged, Jenna stepped into the familiar hallway lined with framed design blueprints. Her office sat at the end of the corridor. The door still had her name etched in gold script: Jenna Carter, Lead Project Designer.

She pushed it open slowly.

Everything was exactly as she had left it.

The drafting table is near the window. The framed photo of Noah and the kids is beside her monitor. The coffee mug that read "Built With Purpose" still rested on her desk.

She placed her bag on the chair and stood there for a moment, not moving.

Then she heard a soft knock.

It was Colleen, her assistant and longtime friend.

"Hey," Colleen said with gentle eyes. "I didn't want to rush in, just wanted to say… welcome back. We missed you."

Jenna gave a small, grateful smile. "Thanks. I wasn't sure I could come back."

"Well," Colleen said, stepping inside, "take it one hour at a time. No one expects you to be full throttle right away."

"I don't even know what full throttle looks like anymore," Jenna replied honestly.

Colleen reached over and set a folder on her desk. "Just a few updates on the Southside Mall expansion and some notes from last week's client meeting. Nothing urgent. I wanted to keep you in the loop."

Jenna nodded. "Okay."

"And Jenna," Colleen added before leaving, "it's okay if you need a break. Or a cry. Or nothing at all. Just... be here how you can."

The door closed softly behind her.

Jenna sank slowly into her chair.

She opened the folder, scanned the first few lines of the project specs, and reached for her mechanical pencil, but her fingers froze.

Her eyes drifted to the picture frame.

Noah, grinning at her in a blue sweater, his arm around her shoulders. It had been taken after her promotion last year. He'd surprised her at the office with flowers and a homemade sign from the kids that read "Mom: Architect of Our Hearts."

The memory hit her like a wave.

She pressed her hand over her mouth and leaned forward, bracing her elbows on the desk.

Tears spilled grief silently in its rawest form.

But she didn't leave.

She didn't run.

After a few minutes, she wiped her eyes, straightened the picture, picked up her pencil... and began to sketch.

The lines weren't perfect.

But they were honest.

Just like her.

The air was warm and breezy as the last bell rang at Chelseaville Academy. Children spilled out of the buildings, their backpacks slung over their shoulders, eager to share their stories.

Grandma Rose waited patiently in the pickup lane, her floral scarf tied neatly and her holy scriptures resting in the front seat beside her.

Owen was the first to spot her.

He walked toward the car quietly, his hoodie tied around his waist, and slid into the back seat with a heavy sigh. Moments later, at Chelseaville Elementary, Mya came skipping out with her energy a little softer than usual, but her face lifted slightly when she saw Grandma waving.

"Hi, Grandma!" Mya chirped as she climbed into the backseat beside her brother.

"Hey, sugar," Grandma said, smiling through the rearview mirror. "How was the first day of school?"

Owen shrugged. "Alright, I guess. My teachers are nice. I got a locker this year."

"Mine was good," Mya said, kicking her feet. "But I didn't sing. Not even during music class."

"That's okay, baby," Grandma said gently. "Just showing up was brave enough."

The car ride was quiet after that. Comforting. Simple. Like old times, trying to break through new pain.

Later that evening, the table was set with oven-baked chicken, jasmine rice, green beans, and homemade cornbread. The scent filled the house, welcoming everyone into the warmth of togetherness.

Jenna had made it home just in time to light the candles before dinner.

Levi walked in from football practice, his cleats thumping down the hall as he headed to wash up.

By 6:15 p.m., the whole family was seated at the dinner table...something they hadn't done like this in weeks.

Jenna looked around at her children and mother-in-law, a fragile but present smile resting on her lips.

"So," she said, folding her hands, "tell me about today."

Owen spoke first. "We got assigned science partners. Mine's a kid named Brandon who says he wants to build a robot."

"Sounds like fun," Jenna said. "You like robots, don't you?"

"I guess," Owen muttered, poking at his rice. "Just... not the same without Dad asking all those weird questions about it."

A pause passed at the table.

"I know, baby," Jenna replied softly. "We all miss his questions."

Mya looked up from her plate. "Ms. Henry asked if I wanted to sing a solo in chapel next month, but I told her no."

Everyone looked toward her.

"Why's that, sweetheart?" Grandma Rose asked gently.

Mya swallowed hard. "Because Brittany said I don't sound the same without Daddy watching. And maybe she's right."

There was silence, then Grandma set her fork down, eyes firm.

"Honey, your gift didn't come from your daddy watching. It came from God. Your daddy just happened to be your biggest fan."

Mya nodded slowly, her eyes glistening with tears.

"I'm proud of you for saying how you feel," Jenna added. "But you don't have to stay silent forever. When you're ready, your voice will still be there."

Levi reached over and gave her a gentle nudge. "I heard you humming in the shower yesterday. You still got it."

Mya finally smiled, a small, soft one.

Grandma Rose turned to Levi. "And how was practice?"

"Good," he said, taking a bite of cornbread. "Coach says scouts from Winslow State and Cozy State are coming to our next two games."

"That's big," Jenna said with a proud nod.

Levi shrugged. "Yeah, but I kept thinking about Dad. He was supposed to be in the stands this season."

"He will be," Grandma Rose said quietly, placing her hand over his. "Just not the way we expected."

As they continued eating, the conversation lightened.

They laughed about Grandma Rose mixing up Owen's lunch with Levi's gym socks, which she denied, and Mya made silly faces out of green beans.

It wasn't perfect.

But it was peace.

A table full of broken hearts… slowly learning to beat again.

Chapter 19
Six Years Later

Time passed, but grief never asked for permission to leave.

It had been six years since Noah Carter took his final breath, yet his presence lingered in every photo, every quiet Sunday, every unspoken word.

The Carter home had changed. The walls had been repainted, furniture rearranged, but the air still carried the weight of what was lost.

Theo, now 24, had recently walked the stage at the college in Kentucky with a master's degree in finance, already making a name for himself on Wall Street. He lived in a one-bedroom apartment in Brooklyn, sent money home without being asked, and called every Sunday to check on his mom, Grandma Rose, and Mya.

Levi, 23, now lives in Chicago and works as a financial consultant at a top firm after earning the same degree. He still wore his high school championship ring. He stayed connected to his younger siblings, especially Owen, who was 20 now and finishing his junior year at a top university in Ohio, majoring in Biology with dreams of becoming a pediatric surgeon.

But the youngest of the Carter children, Mya, stood at a very different crossroads.

She had just turned 14, a freshman at Chelseaville Academy, the same school her brothers once dominated on the football field and golf tournaments. Her voice, once soaring and radiant, had been silent since she was eight. Her body had changed too, softening under the quiet burden of emotional weight, growing in places that made her feel unseen or, worse, mocked.

She hadn't sung in six years.

She hadn't even dared to hum.

It was the first day of high school for Mya, as Jenna stood at the stove stirring a pot of oatmeal, her hair pulled into a sleek ponytail, her eyes scanning the day's architecture drafts on her phone. Her presence was stable—routine-driven—but distant, like a ghost doing chores.

"Breakfast is ready," she called out, not looking up.

Mya shuffled into the kitchen, her backpack already strapped on, oversized hoodie draped loosely around her body. She had grown tall like her brothers, but with a slouched posture that begged not to be noticed.

"Morning," she mumbled.

"Morning," Mom replied flatly, setting a bowl on the table.

They sat in silence, no scripture readings. No music. No laughter. The house, once full of joy and harmony, was now a museum of survival.

Jenna didn't notice Mya's hesitation before eating.

She didn't seem to notice how she picked at her food.

Didn't notice that Mya had packed her lunch, just water, celery sticks, and half a protein bar.

Outside, Grandma Rose honked the horn. She had taken over morning drop-offs after Jenna's workload had increased.

Mya stood up, grabbed her lunch, and offered a quiet goodbye.

As she stepped outside into the late August heat, sweat immediately clung to her long sleeves. But she kept them on. She always did. The fabric felt like armor.

In the car, Grandma Rose gave her the usual morning blessing, "You're the head and not the tail, baby. Go be excellent today."

Mya smiled weakly, then turned her face to the window.

She had no idea what the day would bring.

Or that the past, the one she buried at age eight, was waiting in the cafeteria with a familiar smirk and a new voice.

Never with her heart thudding so loudly she could barely hear the morning announcements. Never with sweat collecting under the sleeves of her oversized hoodie, even though the air-conditioning was on full blast. Never with so many eyes around her, and none of them familiar.

The little sister of the legendary Carter boys, whose last names still echoed through the trophy cases in the athletic wing. But today, none of that mattered.

Today, she was just... alone.

She made it through her morning classes in silence, nodding when called on, and keeping her head down as teachers mispronounced her name and students brushed past her as if she were invisible.

But then came lunch.

She stood near the cafeteria entrance, her tray in hand, scanning the room for an empty seat. Her heart picked up speed. The buzzing noise of laughter, chairs scraping the floor, and cliques gathering at familiar tables wrapped around her like a fog.

That's when she saw her.

Brittany Abraham.

Mya's stomach dropped.

The face she had buried for six years was suddenly no longer a memory; it was real. Older, taller, and even more confident than before. Her curls bounced as she walked. Her makeup was perfect. She laughed effortlessly, as she'd already conquered the school.

And she had an audience.

Brittany sat with a group of juniors in the center of the cafeteria, drawing attention like a magnet. Mya tried to step past her without being seen, but it was too late.

"Wait a second..."

Brittany's voice was sharp and sugary. Loud enough to make people turn.

Mya froze.

"Oh my gosh...is that Mya Carter?" Brittany said, eyes narrowing.

Mya slowly turned her head, already shrinking inside.

"It is! Wow. I didn't recognize you," she said mockingly, glancing her up and down. "You've... filled out."

A few sneakers rose from her table.

Mya didn't respond. She clutched her tray a little tighter, trying not to look at anyone. Her throat burned.

"What's wrong, Mya?" Brittany teased. "Still too scared to sing, or is your mouth just too full these days?"

The laughter got louder.

Mya stood still, her face flushing, every muscle in her body screaming to run, but her legs wouldn't move.

That's when a voice cut through the noise.

"Back off."

Everyone turned.

Bonnie Henderson, a petite freshman with thick glasses, long braids, and zero tolerance for bullies, stood just behind Mya, holding her lunch tray. Her eyes locked on Brittany, unblinking.

"I said Back off," Bunny repeated.

Brittany scoffed. "And who are you supposed to be?"

"Someone who's not scared of you," Bunny said calmly. "Try picking on someone who cares."

The table grew quiet. Brittany raised her eyebrows but said nothing.

Bunny stepped around Mya and nodded toward an empty table in the corner. "C'mon. Let's sit over there."

Still stunned, Mya followed.

They sat down, trays untouched.

"I'm Bunny," she said, taking a bite of her apple. "And I hate girls like her."

Mya stared at her for a long second, trying to understand what had just happened. She's short, slim, with short black hair and thick glasses. She has a hippie vibe but a fierce, confident attitude. Then a small, reluctant smile cracked her lips.

"Thanks," she whispered.

"Don't mention it. People like her are miserable inside. They don't know what to do with it."

Mya nodded, a tear quietly escaping the corner of her eye before she could catch it.

She didn't say much more during lunch period. After 15 minutes of silence, the bell sounded, signaling an end to the lingering echoes of laughter and conversation in the cafeteria. Students spilled into the hallway like a wave, voices rising, shoes squeaking, lockers slamming shut. Mya walked beside Bunny in silence at first, still trying to grasp what had just happened. She glanced over at her with a half-smile, grateful but unsure how to express it.

"Hey," Bunny said, nudging Mya gently with her elbow. "You okay?"

Mya nodded. "Yeah... I think so. I just...thanks again. For what you did."

Bunny shrugged, brushing a curly strand of hair from her face. "I didn't like what she said to you. No one deserves to be treated like that."

They stopped at their lockers, and Mya's eyes widened. "Wait—this is yours?" she asked, motioning to the locker directly beside hers.

Bunny grinned. "Yep. Locker twins. Crazy, right?"

Mya smiled, a genuine one this time. "I guess it's meant to be."

Bunny opened her locker and began organizing her notebooks. "You got a phone?"

"Yeah," Mya said, pulling her phone from the front pocket of her bag.

"Let me get your number," Bunny offered, holding out her phone.

Mya read off her digits as Bunny typed them in, then Bunny called her, so she'd have hers too. Mya's phone buzzed with the new contact: Bunny H.

Mya chuckled softly. "I like the emoji of the bunny."

Bunny winked. "Gotta keep things cute."

They both laughed, the kind of light laughter that comes when something finally feels right. For the first time in a long time, Mya didn't feel invisible. She didn't feel like a shadow trailing behind her brothers or hiding from mean whispers in the hallway. Standing beside Bunny, she felt seen.

"I'm glad we met," Mya said quietly as they packed up their things

Bunny looked at her, voice sincere. "Me too, Mya. I think we're gonna be good friends."

The late bell rang, and students hurried around them, but Mya didn't feel rushed. As they walked side by side toward their next class, something in her heart settled. It wasn't just a good day; it was the beginning of something she didn't know she needed. Bunny went to science class on the second floor, while Mya went in the opposite direction.

Mya was sitting in the history class, which was the last class on her schedule. She was staring at the clock, which seemed to take forever to strike 3:05 pm. "Finally," she said.

The final bell rang like a shot at a race, and the building sprang to life with energy. Backpacks zipped, chairs scraped, and students burst from classrooms like a stampede. The hallways swelled with noise as kids rushed toward the exits, some weaving to the parking lot, others sprinting to the long line of yellow buses waiting outside.

Mya moved with the crowd, gripping her bag and trying not to get bumped too hard as people pushed past. She smiled when she spotted Bunny standing near the double doors, waiting for her.

"There you are!" Bunny said, linking arms with her like they'd been friends for years. "I didn't want to leave without saying goodbye."

"Thanks," Mya replied, surprised at how much she meant it.

They stepped outside into the late afternoon sun. The warm breeze hit Mya's cheeks as students scattered in every direction. A group of juniors tossed footballs in the parking lot while others climbed into sleek cars and drove off with music thumping from rolled-down windows. Small clusters of first-year students gathered near the buses, still adjusting to the routine.

Bunny glanced around before turning back to Mya. "So, first day back wasn't all bad, huh?"

Mya laughed. "Not how I expected it to end."

Bunny grinned. "Good. That's what I like to hear."

They paused by the curb as one of the buses roared to life. Bunny's ride hadn't arrived yet, but Mya could already see her mom's car pulling up down the line.

"I'll call you later," Bunny said, giving her a playful nudge. "We need to catch up on all the school gossip. You're not escaping that."

Mya laughed again, the sound lighter this time. "Okay. I'll be waiting."

They hugged briefly, and for a moment, Mya just stood still as Bunny jogged off toward her bus stop to wait for her mom. She felt something shift inside her, something warm, something hopeful. Maybe this school year wouldn't be so bad after all.

As she climbed into her mom's car and buckled her seatbelt, she looked out the window once more. Bunny was already waving from a distance, a big smile on her face. Mya waved back.

When Mya walked through the front door, the house smelled faintly of rosemary and garlic. It was peaceful, quiet, even, but not in a warm, welcoming way. It was the kind of silence that made the walls feel too wide, as if everyone were staying in their corners.

Her mom, Jenna, offered a soft "Hey" and walked past without making eye contact, heading straight to her bedroom and closing the door behind her.

Grandma Rose was in the kitchen stirring a pot on the stove while also sliding a plate with a small snack onto the counter. "Hey, baby," she greeted warmly. "Got you a little something until dinner's ready."

Mya gave a polite smile and mumbled, "Thanks, Grandma." She grabbed the plate: apple slices, peanut butter, and a few crackers, and headed straight to her bedroom without another word.

Grandma Rose turned and watched her go, her smile fading. She sighed. Her eyes then shifted down the hallway, where Jenna's door was still closed. She wiped her hands on a dish towel and quietly made her way to Jenna's room.

Inside, Jenna lay curled on the bed, half-dressed from work, staring at the muted television. Her shoulders were tight, her eyes blank. The shadows under them looked deeper lately.

"Jenna…" Grandma Rose spoke gently, like testing a fragile floorboard.

"What is it, Mama?" Jenna didn't look up

"I didn't want to say this in front of Mya, but…" She paused. "Have you noticed she's gained nearly twenty-five pounds since the spring?"

Jenna let out a short breath, not quite a sigh. "She's fine, Mama. She's just growing up. It's normal."

Grandma Rose didn't respond right away. Her eyes narrowed slightly, not in anger, but in sorrow. "There's a difference between growing and grieving," she said softly.

Jenna flinched but didn't reply. The tension in the room thickened like fog.

"I'm not trying to argue," Grandma Rose finally added. "Just… pay attention."

With that, she walked out, leaving Jenna alone again in the dim room.

Grandma Rose moved down the hallway and knocked gently on Mya's door before peeking in. "Can I come in, baby?"

Mya sat cross-legged on her bed, nibbling a cracker from the plate. Her backpack was tossed to the side, and her shoes were still halfway on. She looked up and nodded.

Grandma Rose entered and sat on the edge of the bed. "So... how was your first day?"

Mya's expression changed instantly. "Guess who's back?"

Grandma Rose tilted her head. "Who?"

"Brittany Abraham," Mya said with an edge in her voice. "Why is she here? She tried to humiliate me on the first day. Called me names in front of everybody."

Grandma Rose's brows furrowed with concern. "Lord, have mercy... That girl again?"

Mya nodded. "But Bunny, she's a freshman, stood up for me, right in the cafeteria. She shut Brittany down as if it were nothing. Then we exchanged numbers at our lockers."

For the first time in what felt like weeks, maybe months, there was life in Mya's voice. Her eyes lit up just a little

Grandma Rose saw it and tucked the moment in her heart. She wanted to say more, ask about Bunny, offer her wisdom, but just then, Mya's phone buzzed.

Mya looked down and smiled. "Hey, Grandma, my new friend's calling."

Grandma Rose stood up with a smile of her own. "Well, I won't interrupt that. Go ahead, talk."

As she stepped out and quietly pulled the door closed behind her, she caught one last glimpse.

A smile. Genuine, complete, and effortless.

It was a smile she hadn't seen in a long time.

Chapter 20
Mess With Me First

The second day of school arrived with unexpected energy. Mya woke up before her alarm, stretched under the covers, and stared at the ceiling for a moment. She wasn't necessarily excited for school, but she was excited to see Bunny. That alone made all the difference.

She brushed her hair carefully, choosing a lavender hoodie and jeans that made her feel a little more confident. By the time she stepped out the door, her nerves were lighter, her feet moved faster, and her heart carried a small but powerful sense of hope.

When she arrived at school, Bunny was standing right by the front entrance, waving like they'd been best friends forever.

"Good morning, Superstar," Bunny called out with a grin.

Mya laughed, jogging over. "You're early."

"I had to make sure you didn't try to sneak past me. Plus," Bunny leaned in, "I couldn't wait to tell you what I forgot last night."

They walked inside together, weaving through the crowds of students as if they belonged there, as if they were a unit. It was a feeling Mya had never had before.

"So, remember Billi from lunch?" Bunny said, lowering her voice. "You will not believe what I saw."

"What?"

"She ate a fly," Bunny whispered dramatically. "Landed on her sandwich, and she didn't even see it. I meant to tell you last night, but I forgot."

Mya gasped. "No!"

"Dead serious," Bunny nodded, wrinkling her nose. "I almost choked on my juice. She chewed it."

They both burst into laughter, covering their mouths as they neared their lockers.

But Mya's laughter stopped cold.

Right on her locker door was a photo, a cartoon image of a large, sloppy cow with the words "Mooooove Out the Way" scribbled across it in marker.

The air around her shifted. Her hands froze mid-motion. Her chest tightened.

Bunny noticed immediately. "What the…" she said, pulling the paper down. "Are you kidding me?"

Without a second thought, Bunny balled the paper up and tossed it into the nearest trash can. Her jaw was tight. Her eyes scanned the hallway like a hawk.

That's when they heard it.

"Moooooo."

Then another.

"Moooooo."

Mya stiffened, her back to the hallway. She didn't have to turn around. She knew who it was.

Brittany walked past with her posse of popular girls, all laughing and making exaggerated cow noises. Loud enough for others to notice. Loud enough that students were starting to whisper, looking around to see who the jokes were targeting.

Mya leaned forward and pressed her hand against her locker door, willing herself to disappear.

But Bunny?

She wasn't having it.

She waved her hand in front of her nose dramatically and turned to Brittany. "Whew! What's that smell?" she said loud enough to echo.

The hallway paused. Some students covered their mouths, hiding their giggles. Others flat-out laughed.

Bunny fanned the air. "Oh, Brittany, girl, did something die in your ego? Or is that your attitude decaying again?"

Brittany stopped, glaring. Her posse stopped, too, but no one said anything. Her eyes narrowed at Bunny, who didn't back down an inch.

"If you want to mess with Mya," Bunny said, stepping between Brittany and the lockers, "then you need to mess with me first."

The tension was thick, but Brittany didn't respond. She gave a scoff, turned her head with a flick of her ponytail, and gestured for her friends to keep walking. This time, she didn't bump Mya as she passed. And that said everything.

As the crowd dispersed and the bell rang, Bunny turned toward Mya, who was still facing her locker.

"You good?" she asked softly.

Mya didn't turn around, but she gave a slight nod. Her fingers were still trembling, but there was a flicker of something else, too. Bunny glided Mya away from the lockers to their first-period class.

Once they arrived in Room 107, the fluorescent lights of the room buzzed overhead as they slid into two seats at the back of the Math class. Their teacher, Mr. Carr, was already scribbling equations across the whiteboard like a man on a mission. He didn't even look up as students trickled in and found their seats.

Mya opened her notebook slowly, her mind still stuck in the hallway.

Bunny nudged her gently with her elbow. "Hey," she whispered, leaning closer. "What's the deal with Brittany?"

Mya blinked, hesitant. "What do you mean?"

"I mean," Bunny said, pulling out a mechanical pencil and clicking it like a reflex, "she's older than us. Pretty sure she's a junior. Why's she picking on a first-year student? That's weird."

Mya stared at the top of her blank paper. She didn't want to talk about Brittany. Not here. Not now. But Bunny's tone wasn't teasing; it was real. She wasn't asking to gossip. She was asking to understand.

Mya leaned over a little, whispering low. "I've known her since music school."

Bunny's eyes widened slightly, but she kept listening.

"She was seven. I was five. She used to get all the solos. Her mom would bring in cupcakes for the class. Everybody loved her. She could act, sing, smile on cue, say all the right things." Mya paused. "Until I got the solo one. Then everything changed."

Bunny frowned. "So, she's holding a grudge? Since you were five?"

"I guess," Mya shrugged. "I don't know. She just... she made my life miserable. Every time I'd walk into rehearsal, she'd whisper things. Make up stories. Push me when no one is looking. I quit after a while. It just wasn't worth it."

Mr. Carr turned around, announcing, "We're going to jump into Chapter Two today: linear functions and slope-intercept form. Get your minds ready, this one's a little more real-world."

Bunny gave a small snort. "Yeah, like bullying and jealousy. That's real-world."

Mya cracked a smile, but it faded quickly.

Bunny leaned closer again. "Thanks for telling me. I needed to know so I can watch your back better."

"You already do," Mya said quietly.

Bunny nodded, thoughtfully. "Yeah. But now I know why. And I'm not just here to defend you, I want to help you stand up for yourself too."

Mya looked at her, unsure. "That's not me."

"It can be," Bunny said. "We'll work on it."

Mr. Carr tossed a dry-erase marker onto the desk. "Mya, Bunny, eyes up here. Let's all focus on the real problems for a minute."

The class chuckled lightly as both girls sat up straighter. But even as they turned their attention to the board, the silent pact had already been made.

Mya wasn't just gaining a friend; she was gaining a shield. And maybe even the courage to become one herself. By the time lunch rolled around, Mya was feeling better, lighter. Math had flown by as well, another three classes, and Bunny's promise to help her stand firm kept replaying in her mind like a silent rhythm.

As they entered the cafeteria, the smell of pizza, fries, and cafeteria mystery meat hit them like a wall. The line moved fast, and the girls grabbed their trays. Today's options weren't great, but at least there were chocolate chip cookies.

"Let's just sit anywhere," Bunny said, leading Mya to a table near the windows. "It's too early in the year for territory wars."

They had just settled in when Billi spotted them from across the room.

"There's my girls!" she called, nearly skipping over.

Bunny waved her over. "Hey Billi! Sit with us!"

Billi slid onto the bench and set her tray down, eyes wide with excitement. "I thought I was seeing things yesterday…but y'all… I ate a fly."

Mya laughed, half in disbelief. "Wait…you did?"

"I told you!" Bunny burst out. "She chomped it like it was extra protein!"

Billi faked a dramatic gag, holding her throat. "I nearly threw up in my mashed potatoes when I realized. That's why I skipped dessert. I didn't trust anything after that."

The table erupted with laughter. For once, Mya felt… normal. No one was teasing her. No one was whispering. Just three girls, sharing lunch and stories and jokes that made the weight on her chest feel a little less heavy.

But then, she felt it.

A cold splash.

Milk. All down her hoodie. Her lap. Even her tray

Everyone froze.

Brittany stood just behind her, an empty carton in her hand, lips parted in a fake gasp. "Oh no," she said with syrupy innocence. "I'm so sorry, I didn't see you there. Total accident."

Mya stared down at her soaked hoodie, blinking in shock.

Billi shot up, milk dripping onto her fries. "What are you doing?!" she shouted, voice sharp.

The cafeteria hushed. Heads turned.

Assistant Principal Harris had been doing lunch duty near the vending machines and quickly strode over, eyebrows raised.

"What's going on here?" he demanded.

Before anyone could speak, Brittany was already at work, dabbing at Mya's hoodie with a napkin. "It was just an accident," she said sweetly. "My tray slipped, and the milk went everywhere. Poor Mya…"

Bunny narrowed her eyes, her expression like ice. She didn't speak. She didn't have to. Her stare alone could've melted steel.

Principal Harris looked between them. "Is that true?" he asked, glancing at Mya.

Mya hesitated, then gave a slight nod. "I-it's fine."

He turned to Billi. "You alright?"

Billi wiped her jeans. "Yeah. But it wasn't an accident."

Mr. Harris gave her a look that said enough. "Let's just keep things civil. Mya and Billi head to the restroom and clean up. We'll get you a new lunch tray if you need one."

Without another word, he directed Brittany away from the table, gently guiding her toward the hallway. Brittany gave one last look over her shoulder, her smile smug and victorious.

Bunny stood up too. "I'm coming with you," she told Mya, her tone firm. "Just in case."

The three of them walked off, silent now, but the silence wasn't empty.

The girls burst into the bathroom, slamming the door behind them. The scent of overly floral soap filled the air, and the buzz of the flickering lights echoed off the tiled walls.

Mya stood at the sink, staring down at her milk-soaked hoodie as water ran over her trembling hands.

Billi grabbed a paper towel and tried blotting her pants. "I can't believe her! That wasn't an accident. That was petty and mean."

Bunny rolled her eyes as she rinsed Mya's sleeve under the faucet. "She acts like she runs the whole school."

Mya sniffled, then suddenly slammed the paper towel down on the counter. "I don't like her!" she shouted, her voice bouncing off the walls.

Bunny raised an eyebrow. "We're not going to get along with everyone in life," she said calmly. "But that doesn't mean you get to be a jerk like her."

"Exactly," Billi nodded. "She's the one with the issue, not you."

They all paused for a moment, the emotion slowly melting into a shared breath. Billi reached into her pocket, pulled out her phone, and smiled. "Okay, serious stuff aside, I need both of your numbers. I'm claiming y'all as my girls now. Group chat pending."

Mya cracked the smallest smile as she gave her number, followed by Bunny. Billi added them both quickly and tapped the screen. "Boom. Team Fly Fighters is born."

They all laughed.

But the laugh ended as soon as the bathroom door swung open.

Three girls walked in first, heels clicking, lip gloss shiny. Then Brittany stepped in last, arms crossed and face smug.

"Well, well, well," Brittany said, scanning them from head to toe. "If it isn't Fatty Patty and the Uglies."

Billi and Bunny spun around, eyes wide. "Ugly?" they shouted in perfect unison. "We are NOT ugly."

Brittany didn't flinch. She stepped forward, close, too close to Mya, forcing her back against the sink. "Still hiding behind your new little guard dogs?" she sneered.

Suddenly, the three other girls moved behind Brittany and grabbed Bunny and Billi by their arms, shoving them against the bathroom wall.

"Hey, get off me!" Bunny yelled, struggling.

"What's your problem?" Billi snapped, trying to twist free.

Mya stood frozen, eyes wide, her breathing uneven. Her heart raced in her chest like a caged bird. She had three older brothers and a dad who always protected her. But now, her father was gone. And this felt like a different kind of threat.

"Still scared to sing, huh?" Brittany hissed. "Perfect, little Mya. Always trying to act innocent. I'm so glad you quit music school. I was tired of hearing you anyway."

She jabbed her finger into Mya's chest. "You can't sing. You never could. I'm a better actress. I'm a better singer. That's why I'm getting the lead in the end-of-year play, A Different Echo: Tiny Words. Not you."

Mya's lip trembled. She said nothing. Her throat closed tight. And then... the tears came.

"You're so pathetic," Brittany spat.

Suddenly...

Wham!

Bunny broke free and shoved Brittany backward into the sink. "Get away from her!"

Billi shook off the girl gripping her arm and stepped forward, standing tall beside Bunny. Her eyes narrowed with a silent dare.

Brittany froze.

Her fake confidence wavered for the first time. She glanced between the two girls. Then she lifted her chin, dusted off her sleeve, and muttered, "Whatever. Not worth it."

She turned and walked out, her friends scrambling to follow her like scattered shadows.

Silence returned to the bathroom.

Mya collapsed to her knees, sobbing. "I'm sorry," she cried. "I didn't do anything. I just stood there. I should've said something. I should've fought back..."

Bunny dropped down beside her and wrapped her arms around her. "You don't have to apologize."

Billi knelt on the other side and placed a hand on her back. "You're not weak, Mya. You were scared. But you're not alone anymore."

They stayed there like that for a while, three girls, different strengths, one heart, huddled together in a moment of shared love and loyalty.

Chapter 21
A Thousand Words

The kitchen felt warmer than usual that evening. The soft clatter of a spoon stirring in a coffee cup echoed as Mya sat at the table with her hands folded, her plate mostly untouched. Grandma Rose moved slowly around the kitchen, her slippers dragging with each step. Jenna had called earlier; she had to work late. Again.

"Everything alright, baby?" Grandma Rose asked as she sat across from her, a mug of coffee in hand.

Mya hesitated, chewing the inside of her cheek before the words finally came out. "Something happened today... in the bathroom."

Grandma Rose looked up, calm but alert. "Go ahead. I'm listening."

Mya swallowed. "Brittany poured milk on me in the cafeteria. Pretended it was an accident. Then... later, in the bathroom, she cornered me with her friends. She got in my face. Called me names. Said I couldn't sing. Said she was better. That she's getting the lead in the end-of-year play."

For a split second, Grandma Rose froze mid-sip, then promptly spat out her coffee, sputtering as she grabbed a napkin.

Mya blinked. "Grandma!"

Grandma Rose wiped her mouth, shaking her head. "I'm sorry, baby. I just... Brittany? A better singer than you?" She let out a small, almost incredulous laugh. "That's the biggest lie I've heard all week."

Mya didn't laugh. She looked down at the table, her shoulders shrinking inward.

Grandma Rose's tone softened. "Mya, honey... truth doesn't always need to be said. Sometimes, action speaks louder than any word. You don't need to argue with her. Just let your gift speak for itself."

Mya bit her lip, tears pooling in her eyes. "I met another friend today, her name's Billi. She's tall with a slim body and long brown hair. She's strong, like Bunny. They both stood up for me."

"That's wonderful, baby," Grandma said, reaching over to touch her hand. "Friends like that don't come around often. You hold onto them."

"I want to be strong too," Mya said, her voice suddenly cracking. "But I miss Dad…"

Her throat caught around the words. Grandma Rose's eyes softened with sorrow as she gently rubbed her granddaughter's hand.

"I know, sweetheart. He'd be proud of the young woman you're becoming. Even on the hard days."

Mya wiped her cheek. "She said I can't sing, that I'm not good enough. That she's getting the lead in A Different Echo: Tiny Words."

Grandma Rose tilted her head. "And what do you say to that?"

Mya didn't answer.

"Well," Grandma Rose continued, "you won't know unless you try. It's been a while since you've sung, yes. But that voice of yours, it didn't go anywhere. It's just waiting on you."

Mya nodded slowly, but her eyes began to dim. She pushed her plate forward. "I think I'm done."

"You barely touched it."

"I'm just not hungry," Mya said quietly, standing up. "Can I be excused?"

Grandma Rose watched her walk away with a concerned frown. She didn't push. "Of course, baby."

Mya closed the bathroom door behind her and locked it. She leaned over the sink, gripping both sides, her breath coming in shaky gasps. She turned on the faucet to fill the silence.

Her reflection stared back at her. She looked at her face... her cheeks... her body.

Then the words returned.

Fatty Patty.

You can't sing.

You're not good enough.

Her eyes welled with tears. She touched her face. Her stomach. Her hoodie was still faintly stained from the earlier incident.

"I'm not fat," she whispered.

Then louder, "I'm NOT fat."

But the words didn't settle anything.

She dropped to her knees in front of the toilet, and like the silent scream of pain she'd been holding inside, she threw up her dinner, all of it.

Afterward, she flushed quickly, ashamed. Her chest heaved as she climbed to her feet and looked in the mirror again. Her eyes were red. Her face was pale. And yet, something inside her whispered: Now you're in control.

She grabbed a towel, wiped her face, and turned off the light. She went to bed.

It had been a month since school started, and Mya, Bunny, and Billi had quickly become known as "the trio" by almost everyone in their grade.

They sat together on the wide stone steps outside the school, sharing snacks, trading stories, and laughing about everything from bad cafeteria food to weird substitute teachers.

"Okay, but tell me why Coach Huff thought it was okay to try and rap about fractions," Billi said, mimicking his awkward moves.

"I still have nightmares," Bunny added, doubling over with laughter.

Mya managed a soft giggle but immediately covered her mouth and shifted her weight like something in her body didn't feel right.

"You good?" Bunny asked.

"Yeah," Mya said too quickly. "I'm just... tired. Long day."

"Girl, we all had the same day," Billi said, nudging her. "But you've been looking kinda... pale lately. And I don't mean winter-pale. I mean tired-tired."

Mya shook her head, avoiding their eyes. "I've just been staying up too late. Homework and stuff."

Bunny raised a brow but didn't push. Still, she noticed how Mya kept tucking her sweatshirt tighter around her body. She barely touched the granola bar in her lap. How her laugh never quite reached her eyes anymore.

Billi unwrapped a bag of popcorn and shoved a handful in her mouth. "I swear, if one more teacher says, 'pop quiz,' I'm transferring to an art school."

"Same," Bunny said. "Mya, you'd better start singing again. I'm gonna drag you to the auditorium myself."

At the mention of singing, Mya flinched, just a little.

"I'm not ready," she whispered, eyes downcast.

"Why?" Bunny asked.

"I just don't feel like myself right now," Mya mumbled.

The girls quieted for a second.

Billi leaned back, staring at the clouds. "That's okay. Sometimes we don't feel like ourselves. But just don't get stuck there."

Mya gave a faint nod, pressing her hands together tightly in her lap.

The truth was, she was stuck. For the last month, she'd been quietly excusing herself after meals, at home, at school, even when out with her friends. No one had noticed. Not really. And that both comforted her and broke her at the same time.

It wasn't about the food anymore. It was about control. About silencing the voice in her head that echoed Brittany's cruelty. About making herself smaller and quieter. Invisible again.

As the sun began to set behind the building, Bunny looked at her sideways. "Hey, we're here, okay? Whatever's going on... we've got you."

Mya nodded again, eyes still distant. "Thanks."

Billi stood up and stretched. "Alright, my dad's gonna honk the horn any second now. You sure you don't want me to drop you off, Mya?"

"I'm walking. My house is just a few blocks away," Mya said quickly.

Bunny gave her a quick hug. "Call us later, alright?"

"Yeah. I will."

They waved goodbye, and Mya started the slow walk home.

But as she turned the corner, her stomach twisted—not with hunger, but guilt. She hadn't eaten all day.

And when she finally reached the porch, she slipped inside without a word and went straight to the bathroom.

Again.

The following day at school, Mya requested permission to use the restroom during fourth period. Bunny and Billi exchanged confused glances, as she had already asked a pass during the second period. The school bathrooms were usually loud, buzzing with chatter, gossip, and the constant slam of stall doors. But during the third period, they were almost always empty. Silent.

Just the way Mya liked them.

She rushed inside, barely making it into a stall before she dropped to her knees. Her body was now accustomed to the routine. The feeling in her chest. The burning in her throat. The guilt.

When she finished, she flushed quickly, wiped her mouth, and leaned her head against the cool tile wall. Her arms trembled. Her knees ached.

She didn't hear the door open.

"Sweetheart?"

Mya froze.

"Are you alright in there?" It was Mrs. Green, the school's attendance clerk and unofficial hallway mom. She had a soft voice, but it was laced with concern.

Mya quickly stood up, flushed again out of panic, and opened the stall door, trying to compose herself. "I'm fine," she said, wiping at her eyes. "Just wasn't feeling good today."

Mrs. Green studied her closely. "You've lost some weight."

Mya's mouth opened, then shut again.

"You feeling okay, baby? You look pale."

"I… I had the flu a couple of weeks ago," Mya lied quickly. "Still getting over it."

Mrs. Green's brow furrowed, but she didn't challenge her. "Hmm. A notable aspect of the flu is that it typically doesn't last a month. You sure you're not hiding something?"

Mya's throat tightened. "I'm just tired, that's all."

Mrs. Green didn't believe her. She could see the way Mya's hoodie hung looser than it used to. The way her eyes looked sunken, her skin was dull. She'd seen this before.

"Come with me," she said gently, placing a hand on Mya's shoulder. "Let's call your grandma. I think you need to go home."

Mya hesitated, but nodded.

They padded down the hall to the primary office. Mya sat in the corner while Mrs. Green picked up the phone and dialed. Her voice was calm and respectful, but her eyes kept darting back to Mya with concern.

"Mrs. Watkins? This is Sharon Green from the school. Mya's not feeling well today. I think someone should pick her up. Yes, she's okay, but I'd like to talk with you briefly when you arrive."

Mya sat still, staring at the floor, twisting the strings of her hoodie between her fingers.

She didn't know what Grandma Rose would say.

She didn't know what she would tell her.

But for the first time, someone had seen through the act.

And now, the truth was coming to the surface, whether she was ready or not.

Within twenty minutes, Grandma Rose pulled into the school parking lot with her heart pounding in her chest. She hadn't even put the car in park before she spotted Mrs. Green standing by the main office doors, waving her over with a look of quiet urgency.

She got out, smoothing her skirt with trembling hands. "What's going on?" she asked as soon as she reached her.

Mrs. Green lowered her voice, gently pulling Grandma Rose aside. "I don't want to alarm you," she began, "but I caught Mya in the bathroom today... vomiting. At first, she said it was the flu, but I've seen enough over the years to know when something's more than that."

Grandma Rose's eyes widened. "Throwing up?"

Mrs. Green nodded solemnly. "She's lost weight. Not the kind that happens from growing tall, either. The kind that happens when something's hurting deep inside."

Grandma Rose felt her knees weaken slightly. "Lord, have mercy..."

"I think she's developed an eating disorder," Mrs. Green added gently. "I'm not a doctor, but I know the signs. I thought you should know."

Grandma Rose put a hand to her chest, her eyes filling with tears, she refused to let them fall, not yet. "Thank you, Sharon. I appreciate you telling me."

Inside the office, Mya sat with her hoodie sleeves pulled over her hands, head down. She didn't look up even when she heard her grandmother walk in.

Grandma Rose didn't say a word. She just walked over, touched Mya's shoulder gently, and whispered, "Come on, baby. Let's go home."

The drive was quiet. Too quiet.

The kind of silence that felt thick, heavy, like it was pressing against the windows. Mya stared out at the trees as they passed. Her throat burned, but not from tears, yet.

When they pulled into the driveway, Grandma Rose turned off the ignition but didn't move.

"Let's go inside," she said softly.

Mya followed her in, dropped her backpack by the door, and sat on the couch without being told. Her fingers trembled in her lap. She didn't want to speak. But she could feel it coming.

Grandma Rose sat across from her, her voice thick with emotion. "Mya... baby, talk to me. Please."

Mya couldn't hold it in any longer. "It started with Brittany," she said, her voice breaking. "She called me Fatty Patty on the first day of school."

Grandma Rose sucked in a breath.

"She put a cow picture on my locker... poured milk on me in the cafeteria... people were staring, and I..." her words caught in her throat. "I just wanted it all to stop."

Tears fell freely now. "I felt disgusting, Grandma. Every time I looked in the mirror, I saw what she said. And no one else noticed. Not Mom... not my brothers... they're always gone or busy or grown."

She wiped her face with her sleeves. "And Mom... she's never home. I know she's working. I know she's tired. But I'm tired too. And I miss Dad so much."

That's when she broke completely.

"I miss my dad," she sobbed. "He used to tell me I was beautiful. He'd cheer for me when I sang. He always saw me. You love me, Grandma, I know you do, but it's not the same. I feel... alone."

Grandma Rose's eyes welled up, and this time, she didn't fight the tears. She crossed the room and pulled Mya into her arms.

"Oh, baby girl..." she whispered. "I'm so sorry. I should've seen it. I should've known."

Mya cried harder against her chest.

"You don't ever have to be alone in this," Grandma Rose whispered into her hair. "We'll get through this together. I promise you. We'll get you help. We'll rebuild your strength. And we'll remind that beautiful heart of yours who God says you are."

Mya could barely breathe through her sobs, but for the first time in a long time, she let someone see all of it.

And in Grandma Rose's arms, it didn't feel like weakness.

It felt like the beginning of a healing process.

Chapter 22
The Other Side of Grief

The living room was dim, with only the small lamp in the corner providing light. A soft breeze moved through the cracked window, carrying the faint scent of evening dew and the rustle of tree branches.

Jenna arrived home later than usual. Her heels tapped lightly on the hardwood as she entered, tired and emotionally drained. She was already pulling off her coat when she saw her mother standing in the hallway, arms crossed, expression tight with quiet concern.

"Hey, Ma," Jenna said, forcing a weary smile. "Did Mya eat dinner?"

"We need to talk," Grandma Rose said, her voice firm but gentle.

Jenna stopped mid-step. "About what?"

"About Mya."

Jenna sighed and dropped her coat on the couch. "What now?"

"I picked her up from school today."

Jenna's brows furrowed. "Why?"

"Because the school nurse didn't think she looked well. And Mrs. Green, God bless her, caught Mya in the bathroom throwing up. She's been making herself sick, Jenna."

Jenna froze.

"What?"

"She's been hurting, child, right under our roof. She's lost fifteen pounds in a month. And you didn't notice." Grandma Rose's voice cracked just slightly. "I didn't either. That's what makes this worse."

Jenna slumped into the recliner and put her hands over her face. "Oh God…"

"I told her we'd get her help. Counseling. Support. Something."

Jenna was silent for a long moment. Then finally, she whispered, "I've been going."

Grandma Rose blinked. "What?"

"I've been going to therapy," Jenna said again. "Every Wednesday and Thursday after work. For months now."

"But... why didn't you say anything?"

"I don't know," Jenna whispered. "I didn't want to explain it. I didn't want anyone to ask me how I was doing or remind me that I wasn't doing enough. I just... I just needed space. A way to breathe."

Grandma Rose slowly sat down across from her. "I understand needing space. And I understand grieving differently. But Jenna..." her voice softened, "you could have told me. I would've helped more. I am helping. But you didn't have to carry that by yourself."

"I didn't think about Mya," Jenna said, eyes filling with tears. "I mean, I did, but not like I should have. I was so focused on my pain. On surviving every day without Noah. I didn't even stop to ask if she was surviving."

Grandma Rose inhaled sharply at the sound of her late son-in-law's name. "I miss him too," she said quietly.

"I know, Mama," Jenna whispered. "He was my husband. But he was her father. And I forgot what that meant."

Grandma Rose reached out and took her daughter's hand. "You didn't forget. You're just trying to hold your broken pieces together."

Jenna nodded slowly, tears spilling down her cheeks. "I should've included Mya and brought her with me to one of the sessions. Or asked the counselor if they saw kids, too. I didn't think..."

"I know, baby," Grandma Rose said, her tone softer now. "But it's not too late."

Jenna looked up. "Do you think she'll forgive me?"

"She's already trying to," Grandma Rose replied. "She still loves you. She needs you to show her you see her again."

They sat in silence for a long moment. Two women, one grieving a husband, the other grieving a son-in-law, both finally realizing that a young girl had been suffering alone between them.

"We'll find a counselor for her," Jenna said quietly.

"And maybe a family session," Grandma Rose added. "Together. All of us."

Jenna nodded. "Yeah. All of us."

It had been four days since Mrs. Green pulled Grandma Rose aside and gently spoke the words no guardian ever wants to hear: I think she has an eating disorder.

Since then, the school hadn't changed, but Mya had.

Everything around her kept moving: bells ringing, books slamming, laughter echoing in the hallways. But inside, her world was quieter. Heavier. The teasing still lingered in her thoughts. Her appetite had vanished completely. And though Bunny and Billi still walked her to class and saved her a seat at lunch, she felt like a ghost trapped between who she was and who she was supposed to be.

She didn't know what to expect when Grandma Rose told her they were going to talk to someone. "Just a lady with a chair and a notepad," she'd said. "Nothing scary."

But Mya's hands still trembled in her lap as they sat in the waiting room of the small counseling center on 10th Street.

The walls were painted soft beige, and the air smelled faintly of lavender. Across from her, a wooden shelf held books to support young girls, provide emotional support, and offer healing. The ticking of the wall clock made the silence louder.

"Miss Mya Carter?" a voice called gently from the doorway.

Mya looked up. A tall, kind-eyed woman with tight curls and a burgundy blouse smiled at her. "Hi, Mya. I'm Dr. Rivers. Would you like to come in?"

Mya glanced at Grandma Rose, who nodded with a warm, reassuring smile. "I'll be right here, baby."

She slowly stood, her legs stiff, and followed Dr. Rivers into a small room with two cozy armchairs, a rug with colorful swirls, and a single window that let in filtered sunlight.

"You can sit wherever you'd like," Dr. Rivers said.

Mya chose the chair farthest from the door.

Dr. Rivers sat across from her and set a closed notebook on her lap. "We don't have to talk about anything you're not ready to. But if there's anything on your heart, I'm here to listen. This is your space."

Mya shrugged, staring at her shoes. "I don't know what to say."

"That's okay. Want to start with how your day was?"

"Normal, I guess." Her voice was barely above a whisper. "School. Class. Lunch."

Dr. Rivers tilted her head kindly. "Did you eat lunch?"

Mya hesitated. "Some of it."

"Was that hard to do?"

A lump formed in Mya's throat. "Kind of."

They sat in silence for a moment. Dr. Rivers didn't rush her. Didn't press.

"Can I ask you something?" Mya finally said.

"Of course."

"Is it… Weird to miss someone so much that you start doing stuff that doesn't make sense?"

"No," Dr. Rivers said gently. "That's not weird at all."

Mya's eyes filled with tears, but she kept her voice steady. "I miss my dad. I miss him every day. He always said I was beautiful. That I had a voice meant for big stages."

A tear slipped down her cheek.

"But now I don't feel beautiful. I don't even feel normal. People call me names, make fun of me, and I want it to stop. So, I stopped eating. And when I did eat, I didn't want it to stay."

Dr. Rivers leaned forward just a bit. "Mya... thank you for saying that out loud. That takes more courage than most adults have."

"I didn't want to tell anyone," Mya admitted. "Not even Grandma. And my mom, she's always working. She's barely home."

"I hear you," Dr. Rivers said. "It sounds like you've been carrying a lot... all by yourself."

Mya nodded slowly, another tear falling.

"Well, you're not alone anymore," the counselor added. "I'm proud of you for coming. This is where the healing begins."

Mya wiped her face with her sleeve, surprised by how much lighter her chest felt, even if just a little.

"Can I come back again?" she asked softly.

Dr. Rivers smiled warmly. "As often as you need."

A week had passed since Mya first stepped into Dr. Rivers's office.

Outside, late-October wind rattled dry leaves along the sidewalk as Grandma Rose walked her inside for a follow-up appointment.

Dr. Rivers greeted Mya with the same warm smile, but today she set two small index cards on the coffee table between them.

"On this one," she said, sliding the first card forward, "write a word you believe about yourself right now."

"On the second, write a word you want to believe."

Mya hesitated, then wrote "broken" on the first card and "enough" on the second.

Dr. Rivers nodded. There's no judgment, only understanding.

They spent the next thirty minutes exploring the space between those two words: the ache of missing Dad, the sting of Brittany's insults, the pressure she felt to be "okay" for everyone else. Mya talked more than she'd planned, and when the session ended, Dr. Rivers gently asked:

"Could you carry enough cards with you this week? A small reminder that the girl inside you is still worthy, no matter what your mind, or anyone else, tries to say."

Mya slipped the card into her hoodie pocket, fingers tracing the ink like a secret promise.

Later that day, the school noise crashed back over her the moment she stepped off the counseling center steps and onto the bus. By the fifth period, she felt hollow again. At lunch, Mya picked at a single carrot stick while Bunny and Billi swapped stories about tomorrow's pep rally. They noticed her barely touched tray, exchanged a glance, but said nothing yet.

When the bell rang, Mya mumbled something about the restroom and hurried off.

She barely made it into a stall before the nausea, half-habit, half-panic took over. Moments later, the toilet flushed, and she leaned against the wall, dizzy and ashamed.

A knock sounded on the stall.

"Mya?" Bunny's voice was gentle but firm.

"We're coming in," Billi added.

Mya opened the door a crack, eyes red. Bunny and Billi stepped inside, concern etched on their faces.

"Why are you doing this to yourself?" Bunny whispered.

Tears spilled over as everything she'd held back poured out:

Dad's empty chair at dinner.

Brittany's Fatty Patty taunts still echo a month later.

The secret counseling sessions, how Dr. Rivers understood, but the pain didn't vanish overnight.

The crushing fear that even her best friends could never really get it.

"I thought you wouldn't understand," she sobbed. "I thought you'd think I was weak."

Billi wrapped her in a steady hug. "Weak? Girl, none of us is walking around perfect. My dad was in rehab last year, did I tell you that? People helped me breathe when I couldn't. Let us do that for you."

Bunny grabbed an index card from Mya's backpack and pressed it back into Mya's palm. "We see you looking at this card a lot. We're not letting you forget this word. We'll remind you every time you try to disappear."

Mya clutched the card, shaking. For the first time since her father died, she let someone other than Grandma see all the messy pieces, and they didn't look away.

She wasn't fixed. She wasn't finished. But in that cramped, echoing bathroom, something shifted:

She was held.

By the end of the school day, Mya felt drained not just physically but emotionally, as if her heart had been stretched open and poured out.

The bathroom confrontation still echoed in her mind: the tears, the fear, the way her voice shook when she confessed the truth... and the way Bunny and Billi stood beside her without hesitation.

She half-expected them to pull away after that to see her differently, like she was broken or fragile. But instead, they walked her to the office and sat with her until Grandma Rose arrived.

Now, as Mya buckled her seatbelt and the car rolled away from the curb, she stared out the window, her voice soft.

"Grandma?"

"Yes, baby?"

"I told them. Bunny and Billi... I told them about everything."

Grandma Rose looked at her quickly, surprised. "Everything?"

Mya nodded, her voice trembling just a little. "That I've been throwing up, I'm in counseling. That I miss Dad so much, I don't even know how to say it sometimes."

Grandma Rose's hands gripped the steering wheel tightly, but she stayed silent, letting Mya speak.

"I thought they wouldn't get it. I thought they'd walk away or think I was too much. But they didn't. They were quiet at first… but then Billi hugged me and told me about her dad being in rehab last year. And Bunny…" she paused, blinking tears away, "…she gave me back the card Dr. Rivers gave me… the one that said *Enough*. She noticed it."

Grandma Rose's eyes glistened, but she didn't interrupt.

"They said they're going to help me get through it. Not fix me… just be there. I didn't know how much I needed that."

The car came to a stop at a red light. Grandma Rose reached over and gently held Mya's hand.

"I'm proud of you," she said. "Not because you told them. But because you finally let someone else carry a little of the pain with you. That's not weakness, that's wisdom. That's healing."

Mya stared at their hands, small and strong together. "I still miss Dad every day."

"I do too," Grandma whispered. "Some days it still hits me like a wave. But I know he's proud of you. You're facing things that most grown people don't know how to face."

The light turned green, and they drove the last few blocks home in thoughtful silence.

As they pulled into the driveway, Mya turned to her grandmother. "Do you think… I'll get better?"

Grandma Rose looked at her with eyes full of love. "I know you will. Because you're not doing it alone anymore."

Chapter 23
The Voice Returns

The scent of garlic, onion, and fresh thyme filled the house as Grandma Rose moved gracefully between the stove and the counter, humming softly while stirring a pot of chicken and dumplings.

Mya sat at the kitchen island, notebook open and pencil in hand, but her math homework was taking a back seat to her video call. Bunny and Billi's laughing faces lit up the screen, propped against a jar of jellybeans.

"I swear," Billi said between bites of popcorn, "Ghit Bouston had a voice that could melt paint off a wall."

"She was unstoppable," Bunny added. "A whole legend."

In the background of Billi's screen, the unmistakable intro to "Love Only Me" played from a Bluetooth speaker.

Grandma Rose glanced up from the stove with a smile. "That was your daddy's favorite Ghit song," she murmured.

Billi swayed to the beat, dramatically holding an invisible mic.

Suddenly, without thinking, without even realizing the words were forming in her throat, Mya sang out loud and fiercely.

Her voice soared...clear, complete, unshaken.

Then silence from her two friends on the other end of the phone.

Utter silence from the screen.

Then....

"WHOA!!!" Bunny shouted, mouth wide open.

"Did you hear that?! Did y'all hear that?! Mya! Girl!" Billi nearly dropped her popcorn. "Where have you been hiding that?"

Mya blinked, stunned. Her own heart thudded in her chest as she realized what she'd just done. No fear. No shaking. No shame.

She sang.

Grandma Rose had stopped stirring. She turned, walked over to the island, and sat down slowly, eyes glassy with tears.

"You did it, baby," she whispered. "You sang again."

Mya looked at her, lips parted, voice still floating somewhere between shock and joy.

Grandma leaned forward and pulled her into a deep hug. "My baby is back."

On the screen, Bunny dramatically fanned her face. "That was not just singing. That was testifying. Girl, you're a powerhouse!"

"Forget Brittany," Billi said. "I see why she's so mad. You're a better singer, period, and I haven't even heard her."

Bunny snorted. "Yeah, we don't need to after hearing Mya."

Mya laughed, cheeks burning, eyes shining. Something inside her that had felt buried for so long had just cracked open, and light poured out.

Grandma Rose stood up and returned to the stove, still smiling as she wiped her eyes with her apron.

"Dinner'll be ready in twenty," she called out gently. "But take your time, Superstar."

Mya glanced at her phone screen, two best friends still buzzing with praise, and then down at her notebook. For the first time in a long time, she felt like herself again.

No shame.

No hiding.

Just Mya.

The next morning, the sun lit the school's front steps in soft golden streaks. Leaves crunched beneath students' shoes as backpacks slung over shoulders, and the air buzzed with chatter about homework, sports, and weekend plans.

Bunny and Billi stood near the front entrance, eyes scanning the drop-off lane like hawks on a mission.

"There she is!" Bunny grinned, waving as Mya stepped out of Grandma Rose's car.

Mya smiled and jogged up to them, her curls bouncing and her backpack slightly unzipped, music notes from a sheet poking out the top.

"Look at you!" Billi beamed. "Voice of an angel and a face to match. You're walking in here like you own the place."

Mya laughed, half shy, half grateful. "Y'all are doing the most."

"No, you did the most," Bunny said. "Last night? You snatched our souls with that Ghit note. My mom is still asking if it was a real performance."

They walked down the hall toward their lockers, the usual crowd bustling around them. Mya's heart fluttered a little, but this time not from fear. There was strength there now. Courage that hadn't been there before.

As they reached their lockers, Bunny pulled up a video she'd secretly taken on video chat last night. "Okay, but listen…this note right here."

The phone played.

Mya blushed and covered her face. "Stop!"

"That's what we call a moment," Billi said. "Like, where's your record deal?"

Then came the voice. Cold. Cutting. Sharp like a paper slice.

"Well, well, well…"

Brittany.

She stood a few feet away with two of her friends trailing behind her like shadows, arms crossed, eyebrows raised.

"Poor little Mya's trying to sing again," Brittany mocked, lips curled into a smirk. "That's cute. But let's be real, I don't think so. I'm still number one. Always have been."

The hallway grew a little quieter, as if even the lockers knew something important was about to happen.

Bunny and Billi both turned to Mya, waiting.

And Mya… didn't flinch.

She calmly closed her locker, slung her bag over one shoulder, and turned to face Brittany directly.

"I don't care, Brittany."

Brittany blinked. "What?"

"You heard me, I …don't…. care."

"It was never a competition between you and me," Mya said clearly, her voice steady, her eyes unwavering. "I was never singing to beat you. I sing for the Lord, not for anyone else. And I'm not afraid of you anymore."

The silence that followed felt like thunder.

Bunny's mouth dropped open. Billi clutched her imaginary pearls.

"Girl…" Bunny whispered. "Did that just happen?"

"You better testify," Billi whispered, both proud and shocked.

Brittany's face turned red for a flash of a second, but she quickly scoffed and rolled her eyes. "Whatever," she muttered, turning on her heel. "This school needed a good laugh anyway."

But her footsteps were fast and tight. And she didn't look back.

Mya let out a small breath. Her hands were trembling slightly, but inside, she felt free.

"She said not for anyone else," Bunny repeated with her hand on her chest.

"That part," Billi added.

Mya chuckled, cheeks still flushed. "Y'all better stop hyping me up."

"Nope," Bunny said, looping her arm through Mya's. "Too late. Your season just started. And you're walking in it now."

As they walked down the hall together, students all around them, Mya didn't shrink back this time.

She stood tall, stronger.

Not because Brittany backed down, but because she didn't. As the hallway cleared, the trio gave each other high-fives and headed to class.

By 12:30 pm, the hallway buzzed with chatter as students filtered out of their mid-morning classes. Posters for clubs, tutoring schedules, and sports tryouts lined the bulletin boards…but one fresh sheet of paper drew Bunny's attention instantly.

She paused, backed up, and grinned.

"Auditions for the End-of-Year Play: A Different Echo: Tiny Words."

Sign-Up Sheet Below

Auditions: November 18th – Auditorium 3:30 PM"

Her eyes danced across the list of names already signed up. Brittany's name was there, of course, written in bold letters right at number three.

Bunny reached into her backpack, grabbed her gel pen, and without hesitation scribbled:

#14, Mya Carter

She smiled to herself, practically skipping away from the bulletin board.

By the time she made it to the cafeteria, the lunch line had thinned out, and students were settling into their usual tables. Billi and Mya were already seated, mid-laugh over something one of their teachers had said during second period.

Mya took a sip of apple juice while Billi speared a baby carrot with dramatic flair.

Across the room, Brittany sat at her table with her friends, not even glancing in Mya's direction.

Bunny burst through the lunchroom doors, practically sprinting.

"Slow down before you fall!" called Mr. Huff from his post by the vending machines.

"Yes, sir!" Bunny shouted back, not missing a beat.

She reached their table, panting, cheeks glowing with excitement. She dropped her tray with a clatter, pointed dramatically at Mya, and announced:

"I just signed you up for the audition for A Different Echo: Tiny Words!"

Mya choked on her juice and spat it back into her cup. "You did what?"

Billi dropped her carrot. "Wait…you did what?!"

"No, no, no," Mya said, her eyes wide, waving her hands in protest. "You didn't."

"Yes. I did," Bunny said proudly, sitting down. "You're number fourteen. Right after Marcus and before that girl with the pink eyebrows."

Mya looked like she was about to slide under the table. "I…I'm not ready."

"You are," Bunny insisted. "You just don't feel it yet. But it's in you, Mya. You need this."

Billi leaned in, eyebrows raised, looking from one to the other.

Then she quietly placed her hand over Mya's.

"I know we're girls. We joke, we hype you up, but I agree with Bunny."

Mya looked at her, confused, her breath still shaky.

Billi leaned closer and whispered gently, "Not just to beat Brittany… but for you to heal. To sing again, for your dad."

That stopped everything.

Mya blinked hard, her throat tight, her heart suddenly too full for words.

She looked at her friends, one fierce, one soft, and saw nothing but belief. Not pressure. Not competition.

Just believe.

She swallowed and finally whispered, "Okay… I'll do it."

Bunny gasped and threw both arms in the air. "YES!"

Billi smiled and raised her apple juice like a toast. "To healing. To stage lights. And to the greatest voice in this school."

Mya laughed nervously, unsure, but real. Deep down, she still felt scared.

But for the first time... she also felt ready. At three o'clock, the last bell rang, and school was out.

The school auditorium buzzed with chatter as students filtered in for auditions. The stage lights were dimmed, but a bright spotlight waited overhead like a crown, casting shadows on the empty microphone stand.

Backstage, nerves danced through the air. Students clutched lyric sheets, cleared their throats, and whispered last-minute lines. Brittany was already in the wings, stretching and humming scales loud enough for everyone to hear.

Bunny and Billi stood just off to the side in the front row, whispering excitedly as the choir director, Mr. Vaughn, and music teacher, Ms. Hoffman, reviewed the audition sheet.

"Looks like we've got twenty-three names today," Ms. Hoffman said, scanning the clipboard. "Should be a strong group."

Mr. Vaughn nodded, adjusting his glasses. "Let's see if any surprises walk in."

Right on cue, the doors near the back of the auditorium opened. Mya stepped in slowly, hugging her folder of sheet music, her heart thudding in her chest like a bass drum. She walked toward the stage, every step loud in her ears.

"Oh my gosh..." someone whispered near the back.

"Is that Mya Carter?"

Brittany, already stretching backstage, peeked through the curtains and froze. Her smirk faded slightly.

Bunny stood and waved both hands wildly. "Go, Mya! Number fourteen, baby!"

"Sing like you're already booked and busy!" Billi added, cupping her hands around her mouth.

Mya blushed but smiled faintly. She could barely feel her legs.

Mr. Vaughn and Ms. Hoffman perked up the moment they saw her name called.

"Next up, Mya Carter," Mr. Vaughn announced. "You may begin when ready."

The auditorium quieted.

Mya stepped into the light. The spotlight washed over her. For a moment, she saw only darkness beyond the stage. No students. No teachers. Not even Brittany.

Just her and the mic.

Her hands shook as she opened her music folder, then closed it again.

She didn't need it.

She looked up, took a deep breath, and began. The words were clear, and every note was a perfect pitch.

The moment the first line left her lips, the room stilled.

Her voice was velvet and strength, full of soul, vulnerability, and quiet power. Bunny's mouth dropped open. Billi clutched the edge of her seat like she was watching the finale of a TV drama.

By the time Mya hit the chorus, she wasn't trembling anymore. Her voice climbed high and fearlessly, echoing through the theater as it belonged there.

Applause erupted before she even finished.

Even Mr. Vaughn leaned back in his chair, stunned. "My goodness."

Ms. Hoffman jotted something quickly on her evaluation sheet, then smiled. "That girl has been hiding."

Brittany, still backstage, stared in disbelief. Her jaw clenched. For the first time, she looked... nervous.

Mya finished her final note with grace, then stood silently, blinking in the light.

"Thank you, Miss Carter," Mr. Vaughn said. "That will be all."

Mya stepped down from the stage, cheeks flushed, still catching her breath.

Bunny grabbed her in a hug. "You slayed, girl!"

"Better call Broadway," Billi said, grinning. "That stage was yours."

Later that day, the cast list was posted outside the auditorium. Students crowded around.

Lead Female Role, Elle Phillips: Mya Carter

Lead Male Role, Ethan Phillips: Jay Benson

Supporting Role, George Jenkins: Marcus Hill

Supporting Role, Aunt Helen: Brittany Abraham

Mya stared at the paper, barely able to process it. The trio walked away from the auditorium as students leaned in, squinting at the neatly taped cast list posted on the glass.

Marcus Hill stood near the front, reading the names aloud to his friends. "Whoa, Mya got the lead! That's wild. She killed that audition though..."

Suddenly, a sharp voice cut through the crowd.

"Move."

Brittany Abraham marched up, her heels clicking against the tile. Without hesitation, she shoved Marcus to the side with her shoulder.

"Hey!" Marcus protested, stumbling back.

But Brittany didn't even glance at him. Her eyes locked onto the list.

Lead Role, Elle Phillips: Mya Carter

Supporting Role, Aunt Helen: Brittany Abraham

Her face tightened.

No. 2.

She reread it. Still No. 2.

A flicker of something, anger? Shock? Fear? ...flashed in her eyes, but she blinked it away, tossing her ponytail over her shoulder as if it didn't matter.

But it did.

She stepped back slowly, face unreadable, lips pressed into a thin line.

Behind her, someone whispered, "Did you see how fast she pushed Marcus? She's heated."

But Brittany kept walking. Not a word. Not a smile.

Just silence.

And the quiet realization that Mya Carter was no longer hiding.

Chapter 24
The Spotlight at Home

Mya sat cross-legged on the living room floor, still holding your phone with a picture of the cast list in her hands, as if it might vanish from her screen. Her cheeks ached from smiling, and her heart felt like it was glowing beneath her sweatshirt.

Grandma Rose sat on the edge of the couch, her knitting needles forgotten in her lap. "Reread it, baby," she said with a grin.

Mya beamed. "Lead Role, Elle Phillips: Mya Carter."

Jenna, who had just walked in from the kitchen, gasped and nearly dropped her coffee. "Wait…the lead?"

Mya nodded, her voice catching. "I got it, Mom."

For a moment, the room was quiet, then Jenna let out a scream loud enough to rattle the picture frames. "Oh my God, MYA!" she rushed over and wrapped her daughter in a hug so tight that Mya nearly dropped the paper.

"I told you," Grandma Rose chuckled, wiping tears from her eyes. "That voice wasn't gonna stay hidden forever."

Jenna pulled back, clutching Mya's face with both hands. "This is huge. Huge! I'm calling your brothers. All of them. Right now."

Mya's eyes widened. "Wait…what?"

But Jenna was already dialing. "They're going to see this. May 10. Front row. Suits and ties, I don't care."

Within minutes, her voice echoed through the house as she moved from call to call.

"Theo, don't play with me…. yes, your sister got the lead."

"Levi, no excuses. I'll book the flight for you myself."

"Owen, if you miss this, I'm changing the Wi-Fi password at Christmas."

Mya sat frozen on the floor, overwhelmed, but in the best way.

"They're coming?" she asked quietly, as Jenna finally sat down beside her.

"All of them," Jenna said, smiling through teary eyes. "For you."

Mya looked around the room. The walls hadn't changed. The couch was still faded in the corners. Her dad's favorite old blanket was still folded neatly on the backrest.

He wasn't there.

But somehow… she felt whole again.

Surrounded by her mother, her grandmother, her friends, and now her brothers returning home, she felt seen. Supported. Loved.

Her voice had come back. And so did she.

"Thank you," she whispered.

"To whom?" Grandma Rose asked gently.

Mya smiled. "To God. And to y'all."

A few days later, Mya headed to counseling. Dr. Rivers smiled as Mya entered the cozy office with a lighter step than usual. No hoodie pulled tight. No eyes fixed to the floor. Just Mya, in a soft blue sweater, jeans, and her curls pulled into a loose ponytail.

"You look different today," Dr. Rivers said, motioning for her to take a seat.

Mya smiled as she dropped into the armchair. "I feel different."

"Want to tell me about it?"

Mya pulled the cast list from her phone and handed it to her like a trophy.

Dr. Rivers leaned forward, adjusted her glasses, and read it.

Her face lit up. "Lead role? Elle Phillips? That's amazing, Mya!"

"I sang at the audition," Mya said softly, the words still feeling like magic in her mouth. "In front of the whole auditorium. Bunny and Billi were there. And Brittany was there too."

Dr. Rivers raised a brow. "How'd that feel?"

"At first, I was shaking," Mya admitted. "But when I started singing, I forgot about everyone. I didn't think about what Brittany said or if I sounded good enough. I just thought about... Dad."

Her voice cracked slightly, but this time, she didn't shrink into herself.

"I think I sang for him. For the girl who thought she couldn't anymore."

Dr. Rivers smiled gently. "That's a powerful shift from fear to purpose."

Mya nodded. "I also told Mom. And Grandma. And Mom called all my brothers. They're coming to the play."

"How did that feel?"

Mya looked down for a moment, then smiled. "It felt... like I'm not alone anymore."

She fidgeted with the string of her sweater. "I used to think Mom didn't care. That she was working all the time to avoid everything, but... she's been trying. She saw me this time."

Dr. Rivers paused thoughtfully. "And have you seen yourself?"

Mya blinked. "What do you mean?"

"You've told me before you felt invisible... broken... unworthy. What do you see now when you look in the mirror?"

Mya was quiet. She thought of the way Bunny and Billi clapped when she sang. The way her mom cried when she shared the news. The way her grandmother said, "My baby is back."

"I see someone who's healing," Mya said at last. "I still get nervous. I still miss my dad. But I'm not hiding anymore."

Dr. Rivers smiled and reached into her drawer, pulling out something small: the same index card Mya had written on during her first session.

On one side, still in her handwriting, was the word *broken*.

But this time, the counselor flipped it over, revealing the word Mya had nearly whispered that day: *Enough*.

"Do you still want to carry this with you?" Dr. Rivers asked.

Mya looked at it, then smiled and shook her head.

"No. I don't need it anymore."

As Mya stepped out of Dr. Rivers' office and into the cool December air, she wrapped her scarf tighter around her neck and smiled to herself. The words she'd spoken, I don't need it anymore, still echoed in her heart. For the first time in a long while, she wasn't just surviving. She was growing. Healing. Becoming someone her younger self would be proud of.

And though grief still lingered in quiet corners of her spirit, she had hope now, and a voice that refused to stay hidden.

Two days later, the halls of Chelseaville Academy buzzed with a different kind of energy. It was the last day of school before Christmas break, and the world inside those lockers and classrooms was alive with cheer, glitter, and the scent of peppermint. Students wore festive sweaters, some covered in lights, others layered with glitter and bells, as they rushed to clean out their lockers and bid farewell.

Mya stood by her locker, carefully folding up her books, when Bunny appeared, wearing a fuzzy Santa hat tilted sideways and holding a half-eaten candy cane.

"Do you realize," Bunny said dramatically, "we survived our first semester… without snapping on Brittany, failing math, or quitting school to become social media stars."

Mya laughed. "Barely."

Billi joined them moments later, dragging a mini rolling suitcase behind her. "Okay, but whose idea was it to assign homework over break? Mr. Clayton said, 'Merry Christmas, here are four essays.'"

Bunny groaned. "Girl, the only thing I'm writing over break is a list of snacks I plan to eat while watching holiday movies."

The girls burst out laughing, their laughter echoing through the hallway.

Mya leaned against her locker and smiled at the two of them. There was a time just a few months ago when she would've spent this day feeling invisible, walking out quietly, eyes low, pretending she was okay.

Not anymore.

Not today.

Billi handed her a small, wrapped gift. "Just a little something. Don't open it 'til Christmas."

"Same," Bunny said, handing over a glittery gift bag with tissue paper bursting from the top. "Mine's probably louder."

Mya grinned and handed each of them a small gift box tied with green ribbon. "You'd better not cry when you open it."

"Oh, I will," Billi said, pretending to fan her face. "You're my favorite emotional roller coaster."

Just then, Brittany walked by with her usual crowd, glitter gloss perfect, but her eyes didn't hold the same sharpness. She glanced toward Mya, hesitated, and looked away without a word.

Bunny raised an eyebrow. "Did she just… not say anything?"

Billi smirked. "Maybe she found a little Christmas spirit."

Mya smiled but said nothing. She didn't need Brittany's validation.

She had her voice.

She had her girls.

She had her peace.

The final bell rang, echoing through the school like a call to freedom.

"Let the break begin!" Bunny shouted, tossing her Santa hat in the air.

The three girls walked down the hallway, arms linked, holiday cheer in their steps, and the future full of light.

As soon as Mya stepped out of the car, the crisp winter air greeted her with a sharp chill and the faint scent of wood smoke drifting from nearby chimneys. Her boots crunched along the icy sidewalk as she walked up to the house, her backpack swinging loosely behind her. The house looked cozy from the outside…lights twinkling in the front windows, and the big red wreath Grandma Rose had hung on the door was dusted with fresh snow.

It was finally Christmas break. No more hallways, no more tests, and for the first time in a long time, no more pressure weighing her down. As she stepped inside, greeted by the warmth and the aroma of gingerbread baking in the oven, Mya's heart beat a little faster. Today wasn't just the start of the holidays; her brothers were coming home, all of them.

Knock, knock…. It was her brother at the door.

She bounced from room to room as Mya's brothers, Theo, Levi, and Owen, dragged their duffel bags through the front door one by one, tracking bits of snow across the welcome mat.

"MYA!" Owen shouted as he dropped his bag and pulled her into a tight bear hug, lifting her feet off the ground.

She laughed breathlessly. "Put me down, you maniac!"

Levi ruffled her hair while Theo grinned and handed her a wrapped gift. "Just a little something for the next Broadway star."

Mya's heart swelled. All of them. Home. Just like Mom said, they would be.

Jenna stood in the kitchen doorway, arms crossed, her smile full of pride. Grandma Rose dabbed at her eyes with the corner of her apron.

"We've missed too many moments," Jenna said softly. "But we're not missing this one."

Later that afternoon, with a sky full of soft, gray clouds, the family bundled up and drove out to the quiet cemetery just outside town.

The car ride was still. No one said much. They didn't need to.

When they reached the gravesite, Mya stepped out of the car first. She held a single white lily in her hand. The wind kissed her face as she approached the stone that bore her father's name:

Noah Carter

1972-2015

Loving Husband, Devoted Father, A Man Who Believed in God

Jenna stood on one side, her arms linked with Grandma Rose. The boys stood behind them, silent, heads bowed.

Mya stepped closer.

"Hi, Daddy," she whispered. Her voice wavered, but she didn't cry...yet. "I made the play. I got the lead."

She smiled through the tears now brimming in her eyes. "I sing again. And guess what? I even stood up to Brittany. I think... I think I'm finally becoming the girl you always believed I was."

She gently laid the flower at the base of the headstone.

Jenna knelt beside her and ran her hand along the cold marble. "You should see her, Noah. She's got your strength. And your heart."

Grandma Rose stepped forward and whispered, "We're still holding each other together, just like you asked."

The boys, usually tough and unshaken, quietly placed their hands on each other's shoulders. Owen let out a deep breath. Theo wiped at his eyes. Levi nodded softly, a tear rolling down his cheek.

They stood together, huddled as a family in the cold. Each heart aching in different ways, but united in memory, in love, in hope.

After a few minutes of silence, Mya broke it.

"I don't feel broken anymore."

No one spoke, but everyone heard her.

And as the first snowflake of the evening landed softly on the stone, it felt like a blessing.

A quiet reminder that even after loss, life could still hold warmth, music, and joy.

After 25 minutes of standing at the gravesite, the wind picked up slightly as the family stood in stillness around Noah Carter's grave, their breaths visible in the cold air. No one rushed. No one filled the silence. It was sacred, soaked in memory, love, and the invisible threads that held them all together.

Eventually, Grandma Rose gently touched Mya's shoulder. "Alright now, let's get inside the car. It's too cold for standing still this long."

Jenna gave the headstone one last touch, whispering something too quiet for anyone else to hear, then followed the others back to the car. Theo lingered a moment longer, eyes fixed on his father's name.

"I love you, Dad," he whispered. "Merry Christmas."

He turned, snow crunching beneath his boots, and followed his family down the narrow path back to the car.

By the time they arrived home, the sun had dipped below the trees, casting soft golden shadows across the snow-covered lawn. The house glowed from within, warm lights in every window, cinnamon-scented candles flickering from the dining room, and the sound of holiday jazz playing low on the radio.

Inside, the boys took their shoes off by the door and headed for the living room. Theo immediately built a fire in the fireplace, while Levi began stringing more lights across the mantle.

Owen wandered into the kitchen and lifted the lid off a pot of stew. "Grandma, this smells heavenly."

"You touch that before dinner and your hand's gonna meet Jesus," Grandma Rose warned, wagging her wooden spoon.

They all laughed.

Jenna and Grandma Rose moved through the kitchen like a choreographed duet, preparing the Christmas Eve meal. Mya sat at the kitchen table stringing popcorn for the tree, laughing as her brothers tried, and failed, to do the same without eating it.

It wasn't perfect. Nothing ever was.

But it was good. It was real. It was whole.

Later, as they sat around the fireplace sipping cider and sharing stories about their dad, his terrible singing voice, his famous Saturday morning pancakes, the way he danced in the living room like nobody was watching, Mya leaned her head against her mother's shoulder.

And for the first time in a long time, the ache in her heart felt softer.

He was gone… but not absent. He was still with them. In their stories. In their laughter.

And in her voice.

Chapter 25
Joy in the Morning

The scent of cinnamon rolls and maple-glazed ham filled every corner of the Carter home. Light from the fireplace flickered across the living room walls, casting a cozy glow over the stockings still hanging and the carefully wrapped gifts now scattered and half-torn under the tree.

"Alright, alright," Grandma Rose called out, "if y'all don't sit down and eat, I'm locking the living room."

Laughter filled the room as Mya's brothers promptly moved to the table, discreetly sampling the bacon and servings of grits with cheese. Jenna walked out of the kitchen with a tray of biscuits so fluffy they looked like clouds.

Mya sat between Owen and Grandma Rose at the table, soaking it all in. Laughter, silverware clinking, the smell of peppermint cocoa, and the presence of everyone she loved most. The chairs were full. So was her heart.

"Best Christmas in years," Levi said, reaching across for a second helping of sweet potato casserole.

"Better than last year's microwave pizza," Theo joked.

Jenna rolled her eyes. "Y'all just needed to show up more often."

After breakfast, they gathered around the tree again, tearing open the remaining gifts and taking turns holding up new sweaters, socks, gadgets, and way-too-much cologne.

Mya's favorite gift came in a small, velvet box. Inside was a delicate silver charm bracelet with a tiny microphone, music note, and angel wing dangling from it.

"It's beautiful," she whispered, blinking fast as she hugged Grandma Rose.

"It's for your voice," Grandma said softly, "and the angel who believed in it first."

Mya excused herself for a moment, retreating to the quieter corner of the living room near the window where the morning light poured in. She pulled out her phone and opened video chat.

Two excited faces filled the screen almost instantly.

"Merry Christmas!" Bunny squealed, wearing oversized fuzzy earmuffs and holding up a pink sweater. "Look what I got!"

"I got a gold necklace and these Dug boots that will change your life," Billi added, angling her phone to show her new knee-highs. "I feel like a famous girl star."

Mya laughed. "Okay, okay! Look!" She turned the camera to her bracelet and grinned. "It's from Grandma. Isn't it perfect?"

Both girls gasped

"Aww!"

"That is so YOU!"

They spent the next fifteen minutes showing off jackets, earrings, makeup, and even matching journals that they all accidentally received from different family members.

"You better be writing songs in that journal," Billi warned with a grin.

"I already started," Mya said proudly.

Bunny sat up straighter. "Wait… does this mean you're finally singing again?"

Mya paused, then smiled widely. "Yeah. I think it's time."

As the call continued and laughter bubbled between them, Mya leaned back in her chair, the glow of the fireplace behind her, and the charm bracelet twinkling on her wrist.

This Christmas wasn't about perfection.

It was about presence. After the last ribbon was torn and the final pancake was devoured, the house was filled with the cozy calm that only Christmas morning could bring. Wrapping paper blanketed the living room floor like snowfall, and the smell of cinnamon, butter, and turkey baking in the oven drifted from the kitchen. Mya leaned back against the couch, hugging her new sweater to her chest while video chatting with Bunny and Billi. Laughter echoed from every room. Owen and Levi were already trying out their latest tech equipment, and Grandma Rose was humming a holiday hymn as she basted the turkey.

But Mya couldn't help but wonder, why had Grandma made so much food?

The table had been set with extra plates. She saw more than one ham being warmed in the oven, and two different desserts cooling on the counter. Her mom had even pulled out the lovely serving platters they only used for significant events. Something was up.

Just then, the doorbell rang.

Mya's head tilted. Her mom quickly wiped her hands on a dish towel and walked toward the front door. Grandma Rose followed, grinning as if she already knew what was coming.

"Who could that be?" Jenna said, pulling open the door

In rushed a gust of winter air, and with it, a wave of joyful shouting and familiar faces.

"Aunt Patrice!" Mya squealed, leaping off the couch.

"Hey, sweet girl!" Patrice wrapped Mya in a tight hug, followed by Uncle Darnell and his booming laugh. Behind them came a flood of cousins, great aunts, and uncles. Some carried dishes covered in foil, others held gifts and bags. Everyone was bundled up in coats and scarves, their cheeks pink from the cold, but their eyes glowing with excitement.

Grandma Rose clapped her hands together and laughed. "Well, now the party can start!"

"You knew about this, didn't you?" Mya said, half-grinning, half-stunned.

"I sure did," Grandma said, winking. "I thought it was time for the whole family to be together again. It's been too long."

Mya's heart swelled as she looked around the now-packed living room. Cousins she hadn't seen in years were flopping onto couches, children were already sneaking cookies, and someone turned on Christmas gospel music loud enough to start a sing-along. It was chaotic, noisy, and perfect.

As she stood there, taking it all in, Mya realized something she hadn't before. The gifts were excellent, and breakfast had been delicious, but this? This moment, this house overflowing with love and laughter, this was the real gift.

She walked over to Grandma Rose and wrapped her arms around her waist.

"Thank you," Mya whispered.

"For what, baby?"

"For giving us this."

Grandma smiled and pressed a kiss to her forehead. "Family is God's way of reminding us we're never alone.

As the family gathered in the great room, living room, and kitchen, the aroma of roasted turkey, honey-glazed ham, collard greens, and candied yams filled every corner of the house. Laughter rang through the walls as kids ran down the hallway with holiday hats tilted sideways and jingling bells on their socks. Mya helped set the table, placing forks beside festive napkins and sliding name cards that Grandma Rose had somehow prepared ahead of time.

By the time dinner was served, the room buzzed with warmth and love. Two long folding tables were stretched end to end in the dining room, covered with steaming trays of food. Everyone had a seat, elbows nearly touching, but nobody minded. Plates were passed down. Glasses were filled. Smiles exchanged like gifts.

After the second round of sweet potato pie and peach cobbler, the grown-ups moved to the living room, while the younger cousins stayed behind to play card games and board games. Mya found herself laughing with her cousins over a silly round of Uno, feeling lighter than she had in months.

It was then that Jenna stood up slowly, gently placing her glass on the mantel as everyone quieted down. She smoothed the front of her sweater, glancing around the room with moist eyes and a whole heart.

"I just wanted to say thank you," she began, her voice calm but trembling with emotion. "Thank you all for coming today. It means a great deal to the kids and me. We haven't seen a few of these beautiful faces since... well, since Noah passed."

A hush fell over the room.

Jenna continued, her words soft but firm. "The holidays haven't been easy without him, but today felt different. Lighter. Warmer. And that's because of you. Your presence brought something into this house that we've been missing: hope, joy, and love. So, from the bottom of my heart, thank you. We are truly grateful."

Aunt Patrice stood up next, brushing a tear from her cheek and clearing her throat. "We're grateful to be here too, Jenna," she said, her voice firm yet tender. "And we shouldn't be strangers to each other. We shouldn't wait for grief or loss to bring us together. Let's do better. Let's keep showing up for dinners, birthdays, graduations, or just because." She looked around the room, meeting everyone's eyes. "Let's keep showing up for family."

Murmurs of agreement echoed through the room.

Then Grandma Rose stood up, slowly but with that same grace she always carried.

"We are still healing," she said. "Every one of us, in our way. But there's healing in togetherness. In laughter, in prayers, in breaking bread at the same table. Today reminded me of how far we've come. And how much further, we still need each other. I'm so grateful for family."

A quiet "Amen" rippled through the room.

Jenna raised her glass again, and this time everyone followed suit. Even the kids stood still, holding cups of sparkling juice and hot cocoa.

"To family," Jenna said.

They echoed.

As the final days of December melted away, the house slowly returned to its normal rhythm. The wrapping paper had been cleaned up, the decorations now twinkled a little less brightly, and the smell of pine and cinnamon faded into the comfort of family routines. But excitement was still in the air, because New Year's Eve was just around the corner.

Mya had been counting down the days for something different, something that was hers. When Jenna gave her the green light to host a small New Year's Eve sleepover with Bunny and Billi, Mya's face lit up like a Christmas tree all over again.

"You sure?" Mya had asked, surprised.

Jenna smiled, handing her a grocery list. "Positive. You deserve to ring in the New Year with your girls. Besides," she added with a wink, "your brothers are headed to Bryer's party, so it's all yours tonight. No teasing, no loud games, no wrestling in the hallway."

Mya practically danced to her room to get things ready.

On New Year's Eve, the house transformed into a cozy girl's haven. The living room was covered in fuzzy blankets, bean bags, and glowing string lights. Scented candles flickered on the fireplace mantle, and a playlist of fun music softly filled the background. Grandma Rose had made her famous barbecue meatballs and mac and cheese, while Jenna brought out pizza rolls, mini hot dogs, sparkling cider, and bowls of popcorn in every flavor imaginable.

When Bunny and Billi arrived with overnight bags and matching pajamas, the squealing started immediately. They hugged, laughed, and claimed their sleeping spots around the living room as if it were a magical kingdom.

The night was filled with board games, karaoke, and dance-offs. Mya couldn't remember the last time she laughed so hard. Grandma Rose even jumped in for a round of charades, and Jenna showed off some very outdated dance moves that left the girls in stitches.

Just before midnight, they gathered around the TV to watch the countdown. Cups of sparkling juice in hand, they shouted the numbers together:

"Ten! Nine! Eight…"

When the ball dropped and confetti appeared on screen, the girls screamed and hugged, tossing glittery streamers in the air as Jenna took pictures and Grandma Rose cheered right along with them.

"Happy New Year!"

It wasn't the biggest party in the city. It wasn't flashy or loud. But for Mya, it was perfect because for the first time, she had a night that was hers. A night filled with friendship, fun, and the people who saw her, supported her, and made her feel like she belonged.

As the clock moved into a brand-new year, Mya's heart felt full. A fresh start. A clean slate. And most importantly, a reminder that she was surrounded by love.

The next morning, sunlight peeked gently through the blinds as the smell of sizzling turkey bacon and fresh waffles filled the house. The living room looked like a soft battlefield of pillows, blankets, and half-eaten snack bowls from the night before. Mya stirred first, blinking against the morning light, her heart still glowing from the laughter and memories of the night before.

She glanced over to see Bunny curled up in her sleeping bag and Billi snoring softly on the couch, her hair wrapped in a glittery bonnet. Mya smiled and tiptoed to the kitchen, where Grandma Rose and Jenna were already preparing breakfast.

"Morning, sweet pea," Grandma Rose whispered. "Did y'all have fun?"

Mya nodded sleepily. "Best night ever."

By the time Bunny and Billi woke up, the kitchen table was already filled with waffles, fruit, scrambled eggs, and juice. They all sat in their pajamas, talking about their favorite moments from the night, how Bunny beat everyone at charades, how Billi almost knocked over the lamp during the dance battle, and how Grandma Rose was surprisingly good at karaoke.

As they were finishing up breakfast, Mya stood up shyly and went to her room. She returned holding a small drawstring pouch.

"I made something for us," she said, cheeks pink with excitement. "Three days before the sleepover, I made these. I wanted us to have something to remember this night forever."

She opened the pouch and handed each girl a delicate, handmade bracelet with soft pink beads and a tiny silver heart-shaped charm.

"They match," Mya explained. "So, no matter where we are or what's going on… We'll always be connected."

Bunny's eyes lit up as she slid hers onto her wrist. "This is so sweet, Mya."

Billi gasped. "I love it! I'm never taking this off!"

The three of them held out their wrists and giggled, admiring their bracelets.

Soon after, Bunny's mom and Billi's big sister arrived to pick them up. The girls stood at the door, reluctant to say goodbye. Their bags were slung over their shoulders, but their hearts were still with each other.

They hugged tightly, rocking side to side like they didn't want to let go.

"Friends forever," Bunny whispered.

"Forever," Billi echoed.

They stepped back and did their secret handshake, clap, slide, snap, and a pinky lock, then burst into laughter.

Jenna watched from the kitchen doorway, her heart swelling with pride. Grandma Rose gave Mya a knowing smile.

"God knows how to send the right people at the right time," she said softly.

And as the door closed behind her best friends, Mya looked down at the bracelet on her wrist and smiled.

"Yeah," she whispered. "He does."

Chapter 26
Back to Reality

The buzz of the school bell echoed through the hallway as students filed into Chelseaville Academy, still groggy from the long winter break. Coats were draped over backpacks, and conversations ranged from holiday gifts to who got grounded over New Year's. The school felt the same, but for Mya, something inside her had shifted.

She walked through the front doors with her new pink bracelet wrapped firmly around her wrist. Her curls were pinned neatly, her outfit carefully picked out the night before, and her steps held a quiet confidence. Bunny walked at her side, sipping from a travel mug and humming a song they'd both danced to during the sleepover. The halls looked the same, with linoleum tiles, bulletin boards with New Year's messages, and the faint smell of cafeteria pancakes, but Mya didn't feel the same.

"Think they missed us?" Bunny smirked, eyeing the students streaming by.

"Not a chance," Mya grinned.

They stopped by their lockers, swapping schedules and discussing the end-of-year choir concert practice times and dates, which would be announced later in the week. Mya was already thinking about the songs in the play, "A Different Echo: Tiny Words." Her voice had grown stronger over the break, and so had her courage.

As they headed to homeroom, a familiar voice rang out behind them.

"Well, look who finally decided to crawl out of her cave."

Mya didn't need to turn around to know it was Brittany Abraham, who was still very much the center of attention. Brittany leaned casually against the lockers, her polished nails wrapped around a lip gloss tube.

Bunny turned first, arms crossed. "She was on vacation, Brittany. Like most people with a life."

Brittany rolled her eyes but said nothing more. Instead, she flipped her hair and walked off with her usual group of girls trailing behind her like shadows.

Mya sighed and shook her head. "She's still the same."

"But you're not," Bunny said. "That's the difference."

Mya smiled. That was the truth.

Classes moved along quickly. Spanish felt long, math was tolerable, and history was sprinkled with a few laughs thanks to Mr. Thompson's corny jokes. But in choir class, when Mrs. Jensen announced the upcoming end-of-year concert "A Different Echo: Tiny Words," a thrill went through her. "Class, Mr. Vaughn and Ms. Hoffman just finished posting the practice dates outside the auditorium, but those who do not feel like walking in that direction. Practice is Tuesdays, Wednesdays, and Thursdays directly after school, 3:30 pm to 5:30 pm."

Mya was excited. She couldn't wait to tell her mother and Grandma Rose.

This time, she had the lead part. This time, she wouldn't sit back and watch others shine while she hid in the background.

Later that afternoon, as the final bell rang, Mya, Bunny, and Billie walked out into the cool winter air, arms linked.

"Are you ready for this semester?" Bunny asked.

Mya looked down at the bracelet around her wrist, the beads catching the soft light. "Yeah," she said with a nod. "I think I am."

That Thursday afternoon, the air inside the music hall at Chelseaville Academy buzzed with energy. Students gathered in small groups, humming melodies and flipping through their marked-up sheet music. As the students warmed up and the pianist began playing the first chords of "Don't Forget Who You Are," Mya could already feel the rush. There was something electric about performing, something that pulled the real her out of hiding and gave her space to shine.

After practice, she skipped to the car with Bunny and Billi. Bunny's mom was driving them home. "I'm so glad that we can be together for the concert," said Bunny. "Although it's backstage, we still get to see you perform."

"Yeah, we don't mind being a part of the supporting and casting crew," said Billi.

Her cheeks were still flushed from dancing and singing, and they talked the whole way home, barely pausing for breath.

As Mya said her goodbyes to her friends and thanked Bunny's mom for the ride, she ran inside the house. "Mom, Grandma Rose," she called as she entered the house, dropping her backpack by the door. "I had so much fun at rehearsal today!" excitedly said Mya.

Jenna looked up from the kitchen island, slicing apples for dinner, while Grandma Rose peered over her glasses from the living room recliner.

"That's great, baby?" Jenna asked.

Mya plopped into the chair and grinned. "We're doing A Different Echo: Tiny Words! Isn't that awesome? Rehearsals are three days a week, but we had a mini preview today after school. It's so good. And guess what? The final performance will take place in May at the downtown civic auditorium. That's like... huge."

Grandma Rose smiled warmly. "I know you're gonna light up that stage, sugar. You were born for that."

"You better believe we'll be front and center," Jenna added, handing her a slice of apple. "We wouldn't miss it for the world."

That evening, after dinner and a quick review of her math homework, Mya cozied up on her bed with her phone, headphones in. She called Bunny first, then Billi. The three laughed about how Mr. Vaughn tried to moonwalk during rehearsal and nearly fell into the choir risers. Then they discussed audition plans, and Bunny promised to help Mya rehearse for her solo if needed.

They stayed on the phone longer than planned, replaying moments from their break, gossiping about new semester schedules, and Bunny and Billi were joking about what they were going to wear for the concert, even though it was months away.

As Mya finally lay down for bed, the glow of her pink bracelet caught the light from her nightstand lamp. She smiled.

The following Tuesday afternoon...

The choir room was buzzing with excitement as the first week of A Different Echo: Tiny Words rehearsals kicked off. Folding chairs had been cleared to the sides, and students practiced choreography in the center of the room while others coordinated lighting and prop details for the upcoming performance.

Mya stood front and center in the second vocal line, her heart pounding with anticipation as the group ran through "Don't Forget Who You Are." Bunny and Billi were stationed just offstage, helping move props and jotting down costume changes as part of the supporting crew. They'd volunteered to help behind the scenes, and even though they weren't in the spotlight, their support was anything but invisible.

"You've got this!" Billi mouthed from behind the curtain with two enthusiastic thumbs up

Mya smiled

But that peace didn't last long.

As soon as the director called for a quick break, the clatter of movement paused, and then came that familiar, sharp voice.

Brittany Abraham.

She leaned dramatically against a mirrored wall, sipping from a metallic pink water bottle and watching Mya like a hawk.

"You know," Brittany said loud enough for the room to hear, "some people think one good note means they can lead an entire show."

A few nearby students chuckled uncomfortably, unsure whether to laugh or look away.

Mya froze for a second, then turned slightly to glance toward Bunny and Billi backstage. Bunny gave her a firm shake of the head...Don't feed it. Billi folded her arms, clearly irritated.

Brittany wasn't done. She twirled a piece of her hair and added, "Let's be honest. Some people blend in for a reason."

Before Mya could respond, Ms. Hoffman called out from across the room, her voice sharp. "Brittany, focus on your cues, not your commentary."

The room went quiet.

Brittany huffed and looked away.

Mya took a deep breath, then walked back into formation. As she passed her best friend, Bunny leaned in and whispered, "You're still going to outshine her."

Billi stated, "She cannot change what has already been written. The outcome will be clear on opening night."

Mya's smile returned, small but certain.

She didn't need to say anything. "From the top!" Ms. Hoffman's voice rang out across the auditorium. Mya quickly focused on her instructions and ignored Brittany.

Mya jogged into place as the music swelled in the background. The rehearsal room was alive with motion, dancers stretching in the wings, vocalists practicing lines under their breath, and costume assistants hustling down the aisles with armfuls of sequins and suspenders. Bunny and Billi stood at the side of the stage, clipboard in hand, whispering notes to each other as they tracked cues.

This was week three of rehearsals, and things were getting real.

Mya had been cast in a featured solo line during the ensemble number "Don't Forget Who You Are," a considerable step up from the background roles she used to shy away from. Her hands were a little sweaty as the intro began, but she found her footing. She hit the note. Then another. Her voice wasn't just heard, it soared.

Mr. Vaughn clapped once. "Stronger projection, Mya, but excellent tone. Own that space!"

She nodded, chest swelling with something between pride and disbelief.

From the wings, Brittany rolled her eyes, whispering to another upperclassman, "I guess being loud is all it takes now."

Ms. Hoffman, who'd been marking choreography near the edge of the stage, turned just in time to catch it. "Let's keep the comments constructive, Brittany," she said without missing a beat. "Focus on your performance."

Brittany fell silent and turned her attention to her mirror.

Over the Next Few Weeks...

Rehearsals fell into a rhythm.

Tuesdays: Blocking and vocal drills. Mya worked hard to perfect her solo line. Mr. Vaughn began calling her out in front of the group, not to critique her, but to compliment her. "That's the sound I want," he said one afternoon after she nailed a particularly emotional verse. Mya smiled so wide it hurt.

Wednesdays: Choreography and character work. Ms. Hoffman helped Mya develop a more substantial stage presence, encouraging her to stop shrinking back behind others. "You've got fire in you," she said, tapping Mya's chest gently. "Let it burn."

Thursdays: Full run-throughs. Bunny and Billi worked like pros: setting props, guiding cast members, fixing wardrobe issues. They were the unseen backbone of the show, and everyone knew it.

One Thursday, chaos erupted when the centerpiece prop, a massive football stadium arch, began wobbling mid-scene. Billi rushed in with zip ties and foam wedges, fixing the issue in minutes. Mr. Vaughn nodded in her direction. "Remind me to hire you for Broadway, Billi."

Backstage, Bunny pulled Mya aside during water break. "You're killing it out there," she said. "You're finally seeing what we've always seen."

Mya blushed, sipping her water. "Thanks. I think... I believe it now."

It was the final rehearsal before Spring Break, and Ms. Hoffman gathered the cast on the center stage. "You've all worked your tails off these past five weeks. When we return, it's time for polishing and final dress rehearsals. But tonight? Be proud of what you've built."

Mr. Vaughn added, "This isn't just about music. It's about courage. You're telling a story that matters. Take a break, breathe, and come back ready. This isn't just a play, it's your moment."

Everyone clapped, cheered, and let out collective sighs of relief.

As the group broke off to gather backpacks and water bottles, Mya lingered a little longer on stage. She looked out into the empty auditorium and imagined it being a complete family, classmates, lights shining, hearts listening.

She took one quiet breath, then walked toward the wings.

Chapter 27
Spring Break Adventures

Spring Break had finally arrived, and for the first time in a long time, Mya wasn't spending it cooped up at home or running errands with her mom. This year, Grandma Rose and Jenna had agreed on something special.

"Are you sure you're ready for four whole days away?" Jenna had asked with a teasing smile as she folded Mya's favorite jean jacket into her duffel bag.

"I'm ready," Mya grinned, practically bouncing. "We're going to Greenhaven Adventure Park!"

Bunny's mother, Ms. Earline, had invited Mya and Billi to join them for a girls' getaway in Virginia. With permission from both families and a carefully packed van full of snacks, music, and way too many changes of clothes, the girls hit the road on the first Monday of break.

From the moment they passed the entrance sign at the adventure park, everything felt like magic.

The air was filled with the scent of funnel cakes and popcorn. Screams and laughter floated from towering roller coasters. Vibrant colors surrounded them, flags from different countries, costumed performers, and glittering water fountains.

Their first stop? The Green-Blue-Yellow Coaster was one of the park's tallest and wildest rides.

"Are we doing this?" Billi asked, clutching her ponytail like a lifeline."

"Yes!" Bunny and Mya shouted in unison.

The ride plunged them down 205 feet of steel and adrenaline, their screams echoing into the sky. When they got off, all three stumbled around giggling, their voices hoarse but spirits soaring.

They tried "Escape from Pomp-Area," rode the carousel in kiddie land, devoured turkey legs and snow cones in the jungle, and danced in a rainstorm during the "Celtic Green Machine" show without a care for who was watching.

One evening, Ms. Earline surprised them with VIP passes to the nighttime fireworks and light show. The girls linked arms, bracelets glowing in the soft light, and watched the sky burst into purples, silvers, and golds.

"This is the best trip ever," Mya whispered.

"Best friends. Best ride. Best snacks," Bunny laughed. "We win Spring Break."

On their final day, the girls each bought matching hoodies from the gift shop, bright pink with sparkly letters that read "Greenhaven Adventure Park Besties 2021." They wore them the whole ride home, singing old school R&B and gospel songs while Ms. Earline nodded along at the wheel.

As they pulled back into their neighborhood, Mya's heart swelled with gratitude. She knew life would return to routine soon, school, rehearsals, and the usual drama, but for those four days, she had felt completely free.

Carefree. Confident. Connected.

She stepped out of the car and hugged Bunny and Billi tightly

"Same time next year?" Billi asked with a sleepy grin.

"You already know," Mya said.

Inside, Grandma Rose was waiting with a warm smile and open arms. Jenna shouted from the kitchen and called, "Welcome home, baby!"

Mya dropped her bags by the door, still wearing her hoodie, and whispered to herself:

"Spring Break. That was the greatest show."

"Well, look who finally made it home!" Mom said with a grin.

Grandma Rose was right behind her, arms wide open. "Come here, girl. Let me see your face."

Mya rushed into her arms and gave her a long, warm hug. "I missed y'all."

"We missed you, too," Grandma Rose said, pulling back to look her over. "You done got a little tan out there. I see those cheeks shining."

Jenna walked over and wrapped Mya in a hug of her own. "Now tell us everything. Every detail. What did you ride? What did you eat? Who screamed the loudest?"

Mya laughed, already heading toward the couch as they followed her. "Okay, okay! First of all, Green-Blue-Yellow Coaster? It's massive. We screamed so loud I think I left part of my voice on that ride."

"Mm-hmm," Grandma Rose said, settling into her recliner. "Did you scream louder than Bunny and Billi?"

"Nope. Billi won that one. She screamed like she saw a ghost." Mya giggled. "And Bunny made us go on it twice."

They all laughed.

Jenna leaned in. "Did y'all eat anything healthy, or just park food and sugar the whole time?"

"Park food and sugar," Mya admitted proudly. "But Ms. Earline brought fruit snacks, so that counts, right?"

"You're young. You'll survive," Grandma Rose said with a chuckle.

Mya went on to tell them about the Celtic show, the fireworks, the matching hoodies, and how she almost bought a pet keychain that squeaked when squeezed.

"I've never laughed that hard in my life," she said, settling into the couch cushion with a contented sigh. "It was so much fun. Like... the kind of fun you don't want to end."

Jenna smiled, brushing a curl from Mya's forehead. "I'm glad you had this. You deserved it."

Grandma Rose nodded. "Now you've got good memories to carry with you when things get hard. That's how God works. He gives us joy in between the battles."

Mya looked between them and smiled softly. "Thank you for letting me go. Really. I won't forget it."

"You better not," Jenna teased. "Because now you owe us pictures and videos. Don't even think about hiding them."

"Oh, I've got plenty," Mya laughed, already reaching for her phone.

As the night settled in and they shared clips from the trip, Grandma Rose made tea, and Jenna reheated leftover mac and cheese. It wasn't a theme park or a fireworks show, but it felt just as special.

Spring Break had come and gone in the blink of an eye, and now, Chelseaville Academy was buzzing with new energy. Posters for the end-of-year performance of *A Different Echo: Tiny Words* were taped to every wall in the main hallway, bright with gold stars and bold lettering:

**"COMING MAY 10 CHELSEAVILLE ACADEMY SPRING PERFORMANCE" **

Directed by Mr. Vaughn & Ms. Hoffman

Mya walked through the doors that Monday morning wearing her Greenhaven Adventure Park hoodie, her earbuds in, and her heart beating just a little faster than usual. With every step, the countdown to showtime felt more real.

In the auditorium, the energy was different. Focused. Urgent. No more casual warm-ups or loose run-throughs. This was the final stretch.

"Welcome back, performers!" Mr. Vaughn said, clapping his hands as students took their spots on stage. "No more coasting...we are five weeks out from opening night. That means staging, costumes, lighting, and character prep are now top priority."

Ms. Hoffman stood beside him with a clipboard in hand. "If you're in a lead or featured role, be ready to stay late if needed. Ensemble, supporting cast, tech crew, you are just as important. Everyone in this room contributes to the story. Let's lock in and make this unforgettable."

Mya glanced across the stage to where Brittany was flipping through her script. The two made brief eye contact, Brittany gave her a blank look, and then turned away. Mya didn't care. Not today.

Bunny passed Mya a freshly printed cue sheet from the prop table. "You ready?" she asked under her breath.

"As ready as I'll ever be," Mya whispered back with a smile.

Billi ran past them both, carefully carrying a sequined jacket to the costume rack. "Heads up, Ms. Hoffman says we're adding new lighting cues for 'Don't Forget Who You Are,' so rehearsal might run over today."

"Perfect," Mya said. "I need the practice."

The group began warming up with a complete run of "Football Camps." The boys' vocals were tight, and the choreography was getting sharper. Stage managers are calling cues.

Then came the moment Mya had been both excited and nervous for her solo verse in "Don't Forget Who You Are."

As the music swelled and the spotlight marked its place on center stage, Mr. Vaughn motioned for her to step forward.

Mya took a breath and walked into the light.

She sang.

And this time, she didn't hold back. Her voice rang out with clarity, strength, and conviction. When she hit her final note, the room stayed silent for a split second, then applause broke out. Even a few of Brittany's friends clapped, surprised by the force of her presence.

Mr. Vaughn smiled. "Now that is what I'm talking about."

Brittany stayed quiet.

But Mya didn't need her approval. She had her voice. Her place. Her moment.

As the rehearsal wrapped up, Ms. Hoffman stepped forward. "Great work today. Remember, this week, it's about precision. Next week, costumes. After that, dress rehearsals and final prep."

Billi tossed a towel to Mya and winked. "You're shining out there."

Bunny grinned. "Just wait till May 10. They're not ready."

And neither, Mya thought with a grin, were they.

But the closer they got to opening night, the more the pressure and the drama started to rise.

The auditorium echoed with footsteps, rustling costumes, and the occasional squeak of sneakers on stage. With just two weeks left until the big performance, everything was in the final countdown. Tech crews called lighting cues from the sound booth while Ms. Hoffman paced the front of the stage with her clipboard, watching every movement with a sharp, discerning eye.

"Let's run 'Don't Forget Who You Are' again," Mr. Vaughn called out. "Full vocals, full staging. Places, everyone."

Mya took her mark center stage. Her palms were a little sweaty, but she had grown used to the nerves. They no longer controlled her. Bunny and Billi were tucked backstage, watching with quiet excitement, ready to jump in if any props needed shifting.

The music started.

Mya stepped forward, her voice rising with strength and emotion. She was in the moment until Brittany sidestepped into her space during the chorus, brushing shoulders and causing Mya to falter.

"Reset," Ms. Hoffman called out, her voice tight. "Run that again."

Mya didn't say anything. She returned to her spot, resetting her breath.

They tried again. And again, Brittany drifted into Mya's position, this time turning just enough to make it look accidental.

The music stopped abruptly.

"Brittany." Ms. Hoffman's voice cut clean through the auditorium.

Brittany turned slowly, feigning confusion. "Yes?"

"That's the third time you've stepped out of your blocking zone." Ms. Hoffman walked down toward the stage. Her heels echoed like drumbeats. "You've had this choreography for weeks. What's going on?"

"It's not that serious," Brittany said, tossing her hair. "She's acting like this is a big stage or something."

The room went still. Mr. Vaughn turned in his seat but didn't say a word; he didn't have to.

Ms. Hoffman crossed her arms and stared Brittany down. "And you're acting like someone who wants to be cut from the show."

Gasps rippled from the cast. Mya stood still, not daring to react.

"You're talented, Brittany. But talent without respect, without discipline, is nothing. If this behavior continues, I'll remove you from the cast...permanently."

Brittany's jaw tightened. She said nothing. Ms. Hoffman's stare didn't waver.

"I'm not going to let you disrupt this production or undermine your peers who've worked hard to be here. Either you show up as a team player, or you don't show up at all."

Ms. Hoffman turned back to the cast. "Let's take five. Everyone reset."

As students scattered to the wings, Mya padded to the side, sipping water and focusing on her script. She didn't gloat. She didn't smirk. She just kept going because that's what growth looked like.

From backstage, Bunny flashed her a proud thumbs-up. Billi mouthed, "You handled that so well."

Mya gave a small smile and nodded. She didn't need the spotlight to prove anything. An hour later, Mr. Vaughn clapped his hands once and called out, "Alright, that's it for today. Great work, everyone. Two weeks left, stay sharp and stay focused."

Backpacks zipped, scripts were tucked away, and the students slowly trickled out of the auditorium. The room still carried a charged energy, but Mya let it roll off her shoulders. She had done her part, and more importantly, she had stayed true to herself.

Outside, the late afternoon sun cast a golden glow over the school parking lot. Billi's older sister, Kia, waited behind the wheel of her silver SUV, already bumping soft R&B on the stereo. Bunny and Mya climbed into the backseat, chatting softly about the scene that unfolded just an hour ago.

"Honestly," Billi whispered, "Ms. Hoffman wasn't playing."

"She meant business," Bunny agreed. "I lowkey think Brittany needed to hear it."

Mya nodded, staring out the window. "I'm just glad it wasn't me getting called out for once."

When they pulled up to Mya's house, she thanked Kia, gave quick hugs to Bunny and Billi, and skipped up the steps to the front door.

Inside, the warm scent of blueberry muffins and baked chicken filled the air.

Jenna called from the kitchen, "That you, baby?"

"Yeah, I'm home!"

Grandma Rose appeared from the living room with her holy scriptures still in hand and glasses perched at the tip of her nose. "How was rehearsal?"

Mya dropped her bag by the door and sat on the armrest of the couch. "It was... intense. Brittany tried to block me during my solo, again."

Jenna frowned. "Seriously? What did the teachers say?"

"Ms. Hoffman stopped everything. She told Brittany that if she didn't get it together, she'd be removed from the play."

Grandma Rose gently set her holy scriptures in her lap and looked at Mya with calm wisdom in her eyes.

"Baby," she said softly, "God told us to love thy enemies. Don't let anybody pull you out of character, even when they're trying to bring you down. Love them anyway. That's how you stay connected with His Word.

Mya nodded, taking in the words. "I know. I didn't say anything, I just focused on the music."

Jenna smiled. "That's growth, sweetheart. We're proud of you."

After a brief pause, Mya leaned forward. "Mom, do you think you can invite Aunt Patrice and my cousins to the concert? It's in two weeks, and I'd love for them to come."

Before Jenna could respond, Grandma Rose lifted her hand with a knowing grin.

"I already made the calls."

Mya's eyes widened. "Wait?"

"They all said they're coming. And bringing their cameras."

Mya laughed, her heart suddenly full again. "Okay, then. I guess we are getting ready for the greatest show."

Chapter 28
Blooming Beyond the Stage

Two days. That's all that stood between Mya and the biggest performance of her high school life.

The stage had been set, the lights tested, and the final adjustments made to her costume. The nerves were there, but so was something more substantial: readiness. Mya no longer felt like the shy girl hiding in the background. She was prepared to walk into the spotlight and own it.

That Thursday after rehearsal, the three girls sat outside on the school lawn beneath a wide oak tree, the spring sun warming their skin. Billi reached into her backpack and pulled out three glossy pamphlets.

"I've been meaning to show you guys this," she said, handing one to Mya and one to Bunny. "Blossom Adult Day Center is hosting an all-girls summer camp. My cousin went last year. She said it changed her life."

Mya unfolded the pamphlet slowly. The cover featured a group of diverse teenage girls laughing around a bonfire, wearing matching shirts that read: "Be Brave. Be Empowered. Love Yourself."

The tagline underneath caught her attention:

"Empowering young women to love themselves, silence self-doubt, and rise above negativity."

"It's for girls our age," Billi explained. "They do workshops on confidence, standing up to bullying, understanding jealousy and vanity, and even sessions on body image and identity. Plus, they have horseback riding, swimming, and these cool sister circles at night."

Bunny's eyes lit up. "Wait, this sounds amazing. How long is it?"

"Two weeks," Billi said. "End of June. It's in the mountains…not far from here, all girls. No phones. Just nature, learning, and bonding."

Mya stared at the page, which showed a photo of girls journaling under the trees, smiling and relaxed. Her heart fluttered at the idea of a summer filled with purpose, not pressure.

"You think we could go?" she asked.

"Absolutely," Billi said. "I'm signing up this weekend. I already asked my mom. She's down. And they offer scholarships, too, so we could all apply."

Bunny looked at Mya with wide, hopeful eyes. "Let's do it. After everything this year? This would be the perfect reset."

Mya nodded slowly, already imagining herself under the stars, surrounded by girls who understood what it meant to be different, quiet, bold, or broken, and still growing.

Later that evening, each girl brought the idea to their family.

At Bunny's house, her mom, Ms. Earline, beamed. "A summer camp focused on self-worth and inner strength. Count me in. Let's get the application started tonight."

Billi's sister helped her print out the forms and even offered to help fundraise for the trip.

And back at home, Mya stood in the kitchen while Jenna stirred a pot of spaghetti sauce. She handed the pamphlet to her mother, watching nervously as she scanned the page.

"Blossom?" Jenna said, eyebrows raised. "Sounds like something made just for you."

"You think so?"

Grandma Rose entered from the hallway, peering over her glasses. "Any place that encourages young girls to stand tall and walk in love? Sounds like a blessing to me."

Jenna smiled. "We'll fill out the application tomorrow."

Mya exhaled with relief and joy. The concert was almost here, and now, something even bigger waited just beyond it.

Mya thought to herself that this could be a summer of growth, a new chapter, and a chance to blossom from the inside out.

Later that night, Mya lay on her bed with her legs crossed at the ankles, the pamphlet for Blossom Youth Camp sponsored by Blossom Adult Day Center resting beside her pillow. Her hair was wrapped, and her pink bracelet caught the soft glow of her nightstand lamp. She had just finished brushing her teeth when her phone buzzed.

Group Call: Bunny and Billi

She grinned and answered immediately.

"Heyyy!" Bunny shouted through the speaker. "Guess what?! My mom said yes!"

"Mine too!" Billi chimed in. "She said she was just happy we're doing something meaningful this summer instead of sitting on our phones all day."

Mya laughed. "Same here! My mom said she'll print the application in the morning. And Grandma Rose already gave it her blessing."

The girls squealed in unison.

"This is happening," Bunny said, her voice filled with awe. "Two weeks in the mountains? No distractions, no drama, just growing and vibing."

"And journaling," Billi added. "I heard they have late-night sessions where girls just talk, cry, pray, and uplift each other."

Mya hugged her pillow tighter. "That sounds... beautiful. I feel like this is exactly what we all need."

"Especially after this year," Bunny said. "We've dealt with enough mean girls, self-doubt, and stress. I want to leave all that behind this summer."

"Same," Billi agreed. "Let's make a pact. No comparing. No shrinking. No negative self-talk."

"Only love, truth, and confidence," Mya finished.

"Deal," Bunny and Billi said together.

For a few seconds, no one spoke. The silence wasn't awkward; it was peaceful.

Then Bunny broke it.

"So… do we all wear matching pajamas again for camp, too, or is that just a sleepover thing?"

Mya giggled. "We might need to bring that tradition with us."

They stayed on the phone for another half hour, planning everything from their dream bunk setup to their first-day outfits…even though it was still weeks away. But it didn't matter.

Because in that moment, the future felt wide open.

And for the first time in a long time, each of them believed she belonged in it.

The next day, the auditorium was buzzing with last-minute preparations. Costumes were being steamed, mic packs tested, and stagehands moved like clockwork under the direction of Mr. Vaughn and Ms. Hoffman. The cast was in full performance mode, nervous, excited, and focused.

Mya had just finished her final run-through of "Don't Forget Who You Are" with the full lighting and stage effects. Her heart was still pounding as she slipped away to the bathroom for a moment to breathe. She needed water. Quiet. A second to regroup before the curtain call tomorrow.

As she washed her hands and wiped her forehead with a paper towel, the door swung open.

Brittany.

She walked in slowly, closing the bathroom door behind her.

Mya turned, surprised, but not afraid.

Brittany crossed her arms, her eyes sharp and full of something Mya couldn't quite read. "You think you've got everyone fooled, don't you?"

Mya blinked. "What?"

"You're not the star," Brittany said coldly. "You just had a few lucky moments. And if you had any class, you'd step aside and pretend to have a sore throat. Let someone with real experience lead the show.

Mya's jaw tightened. For a moment, the old fear tried to creep in, but she took a breath and stood taller.

"I'm not going to argue with you, Brittany," Mya said quietly, firmly. "I don't know what you're going through, but you need to love yourself and find peace."

Brittany blinked, caught off guard by the words.

"You're special," Mya continued. "And talented. However, that won't matter if you keep tearing people down. I'm not dropping out of the concert. I've worked too hard to get here... and so have you. But I forgive you. For everything."

She didn't wait for a reply.

Instead, Mya reached into her hoodie pocket and pulled out the Blossom Adult Day Center pamphlet she had brought to show Ms. Hoffman after rehearsal. She placed it gently on the sink beside the soap dispenser.

Then, with her head held high, Mya walked out calm, steady, and stronger than she had ever been.

Brittany remained frozen for a moment, staring at the door.

She glanced down at the pamphlet. Her fingers hesitated... then reached out and picked it up.

She said nothing.

But she didn't throw it away either. Everyone was back on stage.

As the cast took their final bows in the empty auditorium, Mr. Vaughn stood at center stage clapping slowly, his expression proud but firm.

"That's it," he said, his voice echoing. "Final rehearsal. You've done the work. Tomorrow, we perform."

Ms. Hoffman stepped forward, her clipboard finally set aside. "Get some rest. Eat a real dinner. No late-night scrolling. And when you step onto this stage tomorrow, leave your fear at the door."

The cast clapped and cheered, some hugging one another, while others were too nervous to speak. Mya stood quietly in the wings, her heart steady. It was no longer about proving anything. Tomorrow wasn't just about a show; it was the culmination of everything she had overcome.

As she walked off the stage with her costume in hand, accompanied by Bunny and Billi, the weight of rehearsal lifted, and excitement took its place.

Tomorrow was the night.

The night they had all been waiting for.

Later that morning, the sun rose slowly over the quiet streets, casting soft golden light through the kitchen window. Inside, the house was still and calm, like it knew something special was about to happen.

Mya sat at the table in her favorite hoodie, nervously tearing tiny pieces from a slice of toast while the smell of eggs and turkey bacon drifted through the air.

Jenna placed a plate in front of her. "Eat something, baby. You've got a big night ahead of you."

"I know," Mya said with a small smile, picking up her fork. "It doesn't feel real yet."

Grandma Rose, already dressed and sipping her morning tea, looked over the rim of her cup. "It'll feel real when you step on that stage and hear the applause. Don't you dare go up there, afraid. You've got a gift, and tonight, you share it."

Mya nodded, swallowing back a mix of nerves and gratitude.

"I just..." She paused, then looked up. "I want to go see Daddy before the concert."

Jenna's face softened. "Of course. We can go now if you want."

"Can I... have a few minutes alone when we get there?"

Grandma Rose reached over and gently squeezed Mya's hand. "Take all the time you need, sweetheart."

After breakfast, Mya got ready and left for the gravesite.

When they arrived, the cemetery was quiet, the wind lightly rustling the trees as if whispering blessings between the leaves. Jenna and Grandma Rose stood a few paces back, letting Mya walk alone to the gray stone marker nestled beneath a budding dogwood tree.

She knelt slowly, brushing away a few petals that had fallen over the engraved name: Noah Carter.

"Hi, Daddy," she whispered.

She looked around for a moment, then pulled the end-of-year concert program from her pocket and gently laid it at the base of the stone.

"I'm singing tonight," she said softly. "And I'm not scared this time. I mean, a little... but not the kind that makes me hide."

Her voice cracked, but she didn't stop.

"I wish you could be there. I wish you could see me. But I know you're watching. And I know you'd be proud."

The wind picked up slightly, rustling the trees.

"I just needed to come here first," Mya said. "To thank you. For loving me. For believing in me, even when I didn't."

She touched the headstone gently, tears in her eyes, but peace in her heart.

"I love you."

After a moment of stillness, Mya stood up, wiped her cheeks, and turned back toward the car where her mother and grandmother waited.

Tonight, she would walk into the spotlight not just for herself, but for him, too.

Back home, Mya was singing last-minute tunes and notes while talking on the phone with Bunny and Billi. I can't believe the concert's in three hours," Bunny said.

"And we've got to be there in forty-five minutes to help set up," Billi added.

Chapter 29
Don't Forget Who You Are

A few hours later, the sun dipped low behind the horizon, casting a golden glow over the front steps of the downtown civic auditorium. The auditorium, once quiet and familiar, was now alive with anticipation. Laughter and conversation filled the air as guests arrived in waves, some dressed in casual spring attire, others in suits and heels, all carrying flowers, cameras, and big expectations.

Inside, the auditorium shimmered with excitement. The stage curtains were drawn closed, but colored lights peeked from behind, hinting at the show about to begin. Ushers handed out programs that read:

"Chelseaville Academy Presents: A Different Echo: Tiny Words"

May 10, 7:00 p.m. Directed by Mr. Vaughn & Ms. Hoffman

The crowd began to take their seats as pre-show music played softly overhead.

Near the middle rows, Jenna, dressed in a soft coral blouse and gold earrings, held a bouquet of pink lilies in her lap. Beside her sat Grandma Rose, proudly holding a small camcorder she insisted on bringing, even though Jenna reminded her that phones could do the same.

"I like my little camera," she whispered. "Let me feel official."

Mya's aunts, uncles, and cousins filled the row behind them. Aunt Patrice was already dabbing her eyes, and the show hadn't even started.

On the other side of the auditorium, Ms. Earline sat with Bunny's younger siblings, passing out peppermints and telling them to behave. Billi's older sister sat next to her, holding a bouquet of sunflowers wrapped in gold ribbon.

The last to arrive, rushing in just before the house lights flickered, were Mya's three older brothers: Theo, Levi, and Owen.

"We made it!" Theo whispered loudly as he slid into the seat beside Jenna.

"You're late," she whispered back, but her smile gave her away.

"Traffic," Levi muttered, adjusting his tie.

Grandma Rose looked down the row and beamed. "Well, now the whole village is here."

Backstage, Mya peeked through a slit in the curtain, her heart thudding. She saw them all. Her mother. Her grandmother. Her brothers. Her friends' families. People who believed in her.

People who had waited to see her shine.

She pressed her hand against her chest, grounding herself in the moment. Bunny stood beside her, already in position to help backstage, while Billi held a headset and pointed to the tech crew, making sure everything was ready.

"You okay?" Bunny asked softly.

Mya nodded. "More than okay."

Then came the voice over the loudspeaker:

"Ladies and gentlemen, welcome to Chelseaville Academy's End of Year Performance of A Different Echo: Tiny Words. The show will begin in five minutes."

The audience quieted, the lights dimmed, and Mya took her place.

It was time.

The buzz behind the stage was electric. Cast members ran in every direction, adjusting costumes, warming up their vocals, and checking microphones. The deep hum of the audience filled the auditorium, and the stage lights flickered on in full force.

Mya stood near the side curtain, already in costume, her hands lightly trembling, not from fear, but anticipation. Tonight was the night. All the hard work, the setbacks, the rehearsals, the growth, had all led to this moment.

She took a breath and closed her eyes.

"Mya."

She turned at the sound of her name

It was Brittany.

She stood just a few feet away, arms crossed, but her expression was softer than Mya had ever seen it. Her voice, when it came, wasn't sharp or sarcastic. It was small. Honest.

"I'm... sorry."

Mya blinked, caught completely off guard. She opened her mouth, but no words came.

Before she could respond, Mr. Vaughn's voice boomed from down the hallway.

"Places, everyone! Let's go, let's go! Curtain in sixty seconds!"

The cast scrambled. Bunny appeared with a headset, gesturing frantically. "Mya! Come on!"

Mya glanced back at Brittany, who looked like she wanted to say more, but the moment passed.

She offered a slight, stunned nod and turned toward the stage entrance, heart pounding in an entirely new way.

The opening chords of A Different Echo: Tiny Words pulsed through the auditorium, sending a wave of excitement through the crowd. The cast burst onto the stage, dressed in bold reds, golds, and blacks, singing, spinning, leaping in unison. The stage shimmered with lights, and the audience was locked in from the very first moment.

Mr. Vaughn stood in the wings, headset on, arms crossed with pride. Ms. Hoffman hovered behind the curtain, her eyes scanning every movement like a proud mother hawk.

Backstage, Bunny handed off the props while Billi and the stage managers signaled the light cues. Everything was going smoothly, even better than rehearsals.

Then came the moment.

The lights dimmed. The music softened.

A spotlight moved slowly to the center stage.

Mya stepped forward.

The piano introduced the first few notes of "Don't Forget Who You Are."

She closed her eyes for just a breath and began.

"I am not afraid to love...I know who I am...

Tiny words slip from my mouth."

Her voice started soft, rich, and full of emotion. Her hands trembled slightly at her sides, but her posture was tall. As the music swelled, so did her strength.

Her voice soared as she continued, "But these tiny words became bigger, and I heard my voice.... I know who I am. Love yourself."

The audience leaned in, holding their breath. Every word she sang was layered with meaning: her battles, her doubts, her courage, her faith. This wasn't just a song; it was her story.

By the time she reached the final note, the auditorium was still.

Then, an eruption of applause.

Cheers. Whistles. Clapping that echoed from wall to wall.

Mya held the last pose for a beat longer, then slowly lowered her hands.

She looked out into the crowd. Her eyes scanned the darkened room, past the stage lights, and landed right on the familiar row:

Her mother was wiping tears from her cheeks.

Grandma Rose was standing with both hands clasped to her chest.

Theo, Levi, and Owen clapped with proud, goofy smiles.

Aunt Patrice is cheering. Bunny's mom. Billi's sister. Everyone.

They were all there.

Mya took it in with a deep breath and the clearest thought in her heart:

"I belong here," she whispered.

She smiled radiantly, unshaken, whole, and stepped back into place with the cast, ready to finish the most incredible show of her life.

The music transitioned into its final number, "Moving Forward." The whole cast returned to the stage for one last song, the choreography tighter than ever, their voices raised together in unity and joy.

Mya stood near the center, surrounded by classmates who once saw her as the quiet girl, but now danced beside her as if she were one of the stars. The crowd clapped along to the beat, energy bursting from every corner of the auditorium.

As the final chorus rang out, the cast lifted their hands into the air, holding their final pose.

The lights faded.

Blackout.

A heartbeat of silence.

Then…roaring applause.

The audience stood. Cheering. Clapping. Some shouted their children's names, while others wiped away tears. Mya stood on stage, heart pounding, hand in hand with her castmates.

Mr. Vaughn stepped forward to bow, followed by Ms. Hoffman. They both gestured proudly to the students, who took their bows with beaming faces.

Mya bowed low, then lifted her head, blinking away tears of her own.

The curtain closed, and the cast burst into hugs and laughter. Some cried. Others danced. Glitter and makeup smudged from happy tears.

Billi rushed over with a headset still slung around her neck. "You did it, Mya. You owned it."

Bunny ran straight into her with a hug. "That solo? That was everything. I almost forgot to run the lights."

Mya laughed, still breathless. "I can't believe it's over."

"You just began," Bunny said, squeezing her hand.

Just then, Ms. Hoffman walked over, her face filled with emotion. "Mya Carter."

Mya turned quickly, trying to stand straighter.

"I have watched you grow into someone who doesn't just perform," Ms. Hoffman said, "but inspires. I hope you never shrink back again. You were meant to stand tall."

Mr. Vaughn appeared behind her, nodding. "Proud doesn't even cover it.

Mya wiped her eyes. "Thank you. Both of you."

Outside the auditorium, the lobby was filled with proud families and bouquets. When Mya emerged, the roar of her name echoed louder than anything she heard onstage.

"There she is!" Jenna called out, rushing forward with open arms.

Mya nearly collapsed into her mother's embrace.

"You were incredible," Jenna whispered, kissing her cheek. "You took my breath away."

Grandma Rose followed, tears streaming down her face, her hands holding a bouquet of pink roses. "You made your daddy proud tonight, baby girl. So proud."

Theo, Levi, and Owen circled her in a playful group hug, chanting "Superstar! Superstar!"

"Okay, okay!" Mya laughed through tears.

Then came Aunt Patrice, cousins, Bunny's family, Billi's family, everyone surrounding her, showering her with hugs, love, and so many "You did it's" that she could barely keep up.

In the middle of it all, Mya closed her eyes for a moment and breathed.

She had faced fear and forgiven Brittany. She had stood in the light.

And she had found her voice.

Later that night, long after the applause had faded and the flowers were set in a vase by her window, Mya lay awake in bed, still wearing a soft layer of stage makeup and the bracelet Bunny gave her.

She stared at the ceiling, the moon's gentle glow casting shadows across her room.

So much had happened this year.

Pain. Doubt. Change. Growth. Grace. Victory.

And somehow, it had all led here to this moment of stillness, peace, and pride.

She thought of her father.

She thought of Brittany.

She thought of the girl she used to be and the one she had become.

"I'm not hiding anymore," she whispered aloud.

With a deep breath, she closed her eyes, her heart full.

Tomorrow was a new day.

And she was ready to walk into it, not with fear...but with faith.

Epilogue
Three Weeks Later

The summer sun was already high in the sky when the white charter bus pulled into the long gravel driveway of Blossom Youth Camp. Trees stretched overhead, casting shadows on the cabins, open fields, and a wooden welcome sign painted with pink wildflowers and bold white letters:

"Be Brave. Be Empowered. Love Yourself."

Mya stepped off the bus with Bunny and Billi behind her, each of them carrying duffel bags and wide, expectant eyes.

"It's even prettier than the pictures," Billi whispered.

"Smells like pine and freedom," Bunny added, dramatically tossing her hoodie over her shoulder.

Mya laughed, soaking it all in: the fresh air, the smiling counselors, the sound of girls already bonding near the picnic tables.

She wasn't nervous this time.

She wasn't shrinking.

As they checked in and received their cabin assignments, a counselor handed each of them a small journal with the words "Bloom Anyway" embossed on the cover.

Mya held hers tight to her chest.

Later that evening, after dinner and a welcome bonfire, the girls gathered in their cabin. Mya sat near the window, writing in her journal as the others settled in for the night.

Dear Dad,

I made it. To the camp, to the stage, to the other side of everything I thought would break me. Thank you for believing in me before I ever knew how to believe in myself. I'm starting something new here, and I'm not afraid anymore.

Love, Mya.

She closed the journal and looked around at her friends.

They had more growing to do.

More stories to live. More truths to uncover. Just then, a knock sounded at the cabin door.

A camp counselor peeked in. "Hey girls, we've got one more camper joining your cabin."

All eyes turned toward the door. And in walked Brittany.

Her usual confidence seemed quieter, her shoulders tense. She clutched her backpack tightly and scanned the room until her eyes landed on Mya.

There was no attitude in her face, just something almost vulnerable.

"Hey," Brittany said softly. "Didn't know you'd be here."

Mya blinked but stayed calm. "Yeah. Me, Billi, and Bunny."

"I... almost didn't come," Brittany said, her voice low. "But I remembered something you said."

Mya tilted her head. "What's that?"

"You told me to love myself," Brittany replied. "And to find peace."

She looked down. "I figured this might be a place to try."

For a long second, the room was quiet

Then Mya stood and took a step closer.

She motioned to the empty bunk across from hers. "There's room."

Brittany gave a tiny nod and moved to set down her things.

And just like that, something shifted.

Three weeks ago, they had stood on opposite sides of the same stage. Now, they stood on the same ground, ready to grow, ready to heal, and maybe, just maybe... prepared to start again.

Mya sat back down near the window, her journal beside her, heart full.

She wasn't just a girl who had found her voice.

She was a girl learning how to use it, with grace, courage, and love.

The End.